FLOATER

Joseph Koenig

VIKING

VIKING

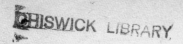

Published by the Penguin Group
27 Wrights Lane, London W8 5TZ, England
Viking Penguin Inc., 40 West 23rd Street, New York, New York 10010, USA
Penguin Books Australia Ltd, Ringwood, Victoria, Australia
Penguin Books Canada Ltd, 2801 John Street, Markham, Ontario, Canada L3R 1B4
Penguin Books (NZ) Ltd, 182–190 Wairau Road, Auckland 10, New Zealand

Penguin Books Ltd, Registered Offices: Harmondsworth, Middlesex, England

First published in the USA by The Mysterious Press, New York 1986
First published in Great Britain by Viking 1988

Made and printed in Great Britain by
Hazell Watson & Viney Limited
Member of BPCC plc
Aylesbury Bucks

British Library Cataloguing in Publication Data

Koenig, Joseph
Floater.
I. Title
813'.54[F] PS3561.03345

ISBN 0-670-81983-2

For Lil

FLOATER

1

The casket sat on the lip of a dark trench etched in shallow Everglades muckland. It was a big bronze number with a red satin lining and angels rising triumphantly from the lid; on 14K a year one of the rare big-ticket items Buck White had lavished on his wife. The others were a self-defrosting refrigerator that was her favorite and the jeweled anklet a West Palm goldsmith had fashioned before the honeymoon. It had set him back a couple of months' pay, Irene's twenty-four-karat cuff; and drove him wild each time he saw it glistening against the warm velvet of her skin. Riding on his hip, it was something else again, as cool as the woman herself. After four years the clasp broke, and Irene stuffed it in a drawer and told him she was tired of it, like a lot of things she once was crazy for but never really became her. What on God's green earth was that supposed to mean? he'd wondered till she filed for divorce and moved in with a frog gigger from Chekika.

He hovered over the grave with his sons at his side. In his fists was a felt cowboy hat, the black mourner's band crushing a peacock feather to the crown like a luminous moth. Behind him somber men, his men, wearing the drab brown of Laxahatchee County sheriff's officers, eyed the crowd, bowed their heads as a spavined black cleric intoned the Twenty-third Psalm. Three decades before, he'd sung with a gospel group that recorded two sides for a race label in the Midwest. Still star-struck, the minister chanted the verse to a dated Motown beat. At his clarion "Amen" the casket was eased into the ground, and White tossed a spadeful of earth after it, a half pound of moist humus and chalky limestone pebbles. Two Mexicans squatting in the shade of a laurel oak brought shovels to finish the job.

Using his thumb, White brushed away the tears of Buck, Jr., who was eight. His other boy, Franklin, three years older, too old to cry, turned away and ran a sleeve under his nose. White fit his hat low on his close-cropped head and hugged his sons close, walked them around the clapboard Free Will Baptist Church to a sun-blistered Ford where his mother held open the door. "Be good now, y'hear," he admonished them. "Mind your grandma."

"We will," Franklin promised, and skittered inside the car.

His brother joined him on the Leatherette griddle of the backseat and wound down his window. "Pa," he called out, "you comin' home for dinner?"

"I'd like to, son, but I still have a lot of work to take care of. You understand what that work is."

"You gonna catch him now. That what?"

"If I can," his father answered.

"You can," Franklin said. "We know you can."

"I guess he doesn't stand a chance, then," White said.

"When you do, you gonna put a hurt on him for what he done? You gonna kill the man?"

"No, boys," White said as a cruiser came by and stopped for him. "You know that's not my job. That's for the courts to—" He backed inside the passenger's seat. "Well, we'll have to see this time."

A cortege of county cars followed the flashing domes back to headquarters.

* * *

That it was a man he was looking for was one of the few certainties he worked with. A white man, the coroner had said, ruling on half a dozen pale filaments woven in Irene's dusky pubic patch. An uncommonly brutal one, judging by the steel guitar string lost in the soft flesh of the throat and not discovered until a second postmortem. The time of death, as well as the location, remained undetermined. The body, nude from the waist down, had been found by a wildlife officer in the virgin cypress swamp of the Fakahatchee Strand behind a Seminole village. Clustered bruises below the biceps showed that it had been dragged there from the road.

In the six days since, the investigation had gone nowhere. Hopes for a quick break were dashed when no one came forward to claim the Laxahatchee commissioners' two-thousand-dollar reward for information leading to the arrest and conviction of the killer. The responding officer's report on the finding of the body, the follow-up by detectives, the crime scene photos and lab work, autopsy results and interviews with potential witnesses were all as familiar to White as a map of the county, a map leading to dead ends at every corner.

When White arrived at his office, a bull-necked man with the square crewcut of a Southeastern Conference football coach followed him inside. He was wearing gray trousers with a military pleat and a tailored navy blazer that was tight across one shoulder. He stabbed out a heavy hand, sundarkened to the cuff, and said, "Sheriff White? Captain Joe Gresham, Florida Department of Law Enforcement."

White felt his grip and released it, pulled up a folding chair. "Pleasure," he said, as if there could be some truth to it. "What've you got for me?"

"The final report from the chief medical examiner's office on the second postmortem, including the killer's blood type from specimens obtained under her fingernails," Gresham said, riffling through a briefcase. "She clawed him pretty good."

"Yes, she would," White said.

"A_1MNRH_1rh, if that means anything to you."

"It doesn't."

"No sickle trait, either. We test routinely for that now," Gresham boasted.

"It's a load off my mind. I was getting used to the idea that he was white. I'd hate to think it was some sick nigger."

Gresham looked up sharply. "Did Mrs. White consort with male Caucasians?" he asked after a pause. "It would help if we knew."

"What about techs?"

Gresham showed White his palms, then brought them together. "And what I know you'll put to especially good use is this psychiatric profile we drew on him."

"I don't give a shit what happened to his pet rabbit when he was seven," White said. "I need a couple of good evidence men to go back in the swamps with me. We don't have the manpower or the expertise to run a comprehensive murder operation here, and we've already lost tire tracks and other good stuff to the weather."

"This is state-of-the-art I'm giving you. Cost a bundle to draw. We brought in forensic psychiatrists all the way from Charlotte."

"Better if they could cast tread marks, work bloodhounds."

"Techs aren't the big deal they once were," Gresham told him. "The psychs feel you'll be better off with this."

"Shows what they know about human nature," White grumbled.

Gresham removed a yellow binder from the briefcase and pressed it against his knees with both hands. "Since the victim had no personal enemies to speak of," he said, "all signs point to a random killer, a serial killer we suspect. Of the fifty-five hundred unsolved homicides in the U.S. annually, ten percent are the work of these animals. At any given time there's at least thirty-five of them running around loose from coast to coast."

"Which one's mine?"

"A strangler, the kind who craves the feeling of power he gets from having a victim die in his hands. For practice he'll choke a woman until she passes out; a wife, girlfriend, anyone'll do. It often takes a while before he works his way up to killing."

"Who is he?" White tried again.

Gresham flipped through the report. "Someone with above-average intelligence . . . a gifted gabber with a knack for worming his way into a victim's confidence . . . He lives a rich fantasy life. When he can't find fresh prey, he may return to the scene of a kill to relive the victory. So what you might want to try is a stakeout of the crime scene."

"In the middle of the goddamn Everglades? Where'll I put my man, in a tree?"

"He's the product of a broken home," Gresham went on. "Quite possibly he resents his mother."

"Pity."

"A lonely man . . . with a smoldering hatred of women . . ."

"No shit?"

"And a criminal history of violent crimes, including sexual assault."

"You came all this way to tell me he's antisocial?"

Gresham worked a finger behind the knot on his hand-painted tie and maneuvered his jaw from side to side. "Tallahassee has only the most rudimentary facts to work with," he said. "Still, you should find this information very useful." He cleared his throat. "Between twenty and forty years of age . . . a heavy drinker . . . likes to move around from place to place . . ."

"What you're giving me fits half the men in this county," White said, pacing the room, "the half that's not already doing time. Forget what he likes on his Wheaties. Tell me what his name is and what he's up to right now. Where do I put my hands on the son of a bitch? What do your shrinks say about that?"

Gresham snapped shut his briefcase and tossed the report on White's desk. "I can't answer," he said, getting up to leave. "Why don't you call and ask them yourself? I'm sure they'll find it interesting talking to you."

Among the few outsiders in attendance at the funeral had been a girl from the *Miami Herald,* a twenty-year-old intern who'd been promised her first byline for a short piece on the frustration of a backcountry sheriff stymied in the hunt for his estranged wife's slayer. The neophyte reporter came away from the ceremony impressed more with "the unflinching dignity of the proud lawman and his shiny-faced boys" and "the Afro polyrhythms of the pastor's baritone dirge, which harkened to the field hollers that were the forerunner of the blues." A rewrite man honed her thirty-five-hundred-word account into a six-inch squib that ran with the obits, next morning, under the headline: BURY SHERIFF'S SLAIN SPOUSE.

In the afternoon White's phone began ringing off the hook.

"This the coon sheriff? We sure sorry 'bout your black bitch, Sheriff Coon. Hear you givin' a cash reward for the boy who done her. We doin' the same, 'ceptin' we paid ours C.O.D. Give him half when he poured her the pork and the rest when she choked on it. What you think of that?"

White slapped his hand against the mouthpiece and whispered into the space between his fingers. "Tyrone, do you have this call traced yet? Fine. Tell the brothers to leave their uniforms in their lockers and load up their riot guns. We're going cracker-crunching tonight."

Click.

* * *

"Sheriff Dewayne White, please."

"Speaking."

"Sheriff White?"

"Yes."

"I have a word for you about the passing of your wife."

"Yes?"

"I know who's responsible, where the blame lies."

"Well . . . ?"

"You, sir. You, yourself, are responsible. The sins of the father are visited on the—"

"Don't preach to me," White said. "I've been washed in the same blood as you. . . ."

"Pardon, Sheriff, I didn't know you were a devout man."

"Asshole."

"Sheriff White?"

"Yes."

"I . . . I really don't know how to begin this."

"Let's start with your name."

"Peter Arquette, sir."

"What can I do for you, Mr. Arquette?"

"Nothing, sir. It's something I'd like to do for you."

"What's that?"

"I'd like to, I mean, I want . . . I have to get something off my chest."

"Oh?"

"Yes, I want to confess to the murder of your wife."

White pulled away to stare at the receiver, then returned it wearily to his ear. "I'm listening," he said.

"It was last Sunday night," Arquette said. "I'd had a couple of beers too many, I guess, and I wasn't feeling myself, and on the way back home I had to use the toilet. The nearest one was in a place called Sports Corner. It's a colored bar in Chekika, do you know it?"

White experienced a gentle pounding, not altogether unpleasant, in his temples. He reached for a pencil. "Yes, I do, Mr. Arquette."

"I was feeling quite relieved when I came out of the bathroom, and as I thought that one more beer couldn't hurt, I ordered a draft and sat down in a corner booth. I was drinking it by myself, as you might understand, when a beautiful Negro girl came in and took a seat at the table closest to mine."

The pounding in White's head turned to hammer blows. "Go on," he said.

"Irene . . . Mrs. White told me about herself," Arquette said. "How leaving you was the biggest mistake of her life and how much she missed her boys, how she hadn't been at peace since she'd run out. . . . Sheriff White? Sheriff White, are you listening?"

In a husky voice White said again, "Go on."

"Well, we sat and we talked, and I bought her a drink. And I must have bought her another one because then it was two A.M., closing time, and the waiters were stacking the chairs on the tables. I offered to drop her off where she was staying, and she accepted very gratefully. We went west on the Trail. As we passed the Fakahatchee Seminole enclosure I pulled onto the road that runs behind it because I had to go to the toilet again. I walked into the trees and zipped down my pants and . . . I don't know how to say this to you, but the next thing I remember is dragging that poor woman out of the truck and tearing off her skirt and forcing her. . . . And after that it gets kind of hazy, but when I woke up in the truck, the strings were missing from my Fender bass, and there were deep scratches on my cheeks and on my arms and on my throat, sir."

"Mr. Arquette, where are you calling from?" White asked. "I'd like to come over and have a word with you in person."

"I'm at my house here in Glades City," Arquette said. "But there's something else you should know about me before stopping by. Mrs. White isn't . . . wasn't the first woman I . . . I've done this to."

"What's that!"

"The Zodiac Killings, Sheriff White, those are mine too," Arquette said tearfully. "I got away clean. And the Stocking Strangler in Columbus, Georgia . . . they tried the wrong man in that case. I did those."

"Bet you're the Chokoloskee Choker too. That right?"

"Yes, sir," Arquette answered. "How did you find out?"

"Sleep well tonight, Arquette," White said. "Confession's good for the soul." But for the soul of a compulsive confessor, poor bastard, not nearly so good as a few stiff drinks.

"White?"

"Who the hell's this?"

"It's been a tough week, eh? Maybe I should call back another time."

"What . . . ? Hector, is that you?"

"So you recognize my voice? I thought perhaps you would not admit it."

"Damn right, it's tough," White said. "It's getting tougher by the minute."

"I'm sorry I could not be there for the funeral. A case came up. . . ."

"I understand, Hector."

"In part, that is why I am calling. I have something to help take your mind off your troubles."

"A nice, juicy mass murder Metro PD doesn't know where to put? Some trip-wire vets with an armor-plated swamp buggy holed up in the glades? Not today, Lieutenant. I don't have the stomach for it."

"No blood, no muss," Hector promised. "All I want is for you to come with me on a ride in the country. Show me around, say hello to a nice man. It will do you a world of good."

"I'm not in the mood," White said. "I buried Irene yesterday, and now I have to get used to losing her all over again. I've been neglecting the boys, working the case myself, and I still don't have a decent clue. Today all the palmetto bugs are crawling out of the woodwork, and each one has my number. A spin in the country . . . uh-uh."

"You'll be doing yourself a bigger favor than me. Get you away from your grief and from your desk. I know how you like to brood."

"Forget it, Hector. The answer is no."

A button lit up on White's phone, and his finger struck at it. He heard adolescent giggles, a squeaky falsetto. "De-wayne, honey, this is your Irene callin' from the grave. . . ."

His finger curled into his fist, and he slammed the fist on his deck, punched back the call from Miami.

"What happened?" Hector asked. "It sounded like we were cut off."

"Where in the country?" White asked.

Lieutenant Hector Alvorado of the Miami Missing Persons Bureau had emigrated from his native Cuba in the tumultuous months before the revolution. He had been back once, in 1961, sailing out of Cudjoe Key in a rust-bucket motor launch, his bronze features shaded with lampblack, out-of-date road maps of Oriente province in his army-surplus fatigues. He returned to Miami two months after a memorial service in his honor, sullen and uncommunicative. Below his left eye was a tic that he kept screened in a blue-gray cloud from a bottomless cache of Have-A-Havanas. His taste in cars was also vintage Havana, running to '59 Chevies, of which he owned three. When he pulled into the lot at Laxahatchee sheriff's headquarters, however, it was an unmarked Oldsmobile from the Miami motor pool that he bottomed on the yellow speed bump.

White was waiting in his cruiser with the engine running. He backed out of his private spot, away from the weathered stanchion with his name stenciled over his predecessor's, and motioned the 88 in. Alvorado slid beside him on the long bench seat and fastened his safety belt, the only cop White knew who used one. "The sheriff's own space," Alvorado said, surveying the near empty lot. "A place of honor."

White snorted derisively. "Two death threats came in after you called. I thought I'd leave them a cheap target to plink at. Anything happens to this supercharged baby," he said, patting the steering wheel, "I'll be gumming my steaks before the commissioners okay another."

"A good thing I didn't take the Chevy," Alvorado said. Usually he pronounced it Cheby, like Habana, and grinned. This time he did not.

"Ain't gonna be anyone's idea of a joyride, is it?" White frowned.

Alvorado let his lower lip protrude. "For you I don't see why not," he said. "For me it's a little work, but not so much to ruin the day. For the man we are looking for . . . it's hard to say."

"Who is he, one of your anti-Castro buddies blown himself to kingdom come? Shit . . . we lookin' for parts?"

"This is not political. The man's name is Madison, Richard I. Madison, which is every bit as Anglo-Saxon as yours. He went missing on a Florida vacation and the Everglades is where the trail ends."

"Where does it begin?"

"Outside of Washington, D.C., in a place called Glen Echo, Maryland. That's where Madison lives with his mother."

"Why didn't you say he was a kid?" White asked. "Waste of time, looking for runaways."

"He's a kid, all right," Alvorado said. "A kid of forty-eight. He was corresponding with a Miami woman he met through a lonely hearts publication. Three weeks ago he flew down to see her for the first time, and that's the last Mrs. Madison heard from her son."

"Maybe the shock killed him," White said. "Did you check the morgue and the hospitals?"

"In fact, I did," Alvorado said. "But I think the girlfriend is a better lead."

"What's the story on her?"

"She's from Key Biscayne, an Alice Rovere. I wasted a week calling her apartment, leaving notes under the door, in the mailbox, with the super. She never phoned back. Yesterday I went out for one last try and to speak with the neighbors. They said she regularly disappears for extended periods of time, often in the company of older men they've never seen before and rarely see again. Where she goes is a mystery to them, but the doorman recalls her mentioning a cottage her family keeps around Everglades National Park. The Laxahatchee phone book shows a Rovere in the right place. I called four times, but no one answered, so the next step is to have a look for myself. Only who can find anything in the Everglades without a guide?"

"A guide? Is that where I fit in?"

"If it injures your pride, call yourself a hunter," Alvorado said. "A great . . . no, White the great hunter."

They left rubber to the end of the parking lot, White punishing the accelerator as though he were afraid the ribbed tracks in the asphalt might reel them back in. They sliced across the highway into a waxy green tangle that parted around a marshy lane. The way was pocked with small craters, bottomless blackwater hazards. Gradually the brush dissolved in a freshwater grass prairie as empty as the Great Plains, the ruler's edge of the horizon violated by gnawed canopies of mahogany and live oak.

A white-tailed deer splashed across the lane, and White crushed the brake pedal. He jumped off it as the doe wheeled and bounded back to where she had come from, hit it again as she changed her mind once more. He glanced at Alvorado taking in the slack in his safety belt.

"These are the 'Glades," he said. "The buzzing in your

ear's mosquitoes. Anything else you want to ask your guide?"

Alvorado cinched the belt around his middle and dug his heels into the floorboards.

"What's the matter, cat got your tongue?"

"The way you drive—" Alvorado slurred and spit a little blood "—I bit it."

They left the prairie land racing south through a precision-drawn grid of avocado trees edged by stately royal palms. The way narrowed, the thin soil perforated by craggy outcroppings that gouged at the cruiser's undercarriage. White slowed reluctantly. The lane asserted itself due west, and he brought down the visor against a swollen orange sun. Discolored by tinted glass, great flocks of birds were coming home to roost. Elegant *V*'s of scarlet ibises, cantilevered beaks probing earthward like divining rods, roseate spoonbills in unnatural green flights, here and there a Cape Sable sparrow, remnants of a decimated species zeroing in on the muhly grass of Taylor Slough.

White switched on his fog lights and opened a conical tunnel in a gray cloud of dust. He heard a light car rattling over the bedrock and came up on a new Mercury Cougar displaying a Florida rental tag. He tailgated it into a break in the trees where it pulled over to let him by. The driver was a gray-haired man whose horn-rimmed lenses magnified uninquisitive eyes. An attractive brunette half his age was beside him on the seat, but not very close. Her hair was almost unfashionably long, and windblown, barretted by sunglasses pushed back on her head. Inside a pastel blouse a simple gold strand mirrored the gentle sweep of her hairline. Dark skin was crafted into precise features with none of the sun's leather, but color-controlled from the cosmetics shelf. What they saw appealed to the different sensibilities of both men.

White braked the cruiser, holding the couple there. "Anyone we know?"

"If not," Alvorado said, "someone we should." He rolled down his window. "Mr. Madison?" he tried.

"Why, yes."

"Miss Rovere?"

"That's right," the woman answered. "How do you know our names?"

"Where have you been hiding?"

"Who are you?" she demanded.

"Yes," Madison put in nervously. "Who?"

"Lieutenant Hector Alvorado, Miami police. I'm with missing persons. This is Sheriff White."

"Missing persons?" Madison asked. "Who are you looking for?"

"It's none of our concern, Dick," Alice Rovere said. "Just ask the gentlemen if they'll let us on our way."

"For you, sir," Alvorado said. He was looking at the woman.

"He's hardly what you'd call missing," Alice answered.

Madison laughed uneasily. "Hardly," he echoed.

Alvorado did not return the laugh. His eye was starting to throb. "It is well for you to tell me that. Tell your mother too. Call her and say you're all right. You have her worried."

Madison removed his glasses and blotted his forehead with a handkerchief.

"And if first you will also tell me where you were hiding—"

"He wasn't doing anything of the sort," Alice interrupted. "I was. I was hiding him."

"Is that right?" Alvorado asked. "From who is he running?"

"From my girlfriends, from my neighbors, from a lot of people who find him as fascinating as I do and who'd keep us from being alone." She snuggled a little closer to Madison. "From the prying eyes of the law and its long arm. You understand."

"Not really," Alvorado said. "If you will enlighten me some more . . ."

"If I do, all of us will be disappointed." She smiled at Madison. "And two of us will be very embarrassed."

"Which two?"

"You and the sheriff, of course."

"We are both grown men."

"Is that why you're behaving like a couple of schoolboys, asking intimate questions of us for your own amusement? Does it excite you? Good afternoon, Lieutenant. The two of us would like to thank you for finding us and for losing us again."

"As soon as you tell me where you've been. I've come a long way to find out."

The woman petitioned White with vulnerable eyes but got no help. "I don't see why you can't just let us go."

"I try to learn all the new places to go hiding," Alvorado explained. "It makes my job so much easier."

"If you must know—" Madison said.

Alice cut him off with a hand on his arm. "No offense, Lieutenant, but it's none of your business."

Ruddiness spreading across her cheeks like a wound told White that she was more chagrined than annoyed. "Don't tell him, Dick," she said indignantly.

"If I do, maybe they'll leave us alone," Madison said. Then to Alvorado: "We've been vacationing at the Sea Isle Club in Palm Beach, and now we're going to spend a few days at our retreat in the Everglades before announcing our engagement . . . if that's all right with you."

"My congratulations."

"Perhaps you can do us a favor now," Alice said.

"At your service," Alvorado said, slipping the gold band from a Have-A-Havana and biting off the end.

Alice opened her pocketbook and fanned the heavy air with an envelope. "If this doesn't reach the right party soon, I don't know what they'll do."

"What is it?" Alvorado asked. He unfastened the safety

belt and hurried to the Cougar, snatched the envelope from her hand, and held it to the waning light.

"My phone bill," Alice told him. "I've been meaning to mail it, but we were just so busy. And I don't know when we'll see a mailbox again."

In the cruiser White looked the other way, trying not to laugh out loud.

Alvorado brought two fingers to his eye and massaged the pulsing flesh. "It will be my pleasure to mail it," he said, and stuffed the envelope in a pocket. He went slowly to the cruiser, chewing on the unlit cigar, then turned back. "Remember, Mr. Madison," he tried again, "your mother is worried."

"Whose isn't?" Alice asked.

Alvorado squirmed onto the seat and mashed the cigar in the ashtray. White swung the wheel as far as it would go, brought the big car back the way they had come, and said, "Whew, we're lucky to be gettin' away with our skins."

"It was an education, being toyed with by that woman."

"Pity poor Madison."

"I would rather trade places with him," Alvorado said, "and complete my education. And there are things I would enjoy teaching Miss Rovere." He retrieved the crumpled cigar and began bending it back into shape. "But I would not send out my tuxedo to be pressed; not just yet."

"You think she's playing him for a sucker?"

"Whatever she's playing, he's enjoying every second of it. Being with a beautiful woman like her, he wins even when he is a loser."

"He's in over his head," White said. "If she's bleeding him dry, it stops being a game. There's laws against that sort of stuff."

"What stuff? Those laws are not for women like her, nor to protect men like Madison. He can afford it. His mama told me he's worth two million dollars."

"That why you were so hot to find him?"

"Money like his," Alvorado said, "should always stay in touch."

A full moon lit the way back to headquarters. White swept the lot with his high beams and picked out Alvorado's car listing to the driver's side over two flattened tires. "What'd I tell you?" White asked.

"Now what do I do?" Alvorado asked. "Call a cop?"

"I've got some liquid puncture seal. Let's get you to the nearest gas station. And you were right, Hector. It was good to get away."

When the Oldsmobile had limped off, White sat at his desk and put up his feet on an open drawer. Dried mud flaked from his boots onto a yellow binder. He whisked it clean and then glanced inside, reached for his glasses.

"A bright person, glib, literate, articulate," he read, "looking remarkably unremarkable when not in action. Since the killings usually are well under way before investigators recognize that they are linked, he is among the most difficult of criminals to bring to justice. . . ."

He turned the page.

2

Norodny, in almost three years at St. Vincent de Paul, had heard a lot of weird shit, but nothing like the business about the Eskimo. The Eskimo had killed a Mountie in Povungnituk, a settlement on Hudson's Bay, and was rumored to have drunk some of his blood. He hadn't understood when he was placed under arrest, didn't know what prison was till he was given life in the nearest one, one thousand miles south in Montreal. It was early February, and the mercury had been locked below freezing since Christmas; but when his bus reached Chibougamau, where the pavement begins, the Eskimo broke out in a violent sweat. His guards trundled him off to a guest house and put him to bed with ice packs while they hunted for a doctor who diagnosed the problem as heat prostration. On his advice they kept the Eskimo refrigerated until he had regained his strength, wiring ahead that they would bring him the rest of the way gradually, to acclimate him to the balmy Montreal winter. He was due at the orientation center Friday.

In the morning Norodny was sent to the warden's office in a prison-issue suit with a hundred-dollar bill tucked in the breast pocket. His new shoes were of convict manufacture and crimped his splayed toes. The warden, unsmiling, offered him a parole and his hand. Norodny gripped both tightly.

"Kicking me out so soon?" he asked. "Well, now that the door's open, I'm in no hurry to go. I want to be here when that Eskimo shows up, so I can ask him if he lends his wife out to strangers and combs his crap in his hair before it freezes."

The warden, who did not speak much English, shrugged and gave Norodny his papers. Among them was a deportation notice ordering him out of Canada within seventy-two hours.

An hour later he sat on a bench in Central Station reading a damp, day-old *Gazette*. He was wearing a new flannel shirt, stiff blue jeans, a shoddy imitation down vest, a gray vinyl parka with a hood ringed in fake wolf fur, and tennis sneakers in which his numb toes were slowly thawing. In his pockets were $8.59 and a stiletto, a ten-dollar investment on the Main. When his feet could feel what was under them, he tossed the paper away and went to the ticket counter. How far his money would take him didn't matter, so long as it wasn't across the border. They hadn't forgotten him in the States—and wouldn't until certain statutes of limitations had run their course.

He paused at the shoeshine stand where a cleaner *Gazette*—that morning's—had been discarded. The first two sections, news and sports, were missing, and he was about to drop what was left when a splash of color caught his eye. It was a travel spread on Carnaval, Canada's icebound Mardi Gras celebration, which was getting under way in Quebec City.

The writer was unimpressed with the food and had nothing much to say about accommodations. But he couldn't stop raving about the women. He'd never seen so many beauties in one place before, of every size and nationality, young, middle-aged, and even old ones, beauties for every taste, for every man. Norodny put down his money for a ticket. He saw no reason to doubt that his type would be there too. Though he couldn't picture her face, he knew what she'd be like—quiet and lonely and rich, especially rich—knew because he'd had experience with her before.

When he boarded the day coach and tore his ticket for the conductor, there was only a jingling in his jeans to remind him of the money he had been given in prison. On an impulse he made up his mind to blow it all during the layover in Trois Rivières, a dying port on the north shore of the St. Lawrence. Wandering away from the platform in the early darkness, he felt a more compelling urge, and when he came back to the train, his shirt was bulging around eight hundred dollars in small-denomination bills and traveler's checks and two round-trip tickets to Hollywood, Florida. Inside his sock a crimson smear ran the length of the stiletto, discoloring the artificial bone handle. At a BanQuebec automatic teller behind the station, ambulance attendants were stanching the wounds of a dairy farmer from Shawinigan more concerned with how to tell his wife that there would be no Florida vacation this year.

Norodny arrived in Quebec while the prudent merchants of the walled city were barricading plate-glass windows behind plywood slabs and opening attics and guest rooms to out-of-town relatives. On Rue St. Therese, Bonhomme Carnaval snipped a pink ribbon as he announced, *"Je declare le Carnaval ouvert."* Outside the walls, two burly Japanese in earmuffs and short sleeves brandished chisels against the deadline for the international ice-sculpting competition. Through a blizzard of milky slivers Norodny watched the battle of the Alamo take form around a slant-eyed Davy Crockett swinging his rifle at Santa Ana's frostbitten infantry. But it wasn't the sculpture that held his interest. All that shaved ice was giving him a terrible thirst.

Evening's bitter cold brought out vendors of *cariboo,* vodka and red wine antifreeze. They served it up in hollow plastic walking sticks, which, quickly drained, provided traction on suddenly treacherous sidewalks. Norodny peeled a five from his roll, then snatched it back to search for the sedentary warmth of a blind pig. In a loud basement under Rue Montmorency he achieved a beery oblivion that saw him through the night.

After a breakfast of more beer and pizza (something he'd dreamed about every night at St. Vincent de Paul) he went back to the train station for a shave and an icy shower. Toweling off in the stark fluorescence of the men's room, he totaled the damage of three years in stir. The stomach was hard, harder than when he was sent up. But so was the face. A fading scar on his chin showed where he had bruised it against authority. At thirty-four, his hair was black and full and combed straight back from an unlined forehead. His hazel eyes, set deep behind heavy lids, were clear and unworried. The effect was a toughness he could do without. It had served him well on the inside, keeping the fags and psychos at bay. Now he was afraid that it was indelible. At least he hadn't learned to shuffle like a con.

It was going to be a warm day by Carnaval standards. At eight-thirty the thermometer inched above zero with the promise of an hour or two of late-afternoon sun. Brushing away the tiny icicles that sprouted from his eyebrows, he forgot that he had planned to stop at an army-navy store for thermal underwear.

In a park overlooking the river he fell in behind a mob of college girls shouldering a maple toboggan. When they paused to adjust the load, he edged closer, racking his brain for a promising line, something that wouldn't type him as an antique. Strangers, strange women in particular, often didn't appreciate his attentions when he hadn't shaved. But the smooth skin told him he looked safe. If there was any doubt, it evaporated when a slim blonde smiled at him with crystalline eyes.

"*Voulez-vous l'essayer*?" she asked, making room for him under the sled.

Dumbfounded, he groped for the few words of French

that had seen him through prison. But most of what he dredged up was obscene, the rest simple commands or crude descriptions of necessities. Nothing was suitable for conducting a romance.

"Speak English?" he tried.

"No, I do not," she answered, her accent so perfect that it fanned fresh hope. And then: "*Quelle dommage*! *Vous êtes certain que tu ne parle pas français*?"

He went away without looking back. At St. Vincent de Paul he had decided early on to cut himself off from the other cons and had made a point of not learning their language. Now he'd found another reason to curse the wasted years. He would have plea-bargained with the devil for a night with the blonde or any of a dozen other women he had seen that morning. Being unable to communicate made him feel powerless around them, and he hated it, for it wasn't his way. In fact, it was quite the opposite.

Buck White stepped softly into the boys' room and turned down the air conditioner. There was an understanding between them that he didn't object if they ate him out of house and home. Try to freeze him out and it would be war. He'd remind them in the morning. For the hundredth time.

He raised the shade and opened the window. A blade of light fell across Franklin's relaxed features, and for an instant he was looking at Irene, at her angular cheeks, the same firm mouth. Irene had liked to boast that she was one quarter Indian, and he'd teased her that it was her spare hindquarters she had to be talking about. But he'd seen it clearly in her bearing and in her dogged insistence on having her own way. And Franklin wore it well. White leaned over the pillow, hesitating as the boy turned onto his side. Franklin was getting too big for kissing, anyhow.

He looked at the other bed, toward Buck, Jr., who favored his side of the family. He was moon-faced with plaited hair, and for an eight-year-old he was immense, carrying as many pounds as his brother on an inch shorter frame. Three months before tryouts, the coaches of the Glades City Pop Warner football team had him penciled in at first-string center. But he was not the better athlete of the two. If Franklin ever put down his clarinet, his father suspected that he would find a play-making guard of real promise standing in his high-top basketball sneakers.

Buck, Jr., scratched at his nose, then opened his eyes and propped himself on one arm, watching his father curiously. White bounced a dirty look off the clock on the wall. "It's three A.M. What're you doin' up?"

The boy rubbed his eyes with his knuckles. "You shoot him, Pa?"

White shook his head.

"Gonna, ain't you?"

"I don't know who he is yet."

"Know what he looks like?"

"Just an idea."

"Tell me," Buck, Jr., said anxiously. "I see him around the house, you can come get him."

"He has no reason to be here, son."

"But what does he look like?"

"He's a . . ." White paused, then began again. "It wouldn't help much. Lots of folks look like him."

"You'll find the right one. You always do."

White sat on the edge of the mattress resting his elbows on his knees. "No one else ever did anything like he did. It didn't matter much if they let themselves get caught. This one's hiding 'cause he's frightened. Could be he's frightened so bad, I won't find him."

"He scared of you," Buck, Jr., said proudly.

"Of me," his father said, "and of the electric chair. Either way, he doesn't have much to look forward to."

"Then he's crazy to hurt mom. Did she do something to him first?"

"Nothing. I don't think she did anything."

"Then why'd it happen?"

"Not so loud," White said, motioning toward the other bed.

"Why?"

White thought about it for a while. "It was a rainy night and your mother needed a ride back . . . back to where she was staying, and he saw her. And it was just bad luck that he was one of those men. The only time they're happy is when they're making somebody else suffer."

"What was she doing out there?" The voice was deeper, starting to mature. White turned around and saw Franklin leaning against the headboard, wide-awake.

He didn't answer right away. "It's not easy to understand," he said after a while.

" 'Cause we're kids?"

"No, I don't understand it myself."

Buck, Jr., started to say something. His father's somber expression brought him up short.

"I want him worse than you do, boys. If I can't find him, I don't see how I can keep this uniform."

"Have it 'cause you're the best," Buck, Jr., said.

Or the dumbest, White wanted to tell them, dumb enough to risk his neck for a bunch of white trash who didn't give a damn if he died doing it, the exceptions being the ones trying to soak up the courage to make sure he did. "Were you boys good today, not get in too much trouble?" he asked.

"Didn't get in *no* trouble," Buck, Jr., said.

"See you keep it up. Grandma's coming to stay with you, and she needs all the help she can get."

"Why?" Franklin asked. "Where you gonna be?"

"Wherever I have to go to find him."

"You got to?" Buck, Jr., asked. "Couldn't you be lookin' for him here? He so crazy, I'm afraid what's gonna happen when you find him."

White kissed his younger son. "So am I," he said.

3

The willowy redhead crossing the river from the city of Levis shook out her bag again for the phrase book. In two days in Canada she had experienced more difficulty with the language than in as many years all over Europe after college. Although the Quebecois made maddeningly perfect sense of everything she said, she could only stab at the peculiarly accented French in which they answered. They spoke too fast, or else garbled their words, resonating them far too long before letting them out in an incomprehensible drone. The phrase book's only value was as a badge warning anyone who would speak with her to go slow.

When the ferry pulled into the slip, Merry Belson was first off the gangway. Eager to begin the search for a hotel, she surrendered her bag to one of an army of shabbily dressed men camped at the pier. There was a gamy scent about him that puzzled her. To his perplexing Gallic babble she responded with polite smiles. She did not protest as he led her past a taxi stand to his rattletrap *calèche*, a horse-drawn tourist cab.

They rode as far as St. Jean's Gate before Merry, shaking with cold, found herself back across the street from the ferry slip. The winter sun, drained by its push across the heavy sky, offered little warmth. She gave her bag to the driver, who planted her on the icy sidewalk as he added up the fare.

"Forty dollars," he said.

And though he put the accent on the final syllables, she had no trouble catching on.

"Forty bucks? You must be out of your mind. I'll be damned if I'm going to give you forty bucks for a round trip to nowhere."

Merry's outburst triggered a noisier response from the driver. Because she didn't understand the specifics, she looked the other way. Sensing a victory, he screamed louder.

Impeturbability was Merry's most formidable weapon, and she trained a full arsenal on the driver. Immediately his situation began to deteriorate. A crowd of passengers from the four o'clock boat gathered around to referee the confrontation. It was plain that they were not partial to the home team. "*Va t'en donc*!" someone yelled at him, and his hair prickled all the way up the back of his head.

To scattered applause Norodny shouldered his way into the small space where the girl stood off her foe. He wondered if the cheers were meant for him or were merely in anticipation of some excitement. In either case he didn't intend to let the crowd down. He stepped between the two of them, wanting nothing so much as to make himself look good.

What was bringing him to the girl's defense was something he couldn't spare the time to figure out. But it wasn't her looks. Despite an economic voluptuousness, the athletic lilt, and the almost translucent skin he found fatal, she did not stand out among the heavy hitters in Quebec City for Carnaval. He had an aversion to redheads, especially of the bottle variety. Later, when he was forced to give it a lot of thought, he decided that it had been her voice: It spoke English.

"It's all right now," he said to her. "What seems to be the problem?"

He missed the answer. He saw what was coming and was sizing up the driver, a tall man whose muscles lent shape to bulky clothes. A saddle nose hinted at indifferent experience with his fists, which were large and bruised. The whip in his hand added more size.

When Merry paused to catch her breath, he offered the driver equal time. But if he had no patience for the girl's story, he was less enthusiastic about hearing it in French.

"For Christ's sake, speak English," he snapped, prompting a faster barrage from the man with the whip. The crowd laughed at Norodny's discomfort, and warmth crept behind his ears. Again Merry tried to explain. The driver drowned her out.

Norodny wouldn't remember lunging for the whip, or missing it, or the handle coming down across his nose. The account of the incident in the morning *Soleil* recorded how he swabbed the blood with his sleeve, examined it, turned to run, then sucker-punched the driver in the Adam's apple. As the big man crumpled against the carriage Norodny wrenched away his whip and tossed it to the crowd. Then he kicked him in the heart. His foot moved less than six inches, but he heard ribs crack and he winced. The driver was subdued, more subdued than was needed. And that wasn't the way to make points with the redhead.

He dived into the crowd, barreling toward the river. He felt a sharp tug at his sleeve and made another fist, whirled around, opened his hand in embarrassment. "I wasn't trying to hurt anyone," he said. "I only wanted to help."

"I could have handled him," Merry Belson said.

"I saw. I was trying to rescue him. He misunderstood."

"Just the same, I'm grateful," she said.

He began moving again. "Don't think I wasn't more scared than you. I'm no tough guy."

"Whatever you are, it's fine with me. I'd like to show my appreciation."

"That isn't neccessary. It was my pleasure . . . helping you, I mean."

She hurried around him, backing toward the pier as if following his lead in a flat-footed fox-trot. "Still, I wish I could do something."

"You can start by letting me on the boat before the *flics* come and throw me in the slammer."

"If you're in trouble, it's my fault. Let me go with you. They won't be looking for a couple."

"I have nowhere to go."

"Me, neither," she confessed. "Can't I still be grateful?"

And since that had been the point of it all, he grabbed her bag and shoved her onto the waiting ferry.

Over a Mexican dinner they traded history. Merry's began with ancestors who, having missed the *Mayflower,* booked passage on the next crossing or the one after that. Chagrined at their tardiness, generations of Belsons had made certain never to miss the boat again. They succeeded beyond their dreams, establishing a small empire as fur traders and later as clothiers in Philadelphia. Until its sale by her late father and mother, Belson's was *the* Main Line haberdasher.

About herself there were few specifics. She was twenty-four and unattached, excruciatingly so. She had returned to Philadelphia from a couple of years hitching around Europe to find all her friends married or enmeshed in starting up careers. She had no job, no place to live. Her most recent address was the Society Hill town house of a former college beau she had walked out on in a huff. A week at Carnaval was going to be her reward.

Norodny told her that he was Ivan Novotny, an investment broker from Los Angeles visiting Quebec to scout locations for a feature film a friend was going to direct. As corroborating evidence he brandished his bankroll when the waitress presented the check.

"I would never have guessed that you worked behind a desk," Merry said. "The way you took care of yourself at the pier, I assumed you made your living with your hands."

"You mean my fists." He smiled. "Uh-uh, that was a lucky punch."

"Lucky for me," she told him. "Lucky you don't like to see someone taken advantage of."

"Can I tell you a secret? I had no problem with what he was doing, just that he was doing it to you. I can appreciate scuffling for one dollar more. It's the only one worth having, no matter how many of the others you've piled up." He put three twenties on the table. "I'm still scuffling."

"Is that what you call it? I admire that," she said. "What I do best with my hands is sit on them."

A beauty to suit every man's taste. He had to laugh. He'd been promised a good-looking woman, and he'd found one without really trying. But the deepest thing about her seemed to be her pockets. He laughed. "If you feel comfortable like that, you'd do nicely in commodities."

"Am I missing a joke? I don't get it."

"Most of my clients are more interested in action than in profits," he said. "Patience, that's the rarest commodity of all."

She couldn't have looked less interested. "Where are you staying?" she asked hopefully.

"I was about to ask the same thing. I was bumped from the Chateau Frontenac this morning. What with Carnaval, there's not a vacant room for fifty miles around."

"Do you have a car?"

"Uh-uh."

"Fifty miles, that's a long walk."

"Not really," he said. "We'd probably freeze to death before we made it out of town."

They kicked a trail through a dusting of snow along deserted downtown streets. Merry, wearying of the hunt for bright lights, reported that she was turning blue. He brought her back to the river as the ferry was squeezing into its berth. They waited for daylight in the overheated cabin, shuttling across the St. Lawrence.

At six A.M. they got off in Quebec and taxied to the train station. A porter let them inside the quiet building. The ticket windows were empty. Merry scooped up a pile of tourist literature from the information kiosk and dealt out a full hand.

"Where to?" Norodny asked.

Merry yawned. "Why don't we leave that up to you?" She stood on her toes and stretched, raising her arms over her head and puffing out her chest to his satisfaction. "I'm free—too free, maybe. I should be easy to please."

"If I had that kind of freedom, I wouldn't be giving away bits and pieces. It's valuable stuff."

"It's also a lot of time to kill without help." If he had to know.

He fanned the glossy brochures. "How about someplace sunny, where there's palm trees and piña coladas all the time?"

"How about being realistic?"

"It's too cold for that," he said, opening a Canadian Atlantic timetable. "Hey, you know what comes through here at ten o'clock? *The Honeymooner* to Niagara Falls."

"Don't be silly. Without a marriage license they'd never let us on board."

"The *Southern Cross* to Miami?" he asked. "I hear they're not so fussy down south."

"Maybe if we tell them we're going steady—"

"I'm serious," he said, producing the Florida tickets from his parka and waving them under her nose with the bravado of a scalper. "We can make connections in New York and be barefoot on the beach day after tomorrow."

"Let me see those," she said, and snatched them away. "Do you do this all the time? Why are you holding two train tickets to Hollywood, Florida?"

"Because," he told her, "I'm afraid to fly."

* * *

After breakfast they explored the privacy of the observation car. Wet snow coated the tinted glass so that they barely made out the power line at the edge of the right-of-way. Merry yawned again. Excusing herself, she stretched out in the reclining seat and shut her eyes.

She adored trains, the acquired pleasure of slow travel. Where she was going was not so important as its distance from where she had been before and the amount of time it would take to get there. Destinations, like points of departure, were places to be avoided, places that inevitably let her down. The best part of a trip was the pursuit of the mysterious middle ground of unlimited possibility, the rest an anxious wait to get it over with. Because she was happiest in between, she had given her life to a slow flux whose anchor was the need for someone new and provocative, who wouldn't bring back past disappointments.

And though they never spoke of it, he would have said he felt the same.

They pulled into Manhattan forty-five minutes late, victimized by an optimistic timetable and frozen switches. Three platforms away, the *Southern Cross* was taking on foodstuffs, its chromium-steel exterior a rolling showcase of spray-paint graffiti. Norodny ran into the station arcade, to a liquor store that was glad to take his Canadian money at half its face value. He caught up to Merry in the dining car, cradling a bulky paper bag in his arms.

"Did you order yet?" When she shook her head, he said, "Let's have a look at our compartment first."

"Can't it wait? I want to see what's on the other side of the Hudson."

"The whole world's on the other side of the Hudson."

He sat on the lower berth and tore open the bag, balled up the brown paper, and tossed it on the floor. "Champagne or bourbon?" he asked, showing off two quart bottles.

"I'm not thirsty."

"Take off your jacket," he tried. "Make yourself at home."

"I'm more comfortable with everything on."

"I wish I was," he muttered. He unscrewed the cap from the bourbon and poured an inch into a plastic cup, tested it on his tongue, his throat, swallowed it, pronounced it okay. He peeled back the spread and absentmindedly inspected the sheets for evidence of more lustful assignations. He stuffed a pillow against the wall, kicked off his shoes, and lay back. "Does this ever feel good."

"I'm sleepy," Merry said. "Do you mind if I take a nap?"

He took another sip. He told himself, *If I get a good buzz off this, it's not a bad day. If she doesn't get undressed in the dark, it's Christmas.*

Merry lowered the shade.

Shit!

And then she was all over him, pushing so hard against his mouth that he thought his teeth would break. He put an arm around her, and she shook it off with her jacket. Her sweater and shirt came over her head in one motion.

Next she attacked his clothes, yanking the shirttails out of his pants, clawing at resisting buttons and zippers, mixing everything with hers in a heap on the floor. She flipped the bed covers, and they were lying on abrasive sheets. She got on her knees, pummeled him with sharp hips.

Two days with hardly any sleep, three years of calling a bunk—and worse—a bed took the sag out of the overworked mattress. Merry stood his snoring for twenty minutes, waking him with kisses and the heat of her body. She wanted him on top, but he was feeling logy and uncooperative. He shut her eyes with his fingers and tangled himself in her arms. She let him sleep forty-five minutes, an hour the next time, two hours after that.

Later: "You don't take prisoners, huh?"

"I let you off easy this time," she warned.

"Now this calls for a drink. Champagne?"

She swatted the bottle away. "The upper," she said. "Let's try the upper."

Merry demonstrated that she was not inhibited by tight spaces, downshifting to taut thrusts whose staccato rhythms were sweetened by the gentle rocking of the train. When it was time for her to light up, Norodny lifted the shade and glimpsed a colony of summer cottages snowbound on a lakeshore ringed with tall pines. Merry stubbed the cigarette against the glass, flicked it over the edge of the mattress, and dragged him down on top of her. They didn't look up again until he smelled smoke.

"Oh, God," he said. "The clothes."

He leapt from the berth to fill cup after tiny paper cup from the sink till the fire was drowned. The only casualty was his vest, which disintegrated into fluffy black ash and saturated the compartment with the aroma of toxic waste.

"Good," Merry said as he collected the remains. "I hated that vest. Now you can buy a decent outfit. I still don't understand how you can travel without clothes."

"I told you, I brought a lot of old rags that turned out to be too cold for Quebec. I was glad to leave them there."

"And not having a bag, it looks so . . . sleazy."

"We'll get matching luggage, too, if it'll make you feel better."

"You don't have to be touchy," she said. Such a temper—it didn't take anything to set him off. And then it was forgotten, just like that. Funny guy but essentially harmless. Nice-looking, too, in that hard, muscular way. She loved brawny men, felt safest in their arms. Her only complaint was that he wasn't bigger, really wasn't big at all. Still, if he ever learned to get a handle on himself, there was no telling where things might lead. "For a grouch you're sweet," she said, and kissed him.

Though he saw no reason to believe her, he let go of the frown.

With exaggerated care she carried a cup of water back to the top berth, setting it down beside the window. She lit another cigarette and made a great show of soaking the match. "I learn everything the hard way," she said proudly. "But I learn."

"More than you can say for most people."

"Are you talking about yourself?" He didn't take the hint. "You never do. I'd love to hear the story of your life."

"Let's wait and see how this chapter turns out."

"It might be too late then. I want to hear it now."

"It starts something like this," he told her, "with my mother and father."

He took the cigarette from her fingers and deposited it in the cup, rolled her onto her back, and began kissing her breasts.

4

The gigger, whose name was Ben C. Lewis, had promised to leave the key. White found it in the mailbox, then went back across the scraped yard for some plastic bags he'd left in the cruiser. He had an hour to clean out Irene's things, more if he didn't mind company. He'd told Lewis that he did, especially his, and wouldn't be longer than twenty minutes.

He felt self-conscious in the empty house, a cedar shack on a limestone reef in the sawgrass everglades, his wife's lover's house. On the kitchen table was an eight-foot pole with four large hooks attached to one end, a dented zinc bucket alive with the fishy frog stink. A brown Christmas tree that had dropped most of its needles stood guard over the bedroom. As he brushed by, a silver globe ringed with red hearts shattered against his gun butt, and he toed the slivers under the metal stand without missing a step.

The bedroom seemed split by an invisible wall, as though Irene had brought pieces of the one she'd put up between them. Her side, the window side, was papered with photos—old black-and-white shots of Irene and her mother, of her brothers, color Polaroids of the boys. In a frame on the dresser he saw a studio portrait of Irene and his sister, Cara, posing stiffly in cap and gown. Tucked against a corner was a snapshot he didn't recognize—Irene standing in front of a Ferris wheel with a plush panda in her arms while Franklin and Buck, Jr., still babies, dozed in their stroller. He slipped the picture from under the glass and studied it at arm's length. It reminded him of one Cara had shot at the Laxahatchee County Fair the year he'd made chief deputy, the first time he showed off his new badge. A sharp white edge indicated where it had been trimmed with a razor blade, leaving only a disembodied arm floating lightly around Irene's shoulders, his hand clutching at air.

He swept the photos into a plastic bag. Then he emptied the top drawer of blouses and shirts, plain discount-store stuff that was the best he'd been able to do for Irene. He examined each item before refolding it and putting it neatly in the bag, looking and folding till the drawer was empty and the bag nearly full.

He found her underwear in the next drawer, the sexy lingerie she'd loved to tease him with, handfuls of cool white lace. Something dark and frilly fell to the floor, and he hooked a finger in delicate silk piping. It was a black teddy, sheer around the breasts, with metal snaps at the crotch. He'd never seen it before. He crumpled it into a tight ball and jammed it inside the bag.

Her jeans were in the third drawer, white ones that fit so tight, they'd looked wet; faded blues and cutoff shorts; her bathing suit. Her skirts and dresses were still in a trunk at the house—something to come home to, she'd once said to his face. Though they were the same size, Cara had been put on notice not to expect much of Irene's. Miami Goodwill would get all the clothes. The jeweled anklet was hers if she didn't wear it when he came by, not for a while, anyway.

He closed the bag with a metal tie and tossed it beside the door. Then he looked around at the tired furniture, grimy walls that had wanted paint for years. When Irene left, her friends had said that it was a deputy's pay that came between them. His friends had tried to console him by saying that the job was his mistress and that he'd left her for it first, that she was only getting even. He'd told them it was just Ben C. Lewis. But they'd all been wrong; he saw that clearly now. What Irene had wanted was her freedom, walking papers from a marriage she'd backed into in her teens to a man fifteen years older. Her friends would smile piously and say that she'd found that freedom. Fuck 'em—they'd never been his friends, anyhow.

There was nothing of hers in the closet. He took out another bag and emptied the bottom drawer of heavy shirts and sweaters, cold-weather things she rarely had call to wear. Underneath was a packet of envelopes held together with a red ribbon knotted in a sloppy bow. The top one was addressed in his own hand. He remembered writing it the day she said she wasn't coming back.

There were five from the boys, others from Ben Lewis—some addressed to her mother's place a year before she'd gone—and a bunch from men he didn't know. There were a few from a friend of his who never mentioned that he was writing. One of these, too, was postmarked before she moved out. If it was evidence he was looking for, he had all he could use. He double-tied the ribbon and opened his shirt, then stopped, weighing the packet in his hand, tearing through the envelopes like a strongman shredding a phone book.

They arrived in Hollywood on a cloudy and moonless night, hazy but not gloomy enough to absorb the neon miasma hovering over the city. Over breakfast at a motel coffee shop Merry outlined their day. They would check into the Poinciana, have lunch at the Stone Crab House, go shopping at Neiman-Marcus.

"What about the beach?" Norodny asked. "This isn't my idea of a honeymoon."

"That was yesterday. You really have to get new clothes right away. You don't know how bad you look."

"Thanks."

"You'll thank me when we get settled in a nice place. My

parents were always glad to pay extra for the best, and that's the way they brought me up. It's the only way, really."

His pancakes, toast, and coffee came to nearly six dollars. What Merry had left most of on her plate added eight dollars more to the check. He separated two tens from the roll of bills and was amazed at how little went back in his pocket.

"I hope everything else isn't as big a rip-off as this restaurant."

"You can afford it," Merry said.

"How do you know?"

"I know. And if I'm wrong, *I'll* pick up the tab."

"Don't let me stand in your way. If you have the cash—"

"Where have you been hiding? No one carries cash. I've got credit cards and my checkbook, and I'm never more than a phone call away from Mr. Dutton."

"Who's he?"

"The executor of Daddy's estate. He baby-sits for my money."

"You mean, you're rich?"

"Only when I have no other choice," she said.

With his little finger he nudged the check to Merry's side of the table, then flipped it back and trapped it beneath his hand. "You can be rich some other time."

Sometime soon, he told himself, when the table stakes were higher than breakfast and the choice wasn't hers to make.

They checked into the Poinciana at ten-thirty and went upstairs for a look at their room. It was more than okay, Norodny conceded, with a sunken marble tub beside a sauna in the john, a terrace with a commanding view of the beach, and a four-poster bed. Merry wouldn't leave until they'd tried out the bed, and it was after one o'clock when they rolled the service cart into the hall and rang for the elevator.

"It's the nicest room you've stayed in anywhere, isn't it?"

"The most expensive," he insisted.

"Today it's my turn to spend."

"You know I can't let you pay for my clothes."

"Try to stop me."

He couldn't believe how easy it was. When they left the department store, laboring beneath stacks of boxes and matched luggage, only his new pigskin billfold wasn't weighed down. On the cab ride back to the hotel he searched for a way to keep his last few twenties from running out on him too. Merry embarrassed him by coughing up the fare and rubbed it in by dropping the change in his pocket.

"Living well," she said at the revolving door, dandling the packages in her arms, "really is the best revenge."

"You've got it backward," he told her. "It's revenge that's the best part of living well."

"You have to twist everything into one of your little mysteries. Revenge on who?"

"It depends on how well you want to live." He took the packages from her and spun the door with his toe. "And who's standing in your way."

"That's not revenge. That's going around with a chip on your shoulder."

"What it is," he told her, "is revenge without the bother of waiting."

"What's your hurry?"

"After you," he said, and followed her inside.

Upstairs, Merry demanded that he try on his new things right away. She dangled the trousers from an Italian suit inches out of his reach, furling a crude veronica as he lunged for them. Suddenly she tossed them aside and grabbed his wrist, pulling him onto the bed.

"Haven't you heard of too much of a good thing?"

"Sure," she breathed, "and when I've had it, you'll be the first to know."

Later he went to the terrace and opened the sliding doors. They stood at the edge of the air conditioning, gazing down on the water where a lone windsurfer wrestled the breeze with a windowed spinnaker. Far offshore a cruise ship out of Port Everglades set sail for the Caribbean, twin funnels hung with colored lights.

"It's the picture on the calendar," Merry said. "I'd do anything for a joint."

She lingered there as he went back inside, then drew the curtain. "Oh, no," she said, "not those rags again."

"It's the last time. I promise."

"But you bought such nice things."

"There's something I have to do, and these are the clothes to do it in," he told her.

"Do what? You don't know anybody here. You can hardly find your way around."

"Then I shouldn't be long."

He skirted the line of cabs idling in the sweeping drive and darted around the corner. A two-fingered salute brought a cruising hack to the curb.

"Where to?" the driver asked. He was a dirty-faced man in a newsboy's cap with a pencil stub tucked against the brim.

"Head up to North Hollywood. I'll tell you where to stop."

They went a dozen blocks along Pompano Avenue, a concrete gorge of high-rise apartments. Two rights put them on Gulfstream, which curved back toward the ocean past new banks with Spanish names. Norodny ordered the driver to stop and broke one of the twenties as easily as if it were his leg. He waited till the cab was lost in traffic before leaving the curb.

He walked past an outdoor tavern and an adult bookstore. He couldn't fathom what would bring someone to the beach to look at dirty pictures and was considering possibilities when the serpentining lights of the Trudeau Wax Museum caught his eye. He ducked beneath a marquee under the protection of a shopworn Sinbad the Sailor. It was seven forty-five by the ticket-window clock. He stepped up to the glass and pushed five dollars at the girl inside.

She was about eighteen, dark-eyed and pug-nosed, with blonde hair, muddy at the roots. She was holding a telephone to her ear with one hand, and with the other she took his money and made change, punched a ticket out of the counter, and slid it toward him. "We close in fifteen minutes, sir," she said without moving the phone away from her mouth. "If you like, you can come back tomorrow and take as much time as you want. Keep your stub."

"This'll be fine."

A boy in a tuxedo guarded the turnstile. Norodny thought he looked effeminate in a ruffled blue shirt and too tight pants, then decided he had something going with the girl, anyway.

"We're only open till—"

"Just tear the ticket," Norodny said.

He dropped the stub and bellied into the dim light of an L-shaped corridor. As his eyes grew accustomed to the dark he found himself before Cleopatra on her throne. On closer inspection he saw that it was Cleopatra as portrayed by Elizabeth Taylor in detail so fine that even the faded tracheotomy scar on the actress's throat had been reproduced in loving verisimilitude.

He passed quickly through the Hall of the Martyred Presidents, whose closest neighbors were Stalin, Hitler, and Idi Amin. In the next room was Jean-Paul Marat, the French revolutionary stabbed in this bathtub in 1793. Hovering over him was Charlotte Corday, his killer, bloodied to the elbow. Marat had been the victim of a painful skin disease from which he sought relief in constant bathing, and Norodny was fascinated with the lifelike sores that covered his body. He parked beside the tub and paid no attention to the adolescent voice announcing that the museum was closing, the hurried footsteps of the other visitors. The lights went off above the presidents and dictators. He didn't budge.

After several minutes the boy in the tuxedo came into the gallery. "I'm sorry, sir. You have to leave now."

Norodny glowered at him and went back to Marat.

"Sir . . ." the boy said.

Norodny turned around, expressionless. A mottled gray knife was in his fist.

"Hey, you ruined the display. Give me that."

But the knife was not Charlotte Corday's. To prove it, Norodny spun behind the boy and poked the blade into the vulnerable flesh behind his jaw. "Don't say another word, you little prick, and you might live long enough to get in Blondie's pants. Give me your keys."

The boy pointed to a silver chain on a belt loop. Norodny heard his breath coming in short gulps and wondered if he had overplayed his part. *I hope the kid's got good self-control,* he said to himself. *The last time I saw someone scared like this, I almost died from the stink.*

Ten minutes went by before a girl called out from the next gallery, "Larry?"

"That Blondie?" Norodny whispered.

The boy didn't answer.

"Your girlfriend from the change booth."

"Yes," the boy said weakly.

"Larry?" She was closer now. "Stop playing games, I want to go home. Oh, my God—"

"Listen good, Toots," Norodny said as the girl stood frozen in the darkness, " 'cause you don't want to fuck up. The three of us are gonna take a nice, slow walk through the museum, and when we get to the exit, you're gonna keep on going. Me and Larry are gonna hang around inside and watch what you do. Which should be real interesting, especially for your boyfriend here, 'cause if you ain't so hot at following instructions, he's gonna eat this knife. What you do is, you go in the ticket booth and clean out the cash drawer and you be extra careful you don't touch the phone. You don't let those beautiful knockers even brush against it. You keep the change. The rest you bring to me. And then, 'cause you been so helpful, I'm gonna do you kids a favor. I'm gonna lock you up and leave you inside."

He thought about what he'd have done if someone had pulled the same number on him when he was a kid. Probably jumped on his head and taken his chances with the knife. Probably, he decided, why no one had tried.

The march through the galleries relaxed him. He was sorry he didn't have more time. At the red exit light he paused before Robert E. Lee accepting the terms of Civil War surrender from a scraggly-bearded Ulysses S. Grant.

"Stop here," he commanded. "You both remember what I told you?"

"Yes, sir," the boy said.

"What about you?"

"I . . . I think so," the girl answered.

"You think so?" Norodny snarled. "You damn well better." He whipped his knife at Grant's head and deftly gouged out an eye. "I'm telling you, sister, you better."

He inched open the door. A family of four in bathing suits was taunting Peter Lorre as Mr. Moto, entombed in glass under the marquee. They stopped again in front of Sinbad and were gone. Norodny shoved the girl outside, tightened his grip on the boy. He watched her walk self-consciously to the glass booth and let herself in, stumbling on the sill. She opened the cash drawer, gathered the bills, and began stacking them in small piles on the counter.

"The hell's she doing," Norodny said, "double-counting it?"

When the piles were neat and even, she fastened them with rubber bands and looked toward the exit. Norodny saw tears in her eyes. He felt others on his hand. He opened the door another six inches. The blonde girl didn't move.

"What's wrong with that bitch? She hate you, she want to see you dead?"

"She's very nervous," the boy said. "I've seen her cry over—"

"Shut up," Norodny yelled.

The girl jumped back and locked herself inside. Norodny cursed and forced his arm under the boy's chin and pressed the dull edge of the blade against his throat. He slid it away hard and fast, and the boy went limp. He tossed him in Grant's lap and went out to the booth.

"Give me the money. Give it to me or I'll kick in the glass and slice your face off."

The girl swept the bills through the slot in the glass, then pushed herself against the wall. Norodny stuffed his pocket and walked away slowly, battling the urge to run. When he looked back, he saw her staring numbly at the phone.

He searched the traffic for a cab, leaping off the curb for one caught at a red light. An open convertible dragging a string of tin cans swerved to avoid him, honking angrily. The horn blared "The Wedding March." The taxi sped away, an off-duty sign on the sun visor.

He hurried along the avenue. Outside a video game room, sirens keened above the electronic clangor. He told himself to stay calm, that it was an ambulance. But as the sound grew nearer he spotted three police cars racing for the museum. He sprinted around the corner. For the first time he noticed that it was drizzling.

A storm-tossed neon water bed marked the entrance to a hotel that offered X-rated films in every room. The sign boasted that afternoon rates began at twenty dollars, and that vacancies always existed. He put on sunglasses and walked into the lobby at a casual, measured pace. "Got a single for the night?" he called into an alcove behind the desk.

The clerk was a balding man in a gray sweater with one elbow gone and the other on the way. He was watching an antacid commercial on a tiny screen and seemed annoyed at the interruption.

"Only one room left," he said. "It's a double, with two beds. Run you sixty-five dollars."

"Nothing cheaper?"

"You're lucky to be getting that."

On the street the sirens choked and died. Norodny slipped the rubber band off a wad of bills, savoring its thickness between his fingers. There was a twenty on top and two more beneath it, but after that, mostly singles. He paid the man what he was asking, thought of a name for the register, wrote it, forgot it, and took the stairs to his room. Sloshing around on an unheated water bed, he totaled what was left of his take. It came to eighty-seven dollars, hardly worth the risk. With the rest of his roll he had less than a hundred and fifty.

He parted the drapes and looked outside. A dirt alley kept the redbrick rear of an Italian restaurant at arm's length. But not the smell. He went out of the room. At the end of the hall a soot-streaked window stared down at the avenue. By pressing his cheek against the filthy glass he could see the wax museum. Uniformed police were scurrying in and out while men in tan raincoats spoke with the boy and girl under the marquee. The blonde had regained her composure and was doing the talking for both of them. The boy kept pointing to his neck.

He needed a drink. He crawled under the covers and spent an hour in the muted glow of a TV that didn't register shades of blue. Half a dozen times or more he went back to the window. When the police finally disappeared from the street, he waited another thirty minutes before leaving the hotel through a service entrance. Taxis were going begging in the rain. Because it was too chancy to take one, he retraced his route from the Poinciana on foot, getting lost only twice on the way.

It was after midnight when the elevator brought him upstairs. The television singed his fingers. He heard snoring and looked around the darkened room till he found Merry curled on an easy chair. He stepped out of his sneakers and was tiptoeing to the bathroom when she woke in a rage. He gave her a few seconds of silent contrition and turned away. She didn't let up until he switched on the light and she saw that he was soaked to the skin.

"You look like you've gone down for the third time, Ivan," she said. "What were you doing?"

"It was a fool's errand," he told her. "And I was the man for the job."

White clamped his hands over Buck, Jr.'s, ears and sent Franklin into the kitchen for a beer. Then he mouthed an obscenity at the blind eye of the TV screen dissolving from the hardwood parquet of the Gainesville Convention Center. With the Florida Gators freezing the ball late in double overtime, the station was cutting away for a news bulletin. White reached above his head to field a sweating can of Budweiser whipped sidearm from the refrigerator door. He jammed it into a Styrofoam holder, peeled back the aluminum tab, and licked the bitter spray from his mustache.

"Uh-oh," said Franklin, belly flopping onto the rug, "we better be goin' down to the cellar, hide under the old mattress."

"What for?" his brother asked.

"Look like the start of World War III. They don't break from the FSU game, it just the President got himself shot again."

"Shhhh," their father said.

The Miami bayfront at rosy dusk materialized behind an announcer wearing a hairpiece lacquered into obedience. He glanced at his copy, and his brow was racked with professional concern. "Good afternoon, I'm J. T. Taylor," he said. "Police in Tampa have announced the arrest of Earl Beverly Taggart, twenty-seven, of Frostproof, sought for questiong in connection with the brutal murders of eight Florida women."

"An' we just missed a three-point play at the buzzer," Franklin said.

"Shut up," his father told him.

"Authorities believe Taggart may be the so-called Gulf Coast Garroter, the sadistic killer whose hallmark is a ligature looped twice around each victim's throat. Taggart was taken into custody as he allegedly tried to force a University of Tampa coed into his car at a shopping mall in Ybor City. Details at six."

The screen went dark, then came to life again in a bare room filled with whooping young men in various stages of undress.

"It's over," Franklin groaned. "They're doin' locker room interviews."

His father shushed him again. He said, "Dial your grandma, bring me the telephone, and kill the sound on that thing." He put his beer between his legs and balanced the phone on the arm of his chair. "Mom," he said, "think you can take another night with the boys? There's a fellow in Tampa I want to talk to."

He took the Ford to the airport and left it in the long-term lot, counting on the scarred finish to scare away strippers. He had no luggage. He walked into the terminal with his hands in his pockets and paid cash for his ticket at the FloridAir counter. He had an hour to kill until boarding time and went to work on it in a coffee shop and then a newsstand. He was paying for a Tampa paper and a tin of mentholated snuff when he spotted a middle-aged man with dull eyes trailing a redcap across the rotunda. There was something familiar about the man, something he couldn't put his finger on. Then he could. "Mr. Madison," he called out.

The dull-eyed man squinted at the crowd. The only one looking back was a towering black wearing a cowboy hat with a peacock feather in the band. "Do I know you?" he asked.

"We met briefly, a few weeks ago," White told him. "You were driving into the Everglades with your fiancée. I was in a police car with Lieutenant Alvorado."

Madison did not seem pleased to be reminded of it. "You're the sheriff," he decided, and sidled away.

"How's things?" White asked, blocking the retreat with the bulk of his body.

"Great," Madison said. "Just great."

"Where you going?"

"Home."

"I don't see Miss Rovere. Is she flying with you?"

"If it's all the same, I'm not in the mood for chitchat," Madison said. "This isn't the Everglades. You can't keep me here this time."

"No one's trying to," White said, and backed off.

Madison took a few steps away and then stopped, emboldened by the distance between them. "That was out of line," he apologized. "Your friend, the lieutenant, gave me a hard time for no reason I could see. It left a bitter taste."

"Miss Rovere paid him back in kind," White said. "Gave him more than he bargained for."

Madison's eyes saddened. "Me too," he said. "Alice . . . she can be so sweet when it suits her. But the real woman is the one you saw sparring with the lieutenant."

"He brings that out in a lot of people," White said.

"I'm not so sure it wasn't the other way around. It got so bad between Alice and me that we had to break our engagement."

"She called it off?" White asked. "Better to find out now . . ."

"Actually," Madison said, looking a little less sad, "I threw *her* over."

"I thought you said—"

"We were going into business together," Madison explained. "Alice said she'd had experience promoting rock 'n' roll concerts in the Miami area, and with my capital and her connections, we'd clean up. The money . . . that's what ruined us. We bickered all the time. Her attorneys were drawing up papers when I took back the ring. It was the only time I saw her cry."

"Might've saved you some tears down the road, tears and money too."

"I'm not sure I understand."

"Mr. Madison," White said, "I don't believe you realize how lucky you are."

"To have loved her? I know it too well. One day maybe I'll try again."

When his plane landed in Tampa, White was met by a couple of Hillsborough County deputies. "Have a good flight?" one asked without introducing himself.

"Can't say," White told him. "I wasn't in the air long enough for the seat-belt light to flash off."

"Ready for another?"

His flip manner put White off. "Where am I going?"

"Anywhere your next lead takes you. Taggart was doing a woman in east Texas the weekend your wife died. He just admitted to that one and six of the other eight."

"I don't have a next lead," White said.

He switched cars at the office, taking the cruiser all the way out to the Fakahatchee Strand. A black-and-brown puppy with a bandanna around its neck squeezed out of the Seminole stockade yipping at his heels. He walked the nature trail into the forest, counting the steps as he always did, the damp boards groaning beneath his two-hundred-plus pounds. Beside a hollow cypress tree he dropped to the ground and knelt between the roots, balanced like a fullback ready to dive into the line.

He dug up a handful of earth, sifting it between his fingers as if it had stories to tell, stories in a language he didn't understand.

"Bitch just don't let go," he said out loud, scarcely recognizing his own voice.

He tossed away a few limestone pebbles and brushed his hands together, went quickly back to the cruiser.

5

Merry sat on her valise at the curb, fanning herself with a Laxahatchee Chamber of Commerce map. "A guest house," she said, turning up her nose. "All the way out in the Everglades. Why?"

"I told you, we've got a bad case of the shorts." He carried the rest of their bags up the steps, past the old folks rocking on the porch. "I'm almost out of cash."

"Isn't there anyone you can call?"

"It's Saturday. Everybody will be away for the weekend."

"I have a few dollars," she said. She went into the street waving her hand as their cab pulled away and headed back to the city.

"It won't be so bad," he said. "You think they're all run by little old ladies in paisley shawls who check your family tree before they give you a key and then poke their nose in everything you do. It's not like that, not here."

He was right about the shawl. Mrs. Webbly, the elderly widow who ran the big house, preferred a light sweater thrown over her shoulders. Otherwise she was as Merry had imagined, a bent, tired-looking woman who proudly informed them that she had lived here all her seventy-three years and expected "quiet, plenty of quiet. . . ."

"You won't have any problem on that score from us," Norodny promised.

"On *no* score, I hope." She sniffed as she opened the register to a fresh page.

The guests were also as Merry had expected. Her favorites were Mr. Bridgeton, who admitted to eighty and padded about in felt slippers and a green eyeshade with a dark meerschaum pipe between his false teeth; and Mrs. Webbly's twin, Edith, who looked nothing like her sister except for wrinkles like accordion folds. Most of the others were transients, retirees and young couples down for the season. All of them were in the dining room for lunch when Mrs. Webbly introduced the new arrivals.

If the guests lived up to Merry's expectations, the old house overwhelmed them. It was a four-story clapboard Victorian with a screened porch on three sides and filigreed gables that left Pythagorean shadows on the patchy lawn. Merry fell instantly in love with the louvered transom over their door, with a featherbed she was forced to admit looked cozier than the four-poster she had made such a fuss about at the Poinciana.

"Think they've heard of indoor plumbing?" he asked.

"There's some in here," she said.

He followed her inside a cavernous room with a tiled ceiling. Light entered through a pebbled window above a cast-iron tub perched on clawed legs. He said something she didn't hear. She was letting the water run, watching it roar from a brass lion's angry jaws. She slipped out of her clothes and waded in. He didn't need a formal invitation.

They sat at opposite ends with their legs straight out, letting the heat soak into their skin. Norodny cradled her feet in his lap and ran his fingers along the soles.

"You're not ticklish?" He peeled the filmy wrapper from a thin bar of soap, wet it, and rubbed it under her feet. He pretended not to see her purse her lips or bite the inside of her cheek, and he acted startled when she broke into raucous laughter.

"Stop," she cried. "If you don't, I'll pee in the water."

He didn't stop right away. Merry had to howl some more before he put the soap back in the dish.

He took her hand and washed his face in it. She moved toward him, but the tub seemed smaller now, and their legs got in the way.

"Will you please hurry up and do something," she said, "before I go out of my mind?"

With great deliberation he reached for the cold-water tap.

"That's not what I had in mind."

He tugged at her ankles. When she didn't budge, he pulled harder. Her hips tensed, then shot forward so quickly that her head slid under water. He let go immediately, and she snapped above the surface, coughing and wiping her eyes.

"You might try being gentle," she said.

"Sorry, guess I didn't realize my own strength."

She went the rest of the way on her hands and heels. She climbed on his lap and wrapped her legs around him and eased him inside. They stayed like that for a very long time, rocking slowly, lost in each other. Then Norodny noticed half an inch of water on the floor and ruined the moment by lunging for the stopper.

"Why must you be so responsible?" Merry asked.

"Look at the floor."

"To hell with the floor. You felt so good."

"We have to do something about this flood. If it starts leaking downstairs, Mrs. Webbly will be up here in no time. She'll have a stroke if she finds us like this."

"It'll be her own fault, the old biddy. Ivan, come back."

He plucked a bath towel off the wall. "One of us had better mop up this mess now," he said.

Merry let the water run some more. It was a minor thing. And yes, he was right about the flood. But it was the little disappointments that ultimately did the most harm to her relationships. She made up her mind never to forgive him.

He dried in a hurry and threw the towel on the floor, steered it through the water with his toe. He swabbed the tiles until they were glistening, then wrang out the puddle in the toilet. He brought his clothes into the other room and was out the door before Merry finished brushing her hair.

Mrs. Webbly was not to be found in her rooms. He tracked her down to the office behind the desk where she was sorting the mail. She took off her glasses when he entered and fluffed her silver hair with her fingertips.

"Yes, Mr. Novotny," she said. "Is there anything you need?"

"Not exactly, Mrs. Webbly, but I do have something of a problem."

"Don't tell me you found a roach. I distinctly told the maid that if she overlooked a single one—"

"No, no, it's nothing like that. I hate to impose, but there's a favor I have to ask of you."

She nudged the glasses back along the worn bridge of her nose. She could see him clearly now, and the concern around his eyes was contagious.

"I'll be away on business for several hours each of the next few days," he explained, "and I was hoping you wouldn't mind going upstairs every now and then to check up on Mrs. Novotny."

"Check on her? I'm not sure what you mean."

"She hasn't been well. I'd feel a lot more comfortable knowing someone was watching her while I'm gone."

"If she's sick, perhaps it would be best if you called a doctor. I can give you the phone number of a very reliable physician."

"I'm sure you can, Mrs. Webbly, but it's not that kind of illness. Merry has . . . well, to be honest, my wife is an epileptic, and she's subject to powerful seizures. They don't last long, a minute or two at the most, but there's no telling what might happen if she's alone. So I'd appreciate it if you'd look in and make sure everything is all right."

"I'm certain that will be no imposition at all," Mrs. Webbly said.

"You're very kind. There's one other thing. She's extremely self-conscious about her condition and would resent it if she knew she was being looked after, so could you please—"

"I'll be *very* discreet, Mr. Novotny. Rest assured."

They were interrupted by footsteps on the runner and Merry's knock on the open door.

"I thought you'd gone without me, Ivan," she said. "Oh, hello, Mrs. Webbly. I hope my husband hasn't been boring you with his stories. I know how hard it can be to get him to stop talking about himself."

"You're a lucky woman, Mrs. Novotny, having such a conversationalist for a husband. I don't find his stories boring at all."

"What was that about?" Merry asked as they waited on the porch for a cab.

"I thought if I got friendly with the old bat, she'd take some of the starch out of our sheets."

"Really, Ivan, you amaze me. What were you talking about?"

"Nothing much. She told me all about the late Mr. Webbly, and I told her about my experiences in the war."

"What war? Were you in Vietnam?"

"No. The Peloponnesian War. I used to do stunts for Paramount."

They went to Miami Beach, to walk along Collins Avenue past doddering Art Deco hotels that were mausoleums for a dead era and a dying generation. Farther downtown blocks of tiled Spanish houses gave way to a faded commercial section of pawnshops and cheap hotels, walk-in law offices, and storefront chapels. As they waited for a light to change, Norodny frowned and said, "You could grow old here and never see a really crummy day."

"What's bad about that?"

"Makes me feel guilty. I haven't done a stitch of work in weeks."

She looked down the side street toward the ocean. An offshore breeze was grouping dark clouds in an ominous sky. "Cheer up," she said. "I think your luck's about to change."

"I don't believe in luck," he said, as if he'd been insulted. "It's a lot of bunk. So's fate. I don't see how any intelligent person can believe in them."

"You found me. . . ."

"I made that happen. I make my own luck."

"The way you came up with a room in Quebec?"

"The way I earn my living." They went across the street. "Most investors will tell you the commodities market is a crapshoot. The good ones know better."

"A little luck couldn't hurt."

"I'd rather be good than lucky," he told her. "And when it comes to the market, I'm very good. If you're sitting on a few dollars you don't need right now, you might let me show you how good."

"Nothing personal," she said, glancing under a pawnshop's gray-and-gold awning, "but there's my idea of a sound investment."

"Trombones?"

"Very funny. I was looking at that diamond brooch."

"Look again," he said, leading her to the window. "These are all cheap sparklers."

"Pretty, though, if you go for costume stuff."

"Do you?"

"Glitter hurts my eyes," she said.

"If you find a diamond you do like, point it out and it's yours."

"As an investment?"

"In us."

Merry looked at the window again, focusing on his reflection. "You're serious, aren't you?" she asked.

"I can hardly bring you back to L.A. without a ring."

"I have a ring. My mother's. Mrs. Webbly was admiring it when she let us have the room."

"Without a ring from me. My daughter would be scandalized if you just moved in on us."

"You have a daughter? Why didn't you tell me?"

"Don't you like little kids?" he asked.

"How little?"

"Eight."

"That's little. But, yes, I adore children."

"Then that's settled. Do you want a ring?"

"A ring would be nice. It's a husband I'm not sure about. When I left Philadelphia, all I thought I'd bring back was a camera from the duty-free shop. You have to give me some time to think about it."

"How much time? Sarah misses me."

"Why didn't you tell me you had a daughter?"

"Some women don't want to know from men with small children. I didn't want to frighten you away."

"I don't scare easily," Merry said, pulling his head down and kissing him. "And I do like diamonds, and children, and you."

"In that order?"

"The whole package," she said, kissing him again. "Especially you."

"Does that mean yes?"

"It means I'm weakening, in the heart if not the head."

She had always known there would be someone like this. Her generation had been so opposed to marriage that she'd come to consider it a form of treason. So she'd constructed a rational defense designed to fall before the man who'd simply sweep her off her feet. She felt full.

"With me it's the knees," he said. "Give me half a chance and I'll lose my nerve. So what are we waiting for?"

"*Right this minute*?"

"Why not? Is there someone you had your heart set on inviting?"

"Not expecially, but . . . but we don't even have the license."

"Worry about that later." He put his hands on her shoulders and steered her away from the window. "How about that chapel across the street?"

"Oh, no, no way. Plastic carnations clash with my dress. I don't mind rushing into things, just so long as they're done right."

"Next time we'll get it perfect."

"What next time?"

"In L.A., with my daughter as bridesmaid and all our friends at the reception. It'll be everything you could ask for in a big church wedding."

"So who needs out-of-town previews?"

"Now that I'm playing for keeps, I can't wait to make it legal. I'm very tradition-minded, you know."

"Yes," Merry said. "I see that."

Their finances dictated a modest engagement, an early movie, dinner, and dancing. At a crowded Coconut Grove disco Norodny threw out his back, and before the band came on, Merry went outside to look for a cab.

"I can't wait to get home," he announced at Mrs. Webbly's. "We'll plant ourselves in the desert till the dry heat bakes the soreness out of my bones."

"I'm not much of an outdoorswoman," she warned him. "Palm Springs is my kind of roughing it in the desert."

"You'd hate it."

"How do you know?" she asked.

"Ever been there?"

"No, but—"

"It's not for us. Phony bastards ruined it, fat-ass doctors and lawyers, the kind who get a hard-on knocking a golf ball around all day, drop a bundle on a house you couldn't give away so they can brag about the zip code."

"You certainly have a strong opinion on the subject."

When he gave her an exasperated look, she laughed and said, "Sounds good to me too."

"You're kidding, right?"

"Uh-uh, I told you I enjoy living well. Where's the fun in having money you can't show off?"

Why did he even listen? Palm Fucking Springs. He'd seen it on TV—Sinatra and that ex-president, the klutzy one, tooling around in a golf cart with Bob Hope, yukking at the old fart's lousy jokes. It made him want to puke.

He went to the door. "Let me run around the corner for some aspirin."

"Where, Ivan?" Digging in, not letting go. "Where's the fun?"

He turned around. He was trying not to yell. "In getting it."

"You know," she said, "before, when you hardly said a word about yourself, I couldn't get a handle on you."

"Now you can?"

"No," she said, smiling like it was a private joke. "Now that we're going to be married, I can't figure you out at all." She went across the room and threw her arms around his neck. "The funny thing is, it doesn't matter anymore."

It would, though; he was sure of it. "I have to run."

"You're not running anywhere," she told him. "I've got some painkillers. Maybe they'll help."

"I'll be right back," he promised, slipping out of her embrace. "And don't give up on tonight. I'm keeping my eyes open for a decent bottle of wine."

Mrs. Webbly intercepted him outside the dining room, where she was supervising the installation of a new pantry. "Will you be gone long, Mr. Novotny?" she asked.

"I hope not," he said.

"Whatever, you can rest your mind about Mrs. Novotny."

"Thank you, Mrs. Webbly. I can't begin to tell you how comfortable you've made our stay."

Mrs. Webbly's stomach was in half hitches before he was gone fifteen minutes. She positioned herself at the window and didn't look away except to glare at the clock. When the pounding in her arteries became more than she could stand, she scooped up some towels from the linen closet and carried them to the third floor. She stopped at the new couple's room and tilted an ear to the door. If anything was the matter inside, she wasn't going to find out like that, not with the water running. She shifted the bundle to her other arm and tapped lightly.

She knocked harder the second time and didn't let up until she heard Merry's "I'm coming, I'm coming." Her relief was tempered with pangs of embarrassment. She wished she could vanish down the stairs.

"Ivan, did you forget your key?" Merry called out.

"It's me, Mrs. Novotny, Mrs. Webbly."

The door opened halfway, and Merry squeezed into the hall. There was a circle of white foam around her lips, a toothbrush in her fingers. "Is something wrong, Mrs. Webbly?"

"I . . . I brought a fresh change of bath linen."

"You're very kind. It could have waited till morning."

"I know, I was just—"

"Did my husband tell you about the little flood we had?" Merry asked, wiping away the toothpaste with the back of her hand. "I'm so sorry. I can promise it won't happen again."

"Don't trouble yourself over it, Mrs. Novotny. I'm just glad everything is all right."

"All right?"

Solemnly Mrs. Webbly handed Merry the towels. She accepted them with a puzzled smile and was backing into the room when the brittle tread of new shoes sounded on the stairs.

"Ivan," Merry scolded as he came into the landing, "you shouldn't have bothered Mrs. Webbly at such a late hour."

"It's no bother at all," the old woman said. "And Mr.

Novotny, *anytime* you need something, please don't hesitate to ask."

"What was that about?" Norodny demanded when they were alone in the room.

"Mrs. Webbly brought fresh towels. It's almost ten o'clock. Really, Ivan, you shouldn't have asked her."

"Is that what she was doing? She caught me on the way out and wanted to know if we needed anything. I must have mentioned that we soaked the towels. I didn't expect her to bring new ones tonight."

"Well, I don't suppose it was such a terrible inconvenience," Merry finally decided. "We'll just have to watch what we say around her."

"Good idea," Norodny agreed.

6

Norodny's back went into spasms overnight, and neither of them got much sleep. At seven-thirty they gave up trying and took a bus into Miami. From the downtown air terminal they trudged to Western Union, where a clerk swore that a telegram sent anywhere in the East would arrive at its destination by ten.

"I want it on Mr. Dutton's desk when he comes to the office," Merry said to Norodny. "The sooner he gets my money off, the sooner we can be in California. How much should I ask for?"

"Everything."

"I can't get all of it, not under any circumstances."

"*Why, why not*?"

"Daddy wasn't especially convinced that I was going to make a responsible adult. His will stipulates that I don't receive the principal till I'm thirty."

"Then have Dutton send whatever's legally yours, say a few thousand by wire, to tide you over, and your bankbooks and negotiables by certified mail. You can transfer your accounts to my bank when we get to Los Angeles. No sense in having to fly to Philadelphia to visit your money."

"I suppose you're right. But I know Mr. Dutton's going to hit the roof."

* * *

There was a note in their box when they got back to Mrs. Webbly's: Merry had received a long-distance call while they were out and was requested to return it immediately. The number was a familiar one, with a Philadelphia area code.

"It's not even ten-thirty," Norodny said. "He doesn't waste time."

"Mr. Dutton is very efficient and reliable, exactly the man I'd want looking after *my* daughter's interests. I just wish he didn't keep such close tabs on mine. What should I tell him?"

"That you're a big girl, that you appreciate his concern, and that you want every cent you're entitled to. Don't make a stink over what you can't get and he'll cough up easy."

It wasn't quite that simple. As Norodny listened in on the extension with a hand clamped over the mouthpiece, Merry was reminded that under the terms of her trust she was allowed to draw up to thirty thousand dollars every twelve months. Already she had spent close to twenty-six thousand. Dutton wasn't obligated to let her have more and wasn't about to volunteer it, either.

"And who is this fellow you say you want to marry? How do you know he isn't some California gold digger?"

"Give me credit for a little good judgment," Merry said.

"Not until you've demonstrated some, young lady. If your father, bless his soul, had known of the harebrained stunts his estate would pay for, he would have left his fortune to the Nature Conservancy."

"I don't see it that way, Mr. Dutton. I'm sure he'd approve of everything I've done. He wasn't half the stuffed shirt you are."

"Perhaps you're right, Merry. Perhaps that's why he turned to me to manage his affairs when he was a young man. Still, the answer is no. Give me your address in Florida and you'll have your four thousand dollars by noon. As for the remainder, you'll be thirty in only six years, and then it's yours to do with as you see fit. Six years isn't a long time. And when you find that money waiting, your opinion of me will have risen in proportion with the principal."

Norodny didn't hang up until he heard Dutton break the connection. "Do you think he'll have it here today?"

"Absolutely," Merry said. "He may not approve of what I'm doing, but he follows his trusteeship scrupulously. If he refused to do something required of him under daddy's will, I could have him removed as executor."

He picked up the phone again and confirmed their flight. The instant he hung up, there was another call for Merry. Western Union wanted her to know that a draft in the sum of $4,150 was waiting in the Flagler Street office.

"Let's go for it now," she said. "I won't relax till I have that money in my hands."

At Norodny's urging she converted the entire amount to cash. They blew four hundred dollars on engagement presents for themselves—earrings for Merry, a digital watch for Norodny—and liked them so much that they wore them back to the guest house.

"Do you think we should tell Mrs. Webbly we're checking out?" Merry asked.

"No rush," he told her. "There could be a hurricane coming. Or an airline strike. The way things work out, both. Let's be sure we're on the plane before we give up the room."

"What do you want to do now?"

"You can start packing while I give these rags of mine a decent burial. Then we'll get ready for tonight."

He put his old clothes in a paper laundry bag, which he deposited in a garbage can in the yard. His knife went down a storm drain when he was certain no one was watching. Back upstairs, he found Merry in bra and panties sitting cross-legged on the floor.

"Lift your right leg over the left and push off with your hands and you'll be okay," he said.

"Shhh. I'm meditating."

"*You're what?*" The crap she expected him to put up with for a lousy four thousand bucks. He'd had it up to here.

Without looking at him she said, "I used to do it all the time. Meditating makes good experiences more intense."

"Then you're gonna love this," he told her, stripping off his shirt.

"Whatever it is—later. Give me fifteen minutes."

He went away, and gradually she realized that what was left of her concentration had been ruined by the sound of running water. He came back and stood over her, nude except for one of Mrs. Webbly's towels around his middle and her own pink shower cap pushed back on his head. "Time's up," he said, and carried her into the bathroom before she could uncross her legs.

Scalding billows rose from the tub, dulling the windows and beading into tears on the metal fixtures. Merry struggled for oxygen, her cheeks ripening as she wriggled out of her underwear. Norodny let her down in the water, shed his towel, and sat facing her. The wet heat pressed against her chest till she thought she was going to faint.

He was more aggressive than she had ever seen him, coming to her in such excitement that the water lapped over the sides. She was frightened by his touch, indignant when he forced her back violently, banging her head against the tub.

"Hey, we have the rest of our lives together, remember?"

If he heard, he didn't show it. His pale rump breached the surface like a small bifurcated whale, and she felt his pelvis grind against her and withdraw in frustration. Dutifully she rolled her hips. He came down heavily, so that she had to fight to keep her face out of the water.

"Ivan, don't be rough."

She considered raking him with her nails but didn't, afraid that it would only arouse him more. She kicked out her legs, and when they found the end of the tub, she was able to arch her back and raise her head a few inches. She remained like that, rigid, unmoving, unfeeling, until he was away from her.

"If you're planning to make that a habit, you can get yourself an inflatable doll," she said.

He lifted her ankle from the water, brushed it with his cheek, ran his lips along the inside of her leg. She leaned all the way back and rested the other leg on his hip. He felt so good when he was gentle. Just letting him touch her was almost more than she could stand.

"That's a lot better," she said. "Promise you'll always be this way."

She tucked a wet lock of hair under the shower cap. Her arms reached out to him. He put both her ankles around his waist and moved closer, hugging her softly, nibbling at the turquoise hoops in her ears. She relaxed completely. Her breath came in languorous sighs. When he felt the stiffness melt from her shoulders, he slid his hands to her face and pressed it under water.

He was amazed at her strength. Despite the fifty pounds he had on her, she bucked him off and kneed him in the stomach, where practiced muscles repelled the blow easily. As her face came out of the water he moved his hands to the top of her head and forced her down. Her fingernails clawed at his chest, tore the skin over his solar plexus, reached desperately for his crotch, tangled in the coarse hair.

She turned her head and pushed her face into the air, sucked at it until his hand came down, stopping her screams deep inside. She bit at his palm and worried the callused flesh. There was the salty taste of blood in the water as she went under again.

She seared her lungs on the soapy water. Unable to cough, she panicked. A reserve of strength fed on her terror, and she brought her leg up into his groin. He rolled off her with a grunt of real pain and backed out of the tub.

"You're crazy," she wheezed. "Out of your fucking mind."

She blinked the water from her eyes. Instead of a raging lunatic there was only the disinterested gaze of a man preoccupied with other things, as if he might be expecting an important phone call.

Making an umbrella of her arms, she scrambled to her feet. He swatted her down and she landed on her side. She kicked at him, but her legs were heavy and had no snap. When she poised the left, he swiped at it and caught her by the ankle. He pulled her close and she slid under again.

He shifted his grip to her feet and raised them over his head, held them there until fatigue began to drag them down. Then he dropped them. She hit the bottom hard, jellying in his hands. He put her legs in the water and flipped her on her back. With her eyes open she looked about the same. He pushed her head under and watched for bubbles. There weren't any. He climbed in the tub with her and let the warm water run against his quivering muscles.

When he was feeling better, he dried himself and tossed the towel in the hamper with her bra and panties. He arranged the body with care, dangling a leg and an arm over the edge of the tub and resting her head on the bottom. He went into the other room for a paper clip, which he used to scrape bits of his flesh from her nails. He spotted a fleck of blood on her cheek, touched it, and watched it float away. The skin beneath it was unbroken.

He pressed the stopper in the drain and lowered the water volume. Remembering the shower cap still on his head, he threw it into the tub. He gathered his clothes and got dressed, took the money from Merry's bag, and stuffed it in his jacket.

He slammed the door as hard as he could, rattling glass louvers all over the big house. Mrs. Webbly, looking extremely annoyed, was waiting on the first floor to see what the racket was about. With her were Edith and

Arlene, the maid. He stopped when he saw them and bent down to tie his shoelace.

"Lucky I didn't break my neck," he said. "Sorry about making so much noise."

"You have to be more careful," Arlene said.

"You can never be too careful." He was looking at Mrs. Webbly, who nodded conspiratorially. "I won't be gone long," he told her.

It was raining again, coming down hard, a rare winter storm. He found a movie theater and paid for a ticket without bothering to see what was playing. He was interested more in the snack bar. He bought a large bucket of popcorn and a box of chocolate-covered raisins and went back for a hot dog and two Cokes. He scarcely noticed the screen. The picture was a musical, something about a young Swede and his brothers and the tropical island where they were shipwrecked and the brown-eyed girls who spent days weaving nets on the beach. A better story was the one coming together in his head, the tearjerker that was going to get him Merry's inheritance. After he finished the hot dog he dozed off.

Mrs. Webbly hadn't gotten over the embarrassment of the last time she had burst in on that nice Mrs. Novotny. She had no intention of repeating the unfortunate experience. On the other hand, she had given her promise to look in on her and couldn't go back on it. What if the poor woman should have a seizure and need help? She'd never forget how she had felt when she saw the foam around her mouth, and the relief when she realized that it was toothpaste.

When forty-five minutes went by with no sign of Mr. Novotny, she decided that the third-floor hall needed cleaning and that Arlene was too busy to bother. It had been years since she'd used the carpet sweeper, and she was surprised at how heavy it had gotten. She pushed it along the runner outside the Novotnys' door and let the murmur of running water settle her jagged nerves. On the way downstairs she ran into the maid carrying the dinner dishes from Mr. Bridgeton's room.

"Arlene, I left the carpet sweeper on the third floor," she said. "Will you put it back in the broom closet when you have a moment?"

"The carpet sweeper, ma'am? I vacuumed there this morning."

She went into the parlor to watch television, taking her usual place on the settee beside Mr. Bridgeton's easy chair. The situation comedy about an immigrant family in proper, turn-of-the-century Boston did little to soothe her. She couldn't understand most of the characters and didn't care for those she did. It was a shame Mr. Bridgeton wasn't there to translate for her, but he hadn't been feeling up to par and was keeping to his room. She had given up on making sense of the show when Arlene came in and whispered, "Mr. Bridgeton says there's a big puddle of water in his bathroom."

"Trouble with the toilet again?"

"No, ma'am, he says it's dripping down from the light fixture in the ceiling. There must be a flood upstairs."

"Oh, my goodness, that's the Novotnys' room."

With Arlene at her heels she ran to the third floor and beat on the couple's door. "Mrs. Novotny . . . Mrs. Novotny. Oh, why doesn't she answer?"

"She's in the bathroom," Arlene said. "I can hear the water running."

"Go downstairs and get my keys. They're on the hook behind the desk."

"She'll hear us if we keep knocking. Here, let me try."

"Do as I say," Mrs. Webbly snapped at her. "Hurry."

Arlene came back, trailed by Edith and one of the retired couples. Soon they were joined by Mr. Bridgeton, looking very out of sorts.

"Those young jerks went out and left the water running," he remarked to no one in particular.

Mrs. Webbly was having a hard time fitting the key in the door. Steadying herself with deep breaths, she twisted the knob. Hot, sticky air poured into the hall. Arlene went inside with her and raised a window.

"She must still be in the tub," Arlene said. "And she must be drunk to let the water run like that."

The others kept a respectful distance behind as Mrs. Webbly rapped on the bathroom door. "Mrs. Novotny, is everything all right? Mrs. Novotny?" She turned helplessly to Mr. Bridgeton. "Oh, what's wrong in there? Now look the other way."

She opened the door and shut it quickly behind her, damming a thin sheet of water that spilled over the step. After a few seconds Arlene went in after her. She emerged, ashen-faced, almost at once.

"Quick, someone call a doctor," she pleaded.

"What's the matter?" Mr. Bridgeton asked.

"Mrs. Webbly's passed out and cracked her head on the floor. She's bleeding badly."

"What about the other woman? What the hell is she doing in there?"

"She's dead," Arlene cried. "Drowned in the tub."

7

Dr. McNab, who lived around the corner and had been Mrs. Webbly's physician for thirty years, came running to the guest house without his galoshes or hat. After a hurried examination of both women he phoned for two ambulances. Mrs. Webbly was put aboard the first to arrive, which maintained radio contact with the Laxahatchee Medical Center. En route, her vital signs were monitored by a resident cardiologist who made a diagnosis of acute coronary infarction and relayed instructions to the paramedics. An examining table was waiting at the emergency room entrance. Nitroglycerin was administered, an intravenous unit installed in her arm and an oxygen tube in her nose, her head was stitched, and she was wheeled to the intensive care ward in guarded condition.

The driver of the other ambulance was ordered to park beside a fire hydrant. As was the case in all instances of unattended death, Merry's body could not be moved until it had been viewed by a pathologist. Dr. Daisy Riley, the thirty-two-year-old medical examiner for Laxahatchee County, was on the scene within half an hour. She went inside the bathroom, consulted with Dr. McNab (who had been her epidemiology professor at South Florida Medical College in Palm Beach), inspected the body again, and called the morgue in Glades City to reserve a slab for the autopsy.

The divorced mother of three sons, she looked to Dr. McNab years younger than when she had been his student. This they both attributed to the braces she had installed on her teeth with the first money she saved and which now rested with her wedding ring in a jewelry box beside her bed. In her trademark lizard-skin cowboy boots, she was a strikingly tall woman lacking only the excruciatingly high cheekbones of professional beauty.

"Such a waste," Dr. McNab said. "It's enough to break your heart."

"She was very pretty," the ME said.

"She was . . . but what I'm talking about, Daisy, is four years of backbreaking work at medical school—and most of it mine. The kind of doctoring you're capable of doesn't do her any good. People need your talents, not the lab."

"Dr. McNab—"

"All right, all right. I didn't say a thing."

Dr. Riley went back to the phone. Her call, logged in at the public safety building, brought Buck White to the guest house less than twenty minutes later.

"Pleasant evenin'," he said, and shook the rain from his jacket. He tipped his hat to Dr. McNab and shook the ME's hand, held it in both of his, reluctant to let go. Once they'd spent a cautious weekend at a Naples motel appraising a future together, stockpiling reserves of an intimacy they'd never share again. "Anyone we know?"

"Not likely," Dr. Riley told him. "Evidently the girl drowned and came here to do it. What led up to it is impossible to say right now, but there are no superficial indications of foul play. The problem is that I can't in good conscience sign a certificate of death without her medical history or a postmortem."

White moved past her into the bathroom, revulsion tugging at the brittle edge of his impassivity. The girl lay on her back in eight inches of water, her shoulders curved inward against the narrow bottom of the tub. A dull film had collected over her eyes, which seemed fixed on the doorway where he stood. He came near, lowered the lids with his fingers, and retreated. She was an attractive girl, which made it that much worse. He was trying not to notice.

He remembered a time when he almost relished such work. What passed for carnage in Laxahatchee County reminded him of nothing so much as what his Army medic buddies in Vietnam had referred to as nicks and scrapes, acceptable losses. By the time he'd made chief deputy, his pre-war sensibilities had been restored, and to keep from going soft he made a point of visiting all scenes of premature death and bloodletting. It never ceased to amaze him that he had campaigned hard for the sheriff's office, that a whim of an exceedingly fickle electorate was forever ruining his digestion.

He heard Dr. Riley say, "The maid tells me Mrs. Novotny and her husband have been staying here about a week. He stepped out shortly before she died. I thought you'd want to talk with him when he returns. Dr. McNab will help me break the news."

"With smelling salts in both hands," White muttered. "I'm glad you're here, Daisy," he said. "Breaking the news is one part of the job I've got no heart for, that and attending at autopsies."

He was interrupted by Arlene. "Mr. Novotny's just come back," she said. "I told him there'd been an accident and he couldn't go to his room yet. Should I let him up?"

"No, I'll go downstairs with Dr. Riley and speak to him," Dr. McNab said. "Sheriff, wait here if you don't mind. We'll let you have him soon enough."

"Buck's got a point," Dr. Riley said in the hall. "If I went in for this sort of thing, I'd have studied for the clergy, not tortured myself on your finals."

A man combing dark, wet hair straight back from his

forehead met them on the second-floor landing, blocking their way.

"Mr. Novotny," the maid called down, "these are the doctors I was telling you about."

"What's this about Merry having an accident? Why can't I go up?"

"I'm afraid we have some awful news for you, Mr. Novotny," Dr. McNab began.

"Did she have another seizure? How bad was it?"

"Very bad, sir. Your wife is dead. It happened soon after you went out. We're sorry."

"What? What are you talking about? Let me see her!" He bulled through them and ran to the room. The door caught on the chain. "Let me in," he yelled. "I want to see Merry."

The doctors were beside him then. "Mr. Novotny, we found your wife in the bathtub and haven't moved the body yet," Dr. McNab said. "You should prepare yourself for—"

"I want to see her."

"Open up, Sheriff," Dr. McNab called out.

The chain rattled against the wood, and Norodny shouldered inside. As he stared into the tub his body began to shake. Dropping to his knees, he cradled Merry's head in his arms. "How could this happen? I was only gone a couple of hours. When I left, she was fine. She was going to take a bath. You're doctors—"

"We know very little at this point," Dr. McNab said.

"That's no answer."

"If you're feeling up to it," said Dr. Riley, "we have a few questions of our own about your wife's health. I'm Dr. Riley, this is Dr. McNab, and this is Sheriff White of Laxahatchee County."

"Sheriff . . . ?"

"The law in Florida specifies that an officer formally release the body for autopsy," Dr. Riley explained.

"I don't want anyone cutting Merry," Norodny said sharply.

"But, sir, we have to find the cause of death."

"I can tell you what killed her, and it's nothing you're going to see in an autopsy. Merry was epileptic. She had fits since she was a little girl. I told Mrs. Webbly about them, and she said she'd look in on her when I was out. Didn't she tell you that?"

"She can't," White said. "Her heart gave out when she found your wife, and she's in the hospital in very serious condition. It's too soon to say if she's going to make it."

"I'm sorry. It never occurred to me she would have to—"

"It's not your fault," Dr. McNab said.

"I can't . . . things are happening so fast. I—" He backed away, buckling as he moved toward the bed. His fall was broken by White, who helped him onto the mattress and put a pillow beneath his head.

"The poor man's overwrought," Dr. McNab said. "And who can blame him? I'll administer a sedative."

"No, no shots," Norodny said. "I don't want a shot."

"I'm not giving you an injection, Mr. Novotny. Just a pill, something to help calm you."

"I don't like pills. Can I have . . . I'd like a drink."

"I'll go look for the maid," Dr. McNab told the others. "I'm sure she knows where Mrs. Webbly keeps her liquor."

He came back with a bottle of brandy and a tumbler. Norodny drank off half an inch and then dangled his feet over the side of the bed. "Thank you, I feel better now. I'm sorry I made a scene."

"There's nothing to apologize for," Dr. Riley said. "If you're ready, we still have some questions about your wife."

"She wasn't my wife."

"How's that again?" White said.

"Not yet, anyway. She was my fiancée. We rushed things for Mrs. Webbly's benefit. We were going to be married this week in Los Angeles."

"You're from California?"

"That's right."

"The same sun shines on your beaches," White said harshly, watching for a reaction. The spouse, the boyfriend, was always a suspect. Always. "Florida's a ways to travel just to have it hang over the other shoulder."

"Coming here was Merry's idea. She's from Philadelphia."

Might as well have asked for the time. "And that's a ways to go on a date."

"It would have been," Norodny admitted. "That's one reason we decided so quickly to get married. We'd just met, while I was visiting back East."

"You originally from the East? That what you telling me?"

"May I?" Norodny took the bottle from Dr. McNab and poured more of the brandy. "What I was saying is that I hadn't known Merry a long time. I don't see what any of this has to do with where I'm from."

"Maybe it doesn't," White said. "Why did Miss Belson come to Florida?"

Dumb, backwoods sheriff had a lot to learn. He took another drink, a long one, and let himself relax. This wasn't going to be as bad as he'd thought. "She wouldn't try on a wedding gown without a perfect tan. How she looked was extremely important to her."

"You should have checked with the Weather Bureau first. The forecast is gloomy, with no end in sight."

"We knew that," Norodny said. "But Merry was a stubborn woman. She thought she could beat the odds."

White needed help, someone for a quick game of good cop–bad cop. A seasoned investigator like Alvorado. No . . . Alvorado always played the bad cop. "Did Miss Belson have anyone in south Florida, close friends or relatives?"

"No, but if you're determined to go ahead with the autopsy, I can tell you who to call in Philadelphia."

"That won't be necessary," Dr. Riley said. "We don't need permission."

"I thought—"

"But we do need your okay to inspect these rooms," White said.

"Why? What are you looking for?"

"Hard to say, till we find it."

"It's another formality," Dr. Riley explained. "Don't be alarmed. We may have to hold a coroner's inquest, and if Sheriff White can look around now, before anything is disturbed, it will save a lot of inconvenience later on. What do you say?"

"Well, I guess so."

"Won't take more than a few minutes," White said. He'd talk to Daisy later. The trick was in getting them worked up, not handing out comfort and assurances. He wanted to talk to her, anyway. "Stick around and watch."

"I'd rather not. I'd like to go out on the porch and breathe some fresh air. And I'd like to be by myself."

"It's up to you."

After he'd gone, White asked, "What do you make of him?"

"You're the sheriff," Dr. Riley said. "All I can tell you is, there's nothing to contradict his claim that the girl died accidentally. No marks on the body, no scratches on his face from a struggle. And if epilepsy was a contributing factor, forget about the postmortem. That doesn't come out under the microscope."

"Neither does the truth."

"Something bothering you about what he said?"

"It's not the 'what' so much as the 'how,'" White answered. "When Irene died, I put my fist through two windshields, ran in every drunk and hooker, every poor bastard going two miles over the speed limit. If this joker was showing all the grief he had for the girl, there wasn't enough love behind it to let a marriage take."

"Too bad we can't test for that before we give out

wedding licenses, the way they do at the Motor Vehicles Bureau." She was grinning at White, who didn't know what to make of her just then. "Make them come back every three years for a renewal."

"And let the sheriff's department ticket violators," Dr. McNab cut in. "Not a bad idea, perhaps, but not a reasonable one. And neither is suspecting a man of a crime because he fails to show the requisite tears."

"Don't bet on it," White said. "Doesn't it strike you as awful convenient that the one person who can say if the girl really was epileptic is more dead than alive, herself?"

"He couldn't have planned Mrs. Webbly's heart attack," Dr. Riley said. "I'll confess it gave me a start when he said they weren't married, but I don't imagine this is the sort of establishment that encourages unwed couples to check in."

"I can't see what he'd hope to gain by posing as her husband, except the opportunity to share this bed," Dr. McNab said. "Can you?"

"Give me time."

"What do you propose to do now?"

"I'll advise the Florida Department of Law Enforcement of what we have here and put in for techs. Not likely they'll send any, so I've requested Rutledge from headquarters. He's a decent photographer when he wants to be, and he'll snap the body before we turn it over to you. After that I'll have a look around the apartment."

Chief Deputy Moses A. "Ma" Rutledge, blow-dried, boyishly slim, and New Jersey–born, was in and out of the bathroom in ten minutes. Though he'd been no closer to combat than a year with the Rutgers University Pershing Rifles, he'd fit himself neatly into the military mold White had rejected. There was a razor crease in his uniform trousers and a spit shine on his shoes. His cap was shaped painstakingly into a high saddle. "Great legs," he said, shaking his head. "Great everything." Because his boss gathered little insight from his observations, he confided them to the medical examiner. "It's a crying shame."

Daisy Riley let her eyes roll into her head. On the day the court had granted her interlocutory decree, she had accepted a date with Rutledge. She had been hungry for the deputy from the first time she noticed him, as he was pummeling a couple of drunks who had set fire to the swings in the crowded playground of the Laxahatchee Elementary School where her youngest was a second-grader. Expectations aroused by his generous smile, the easy lope of the natural athlete had weighed in no small part on her decision to finally leave her husband. On their date he took her to a drive-in movie in a customized van with a fur-upholstered water bed reflected in the mirrored ceiling. She tried not to let it interfere with her assessment of him as a talented cop.

"I've always suspected that you were a necrophile," she said.

"Yeah, I'm getting ready to come out of the closet."

"I'll warn Buck. Next time we don't leave you alone with a stiff."

"What happened to my girlfriend?"

"Bad luck," she told him. "And a touch of epilepsy. Buck won't buy it. He wants to make a federal case."

"He always does, ever since—"

"But this time he's sniffing around the wrong tree."

He stepped back into the bathroom and shut off the light, pocketed the film. "What makes you say that?"

"Don't take it personally, Ma," she said over his shoulder, "but it's not that easy to subdue a healthy, full-grown woman."

"So it wasn't easy."

"It never happened. Neither one of them has the battle scars."

"He couldn't have just pushed her head under water?"

"Did you see her nails? She'd have clawed the stuffing out of him."

"You're in the wrong racket, Daisy. You'd make a good cop."

"Maybe I already have."

"Huh?" He put a new roll of film in the camera. "Damn accidents . . . Next Buck'll want a paparazzo on hand for every parking ticket. Well, got to run. If I don't have these at the drugstore by five, *Playboy* will be on my back all week."

"You're awful," the medical examiner said.

And meant it.

The search of the rooms, conducted around a procession of morgue attendants, turned up a vial of yellow pills, a receipt from Neiman-Marcus for more than four hundred dollars, and little else.

"Been shopping?" White asked when Norodny came back upstairs after the body had been wheeled out.

"Uh-huh. Merry had a good eye for clothes. She was fussy about the way both of us looked. She picked out the suit I have on now. I was going to wear it to our wedding."

"Tell me what these pills are? I found them in Miss Belson's purse."

"It's the first I've seen of them," Norodny said. "Is the bottle from a Philadelphia pharmacy?"

White squinted at the label behind the dark plastic. "Yes it is. You don't mind if I hang on to these? Dr. Riley will be interested. Other than that, I want to offer my condolences and also my thanks for your cooperation. Not likely we'll be bothering you again, but it'd be appreciated if you kept a short halter till the autopsy."

"I'm not going anywhere till your coroner answers a few questions of my own."

"Where will you be staying, the Holiday Inn?"

"I'm paid up here for the next few days," Norodny said.

"Here . . . ? Well, just so long as I know where to reach you."

* * *

"Heartless son of a bitch," White said as he showed Dr. Riley the pills. "I'd sooner bed down in a gator hole than in the rooms where my girl died."

The autopsy performed overnight in the basement morgue of the Laxahatchee Medical Center produced no surprises. At the time of her death, Dr. Riley found, Merry Belson was not under the influence of alcohol or drugs, although there was a trace of Ativan, a muscle relaxant, in her bloodstream. Nor was she pregnant or had a recent abortion. The hyoid bone in her larynx was undamaged, eliminating the possibility of strangulation. A search for epidermal matter beneath her fingernails proved negative. There were no cuts or abrasions on the body; a slight bruise on the back of the head seemed the result of a muscle spasm during the seizure that took her life. The blood chloride levels on the right and left chambers of the heart were unequal, indicating that she still was breathing when she went into the water and dictating the inevitable conclusion of death by accidental drowning. All that remained in the way of an official ruling was the receipt of a medical report from her doctor in Philadelphia.

The boys hadn't gotten up yet when White reached for the phone on another rainy morning.

"I'm sorry to wake you like this," Dr. McNab said, "but I was sure you'd want to know that Mrs. Webbly came around late last night and is going to be all right. As her personal physician, I was called to the hospital by the cardiologist. In the time I was allowed with her, she spoke of little else than the Novotny couple. She said Mr. Novotny confided that his wife suffered from seizures and asked her to keep an eye on the young woman when he wasn't around."

"Did you tell Daisy?"

"I did. She was planning to send for the girl's health record before issuing a statement. But after hearing what

Mrs. Webbly had to say, she didn't feel that the trouble and expense were justified. She ruled it an accident and recommended that there be no coroner's inquest."

"Damn it, I wish she'd spoken to me first."

"I doubt you could have changed her mind. She's a fine doctor but the victim of her own conceit." Dr. McNab laughed. "She doesn't think very highly of anyone's opinion unless he has half a dozen initials coming after his name. Or hadn't you noticed?"

No, he hadn't. "The way I feel about someone's who doesn't have Officer or Deputy come before it."

"What I'm trying to say is, even if there were no history of epilepsy, there wasn't a mark on her. How do you go about suggesting possible homicide when you haven't the faintest idea of how the girl was killed? He didn't pour the bathwater up her nose."

"What do you think, Dr. McNab? What's your personal feeling on this?"

"That it's always in poor taste to contradict a colleague."

"Is that your professional point of view too?"

"Quite the opposite," Dr. McNab said. "In objective diagnosis there are no tools I value more than an informed second opinion and a feeling in my belly that won't go away."

8

"Catching up on your reading?" White asked as he came into the room.

"Oh, this," Norodny said sheepishly, tossing the skin magazine on top of the others spread over the bed. "Not really. I was looking at the cartoons."

"That's what I hand the old lady when she finds me with one. Makes me feel like I got caught with my fingers in the cookie jar."

"I know what you mean." Norodny laughed.

"Oh?"

"You said you had some news for me."

"*Good* news," White said. "First of all, you'll want to know that the doctors say Mrs. Webbly is going to be fine. She regained consciousness last night, and the outlook for recovery is excellent, I'm told."

"That's great. I felt more than a little responsible."

"Don't let it eat you up inside. Dr. McNab told me her arteries were so clogged and brittle, a heart attack was only a matter of time. If it hadn't been finding your . . . well, it would have been something else."

"Is there anything new on when the autopsy will be performed?"

"It's done. Dr. Riley took charge personally and ruled Miss Belson's death an accident. There's not going to be an inquest."

"Does that mean I can leave?"

"Anytime you like." Choking on the words.

"That's a relief," Norodny said. "These have been twenty-four rough hours, hanging around with nothing to do but think of Merry and wonder if I'd have to go to court. I never considered this part of the world unfriendly territory till I realized that I might be involved with the law. It wasn't the most comfortable feeling."

"You've been here before? You didn't mention that."

"No . . . what I meant is that getting involved in police business isn't my idea of a good time."

"It's not mine, either."

"Oh?"

"You'll be heading back to California now?" White asked.

"As soon as I've made arrangements for Merry's body to be sent home."

"That's been taken care of. Dr. Riley contacted Miss Belson's legal adviser, and he insisted on handling everything, himself."

"Then I'll fly to Philadelphia for the funeral. You know, I still can't accept that she's dead."

"I understand," White said, looking at the magazines on the bed.

At the end of an awkward silence Norodny stuck out his hand. "Well, Sheriff—"

"One more thing. On the chance that we want to talk to you again, would it be asking too much for your address and phone number in Los Angeles?"

"Not at all. Let me write it down."

He accepted a pen from White and looked around the room for a piece of paper. Then he tore out the centerfold from an open magazine and wrote a few words where the suntan ended on a girl clad only in a cowboy hat and spurs.

"You'd better copy it somewhere first chance you get. You don't want to catch any flak from your wife."

"Sure don't," White said, and shook his hand.

* * *

"That miserable slime," White growled. "His girlfriend isn't buried yet, and he's slobbering over a mountain of stroke books."

"You know how it is with some men," Rutledge answered, without looking to see where his words went. "When things go bad, they can't stop drinking. With others it's dope. Then there's those of us that have to have a woman." He sat on a wooden bench with his cartridge belt across his lap, wetting a soft rag in sweet-smelling gun oil and rubbing it lovingly against the blue steel barrel of his service revolver, a .32 Smith and Wesson Chief's Special. "Can't blame him for fantasizing, even if it does seem early."

"I'm not so sure," White said.

"You can't, not until you get some laws against bad taste."

As Norodny had suggested, White wrote the address and phone number on a sheet of paper. Dropping the centerfold in a brown envelope, he asked the police operator for a long-distance line and dialed the Los Angeles exchange. He let it ring a dozen times before hanging up.

"What did you expect?" Rutledge asked. "If Norodny is here in Florida, he can hardly be home to answer the phone."

"What I expected," White told him, "was the monkey house at the L.A. Zoo."

Because the cheap rooms at the Mar-A-Lago Hotel had no phone, Norodny spent the morning shooing anyone with a quarter from the booth in the lobby while he waited for Philadelphia to return his call. He was inspecting a takeout menu from the coffee shop when it finally came.

"My secretary informs me that you called at a few minutes past nine," Dutton told him. "I'm sorry to have kept you waiting. I don't often come to the office this late, but as you know, today was Merry's funeral."

"I didn't know. Nobody told me anything," Norodny said. "The body was practically stolen from under my nose, which is a pretty shabby way to treat your client's husband."

"Her husband? I was under the impression that she died before you could be married."

"You were under the wrong impression. There was a wedding three days before the accident."

"Mr. Novotny, I'm sorry. I spoke at length with a Dr. Riley, who assured me that Merry was still single at the time of her death."

"She knew as much as you, not a goddamn thing."

"You have my heartfelt apology. Had I been aware that Merry went through with a ceremony, of course I would have left everything up to you."

"Go easy on me, Mr. Dutton," Norodny said in a softer voice. "It hasn't been fun these last few days. Losing Merry was only the worst part. The police wouldn't release the body without an autopsy, and I went nearly insane making funeral arrangements. Do you have any idea what it's like trying to buy a grave site in Los Angeles? Then there was the death notice the papers printed while they were still running our wedding announcement, and then telling about it to two kids who thought I was bringing home their new mom. When I learned she'd been brought to Pennsylvania, I became physically ill."

"I did what I thought was right. She's buried beside her father and mother in the family plot in Rosemont. Will you be coming to visit the grave?"

"As quickly as I can straighten out my affairs in Florida," Norodny said. "I'd like to meet Merry's family."

"They're anxious to meet you too. They have many questions about how she died. We all do."

He looked at the menu again and settled on the tuna melt. "I thought you spoke with the sheriff here."

"Yes," Dutton said. "And, like the medical examiner, he said something about an epileptic incident. I find that very disturbing. There's no history of epilepsy among the Belsons."

"Seizures," Norodny corrected him. "She had at least three of them in Florida, always in hot, hot weather. I may have used the word *epilepsy* to try to explain them. They were very powerful, very frightening. Merry occasionally fooled around with recreational drugs, you know. I didn't say anything to the police."

"I'd like to hear about that too."

"Why don't we plan a meeting at your office for Friday morning? There's also the matter of some property of mine that you're holding."

"I'm afraid I don't know what you're talking about," Dutton said.

"Merry's estate. As her heir, I'd like to assume control over my late wife's investments."

"Aren't you being premature? The will hasn't been probated yet. In fact, we haven't found one. My feeling is that Merry died intestate."

"You might as well stop looking. Her marriage makes her old will obsolete."

"Not under Pennsylvania law," Dutton said, "especially not when death terminates a union of such short duration. The courts can be very arbitrary about these things. Merry's estate may be in litigation for years."

"That isn't what my lawyers tell me. They say the issue is cut-and-dried, unless someone goes out of their way to put up obstacles." He waved the menu at a waitress and pointed inside when she came by. "You'd be saving both of us a lot of time and expense if you'd try to speed up the process instead of impeding it."

"Don't tell me how to run my practice, Mr. Novotny."

"I'm only trying to say what I think is fair. We went through a substantial chunk of my savings on our honeymoon. I'm sure you know Merry was a high liver, and now I—"

"You want to be reimbursed, is that it?"

"I just want what's mine."

"Mr. Novotny, if I were you, I'd resign myself to a long wait. I didn't like the appearance of this courtship from the start, and I like your money-grubbing less. If you're going to contest my execution of the estate, be prepared to present any new will and your marriage license as well."

"Merry didn't have a chance to change her will," he said. "So what? You know how she felt. You're morally obligated to turn over that money."

"As for my obligations, I have only one—to see to it that her cousins receive the proceeds from her trust."

Norodny slid the door shut. "The courts can be a double-edged sword," he warned in a loud voice. "Merry's cousins will be collecting social security before I drop my claim, unless you stop being a horse's ass long enough to cut a deal that makes everybody happy."

"I'll see you in probate court," Dutton said. "And in criminal court, if you're determined to fight this to the end. Let me tell you that you'll receive not one red cent of Merry's without a police investigation into her death."

"There was an investigation here, and the finding was no foul play. You can't bluff me."

"If you think I'm bluffing, come to Philadelphia. I'm sure I can use my influence to empanel a grand jury to reopen the case. After that we can discuss your claim to the estate. And now, Mr. Novotny, I'm a very busy man, so if you'll excuse me . . ."

"We'll deal, Dutton—" he said, before the crash of the receiver cut him off.

Dutton's second call to Florida, to Laxahatchee sheriff's headquarters, was routed to Rutledge's desk. White was peeling apart a brown bag when the phone started ringing. He jammed a thin sandwich between his teeth and hurried over to get it.

"Sheriff White?" Dutton began. "I just spoke with Ivan Novotny again, and if you had any doubts before that the man was a fortune hunter, you can forget them now."

"I didn't," White said. "What'd he tell you?"

"That he married Merry, after all, and is entitled to her inheritance."

"Wouldn't surprise me if he said they had triplets. Did you ask him why he changed his tune?"

"I didn't see the use. He'd have had an answer, I'm sure. Two or three of them."

"Yeah, and sometimes he gets them straight. Is he going to receive any part of the estate?"

"Not if I have anything to say about it. There's something bizarre about the man, how his mood shifts with his story, as bizarre as Merry had been acting since she met him. I'm sure you're right about his having something to do with her death."

"Where is he now?" White asked.

"Still in your area. I tried goading him into a trip to Philadelphia where I can have him clapped in jail for as long as it takes to complete an investigation at our end. I don't suppose he'll go for it, but you never know. I don't have to tell you how often greed makes men their own worst enemy."

"I think it already has."

Rutledge came back from lunch early, circling the office till White put down the receiver and vacated his chair.

"That was Dutton. He says Novotny's been making a pitch for the girl's money, lying through his teeth about everything."

"So what else is new?" the deputy asked. "Did you get anything you could use to change Daisy's mind?"

"Ever tried that?" While Rutledge was deciding how to answer, White said, "You have any idea what it takes for permission to exhume a body? The Department of Law Enforcement would have to make a formal request to the attorney general, who'd have to contact the authorities in Pennsylvania."

"Couldn't the inquest be held without the corpse?"

"Yeah, on a shitload of fresh evidence."

When White came in the next evening, there was a note on his desk asking him to contact Officer Pooler in the records room.

"L.A. cops responded to your query on Ivan Novotny," Pooler told him.

He was a fat man in a wheelchair, a Canadian who had fought in Vietnam with the Americans and paid for the privilege with his legs. White, who had been wounded beside him at a fire base in the Central Highlands, had lobbied hard for the special ordinance of the county government, which enabled him to join the force. His entry-level salary paid for the department's most diligent officer, and he was White's best friend in uniform, someone to listen to when the conversation turned away from Willie Nelson and the Talladega 500. The ordinance prohibited his receiving a promotion or raise.

"What do they say?" White asked.

"Nothing. They have no record for any Novotny, and there's no listing in the phone book. The number doesn't check out, either."

"Did they visit the address we gave them?"

"They couldn't. It doesn't exist."

"He shouldn't be hard to find," White said grimly. "Just alert the hospitals to keep an eye out for anyone laughing himself to death. I feel like the biggest sap of all time for letting him slip away so easy."

"Cheer up, Sheriff, it wasn't your fault. And if it's some consolation, I think it's time to try Tallahassee again. You shouldn't have as much trouble getting what you want from the DLE."

Over the next several days White threw the meager weight of his office into a campaign for permission to reopen the case. Florida Department of Law Enforcement brass, eager to get him off their backs, dispatched a team of crime-scene technicians from Tallahassee. White met their plane and drove them to Mrs. Webbly's where Arlene informed them that in the week since Merry's death two couples had checked in and out of the Novotnys' rooms.

"You won't find anything," she warned. "I cleaned that suite myself."

"Just the same, we'd like a look around," White told her.

"Help yourselves. But I'm telling you, you're wasting your time."

Then men from Tallahassee spent an hour and a half inside, dusting every hard surface for fingerprints, filling tiny glassine bags with hard-won mounds of grime. When they were done, they followed White downstairs.

"Quite a job you do," one of the techs told Arlene. "There wasn't so much as a smudged print or a strand of hair. If I'm ever in the market for someone to sterilize my place, I'll call you first."

"So that's where it stands," White said. "We don't know who he is or where he's gone, or where to start looking next."

"Why not drop the whole thing?" Rutledge asked.

"Don't tempt me."

"Forget about it for a while. It hardly seems fair that when the tourists knock each other off, we're the ones who have to pick up the pieces."

"We can't be sure he is from out of state. Shit, we can't be sure of anything."

"What you do, then," Rutledge said, "is sit tight. Give 'em enough rope and they always—"

"Whoever said that first ought to be strung up from the top shelf of the records room. Ever figure out how many unsolveds there are in the state each year? Has to be hundreds. Who knows how many more when you consider ones like this that go down as accidents. I *can't* sit tight. There's got to be something to do."

"Well, why don't we collate the evidence we do have?"

White drummed his fingers on the phone. "What the hell," he said after a while. "Give me a manila folder."

He typed a label, pasted it on the flap, and went through his desk for something to put inside. He found a copy of the autopsy report, Rutledge's photos of the body, notes on his talks with Drs. McNab and Riley and Mr. Dutton. "I thought there was more."

"Didn't you have an envelope somewhere?"

"I was keeping it in my top drawer," White remembered, "and then I put it in the evidence locker."

He nudged the rusty tumblers on a padlock that sealed a dented steel cubicle. His reward was a brown envelope. He swept out the centerfold and ruefully examined the address and phone number.

"That all of it?" Rutledge asked.

"Just a lousy sample of his handwriting and his taste in women," White said. "Hold on! What am I saying?"

He dropped the paper as if it were on fire. "I think we have something for the fingerprint men, after all."

"His name's Norodny, Francis Alfred Norodny, which should tell you why he calls himself Ivan. Look here, Ma," White said, "he's got the busiest rap sheet I've seen on a white boy, most of it for hurting women. There's enough aliases to fill a phone directory."

Out of the corner of one eye Rutledge saw their lunch on its way. He rolled the printout from the National Crime Information Center into a tight cylinder and passed it back across the table, dabbed at his knife and fork with a paper napkin, and then put them down beside the fried chicken he would eat with his fingers. He said, "If we're talking about rape, we can get a warrant for failing to register as a sex offender. He was here long enough."

"There's some stat rape," White said, opening the scroll

and reading down three inches. "That was his game as a juvenile, when all it cost was a notation on his record. He gave it up by the time he got to Cornell. No more need to push, I guess."

"Cornell? That's not exactly the school of hard knocks."

"He spent three years there," White said, uncurling some more of the printout. "An economics major. Then he transferred down the road to Attica U, graduating with the class of seventy-four, in fraud, a two-year degree. There's also Rahway, New Jersey, grand larceny in 1977. Next year he was back at Attica for some graduate work, forging and uttering, three counts. He likes to marry women, or promise to, and take them for whatever they have. But his last beef, up in Canada, was for strong-arm robbery and assault."

"Rough stuff like that's way out of line for a bunco artist."

"This isn't: His second time around at Attica, he cried stomachache till he was sent to the infirmary. Someone left him alone for a couple of minutes and he found a pint of whole blood in a refrigerator and gulped it down. When the doctor told him to open wide, he puked it in her lap. She couldn't get him to a hospital fast enough. That night it was bed sheets out the window."

"A Cornell man," Rutledge said, toying with the chicken. "It's a fucking disgrace. My sister applied to Cornell. She didn't go. The family couldn't afford it."

"His could," White said. "His mother's got *beaucoup* bucks." He pronounced it *bookoop*. "They're in the market and in shipping and in hardware and plumbing supplies."

"And he makes a career out of pulling crap like this? He must be out of his skull."

"Just difficult, according to the shrinks who saw him in stir. 'Grounded in reality with above-average intelligence.' That's what they say at Rahway. The verdict in New York is 'Noncertifiable despite severe sociopathic disorder.'"

"Meaning what?" Rutledge asked. "He's only in it for the money?"

"What he'd like to believe," White said. "Probably has a real high opinion of himself. His kind usually does. Hell, he knows he's not loony, not really. How's he admit the money's just an excuse?"

"So he's your regular boy next door who's lost his conscience," Rutledge said. "Or never had one."

"And now mine's not gonna give me any peace till I see the son of a bitch in Raiford. Listen, Ma, I want you to start bugging Tallahassee again. I'll alert the NCIC. If he pops up anywhere, we ought to hear about it soon enough."

"We still don't have a warrant. What do we tell them to hold him for?"

White dumped two sugars in his coffee and brought the cup to his lips. Then he lowered it. "Capital offense," he said. "Disturbing the peace of my mind."

He told the driver to keep the meter running. It had rained every day for a week, and the grounds keeper hadn't sanded the lanes. He moved among the headstones studying the inscriptions, stopping from time to time to scribble a few words in a child's notebook. When he was done, he trudged back through the lonely rows and rode over the bay to his hotel.

Behind a portable typewriter he glanced at the first notation. Albert David Morrison: B 8 26 52 Vero Beach, Fla. D 1 19 53. With two fingers he pecked out a letter whose last paragraph read:

> *Last week my home was seriously damaged in a fire, and all my personal documents including my Social Security card, army discharge papers, driver's license, and birth certificate were destroyed. I am writing today to all the proper agencies and would appreciate it very much if you will send a new copy*

of my birth certificate to my family's temporary residence, Room 657 of the Mar-A-Lago Hotel in Miami Beach.

Sincerely,
Albert David Morrison

He tried various signatures on another piece of paper, duplicating the smoothest at the bottom of the letter. It went into an envelope addressed:

HALL OF RECORDS
257 DODGER STREET
VERO BEACH, FLORIDA 32960

Above other names he sent identical requests to Miami, Fort Lauderdale, West Palm Beach, Hallandale, and Key Largo, then settled down to wait for replies. In five days he received a registered letter from the recorder's office in Hallandale, a Miami suburb. Inside was a photostat copy of the birth certificate of one Sidney Mark Waldorf, born there on November 14, 1950. If the authorities didn't know that Waldorf had died ten months later and was buried in Coral Gables Cemetery, it was none of his concern.

He spent a long afternoon at the Miami Social Security office and then opened a small savings account in Waldorf's name, using it to back up applications for a raft of credit cards. Remarkably active after such a long hiatus, Sidney Waldorf passed a simple road test, which earned him a Florida driver's license.

He received material from the Hall of Archives in Key Largo, the Bureau of Vital Statistics in West Palm Beach, and Miami City Hall. At the end of a hectic month he prepared to check out of the Mar-A-Lago fully documented as any of five men (he had not heard from Fort Lauderdale) whose interrupted lives he was anxious to fulfill.

9

She kept her letters in a Gucci shoe box according to the financial status of her correspondents. The front of the box was for men worth at least half a million dollars. Directly behind were twice as many letters backed up by half as much money. The next place was reserved for writers hard-pressed to scrape together a couple of hundred thousand. They were followed by a large collection of admirers whose fortunes were mainly promise. Although she never wrote back, she enjoyed keeping these for rainy-day reading. A long time ago she had lost count of the number.

The letter from the Miami Beach hotel lay open on the desk. Mr. Waldorf, she thought, you've got a piss-elegant name, and you certainly keep the bucks out in front. Other than that, you sound as exciting as shuffleboard. But who cares?

From a thin folder she removed another letter, badly frayed and tearing along the creases. It was two pages long, without date, salutation, or complimentary close. Because she had composed it herself and sent so many over the years, she rarely looked at it as she put another copy on paper in a strong, precise hand.

Words can't adequately convey the pleasure I received from your letter. For too long I've felt isolated from the larger purposes in life, from love and marriage and a family of my own. With your help it is not too much to hope that these things may one day be attainable.

In answer to your questions, I am twenty-seven years old and have never been married. I was educated in private schools in Connecticut and Rhode Island and have degrees in music and French literature from Pembroke College. I am five feet, five inches tall, weigh 115 pounds, and am in excellent health. I have never been seriously ill a day in my adult life, and there is no history of sickness in my family. I rarely smoke; I drink in moderation and sleep well. I am just as comfortable in the kitchen as in fine restaurants and enjoy travel and good times of any kind. My hobbies center around sports and the arts, and I think you will find that I am a broad-minded individual.

My net worth currently stands in excess of $400,000, most of which is invested in blue-chip stocks and municipal bonds. Please don't consider me mercenary for having inquired in my ad about your finances. I feel vulnerable about being exploited for my wealth and had to assure myself that you were a man of means before opening my heart to you. A detailed statement is not necessary, although if you would like one from me, I will be glad to provide it. I hope you trust me when I tell you that money is the farthest thing from my mind.

Neither should you worry about sending a photograph. If two people share an affinity for the same things and strong feelings for each other, appearances have no right to intrude upon their happiness. However, if you would like to see another picture of me before we get together, I will understand. Let me know and I'll include one in my next letter.

Please write soon and tell me when you are

coming. I feel as if I have been waiting my whole life to meet you and do not want to delay even a day longer. If you would like, I will make reservations for you at a hotel here on Key Biscayne.

Leaving out the final sentence, she signed it, "Yours truly, Alice Rovere," typed out an envelope, and put it with the others. In the afternoon she brought them to the post office. Because of the holiday crush, Sidney Waldorf didn't receive his letter until the day after Easter.

He was as thrilled with Alice Rovere's letter as she had been with his. He preferred not to deal with younger women, who rarely were prepared to attach themselves to him out of desperation. Then again, $400,000 sounded too good to be true. It had been his experience that subscribers to *Rhoda Love's Lonely Hearts Bulletin* overestimated their wealth by considerably more than was fair. Key Biscayne wasn't much of a selling point, either. The heat and relentless humidity were starting to make him nuts.

What troubled him most was the picture that ran with Alice Rovere's ad. It showed a clear-eyed beauty with a dark complexion and an eager smile, the concerned features of a serious woman in a hurry to shrug off the coltish hold of her teens. He found it hard to believe that she had to advertise for a man with a face like that and everything else she had going for her—even if it was a good deal less than $400,000. When he thought about it, it was the picture that had made him write, and that was a hell of a way to do business.

He clipped the letter to the envelope and put it on the other side of the bed. Two had come that day, which made six for the week, only fourteen in the month he had spent in Miami Beach. Except for Alice Rovere's, there was little to choose. Most were from drab widows with barely enough to float the honeymoon. Someone young and pretty and broad-minded (that had given him a laugh) would be a refreshing change of pace from the spinsterish office girls and teachers, the nurse and the legal secretary and the former nun turned dolphin trainer with whom he had been wasting his time. Anyway, he'd had his fill of the Mar-A-Lago and the decaying racetrack at Hialeah. He'd blown a small fortune vying for rich widows with the bookies and touts, and all he had to show for it was Don Shula's autograph on a clubhouse napkin.

He reread the letters, shredding each one as he finished. Then he phoned Key Biscayne. Getting no answer, he took a cab to the track and tried the number again after the second race. Alice Rovere stepped out of the tub and picked up on the third ring.

"Yes?"

"Miss Rovere?"

"Yes, who is this, please?"

"Sidney Waldorf."

"Who? Oh . . . Mr. Waldorf, I . . . I just stepped inside the apartment and my arms are full of packages. Can you give me a second?"

"Take all the time you need."

Letting her bath towel fall, she hurried to the bedroom and opened the shoe box. The letter she was looking for was close to the front. She read it through as she went back to the phone. "Thanks so much for waiting."

"Not at all. If there's anything you have to put in the refrigerator, I can hold on."

"No, no, it's taken care of." She finished the letter. "How are you enjoying your stay in Miami?"

"Very well," he told her, "considering that I've forgotten the last time I saw the sun."

"I've never seen weather like this. It's not supposed to rain in Florida till summer. Will you take my apology?"

"Accepted," he said, "though it's not necessary. I've found plenty of things to keep me busy."

"Such as?"

"The Seaquarium and the jai alai fronton and the Monkey Jungle and one of the most exciting investment opportunities I've ever come across. I'm thinking seriously of relocating here."

"That's wonderful."

"It could be more wonderful. I was brought up in a small town, and there are times I get incredibly lonely in the big city, especially a city where I don't know anyone."

"But you do have a friend in Miami, Mr. Waldorf."

He was struck by her breezy awareness, which made him sound slightly punch-drunk by comparison. As he listened, it became contagious, and he found himself reverting to diction he'd found imperative to hide in prison. It was his professional voice, his natural voice, and as he settled into its easy rhythms he felt as though he'd finally shaken the effects of a lingering cold.

"I'd like to take her to dinner," he said. "Is tomorrow night too soon?"

"On the contrary. I'm starved."

Alice's place was five minutes from the bus stop, a pale brick high-rise on the seven-hundred block of Matanzas Street. Italic lettering on the burgundy canopy proclaimed THE PONCE DE LEON. He ducked underneath and pushed through the revolving door. A doorman in a gilt-encrusted uniform that could have been handed down from a Soviet marshal intercepted him at a horseshoe desk.

"Alice Rovere, please. I don't know the apartment."

Gloved fingers rummaged through the buttons on a metallic console. Norodny rocked on his heels, letting his eyes drift across the lobby. A red light drew them high into a corner where a security camera swept the entrance. Instinctively he tugged his hat over his eyes. The doorman gave him the receiver.

"You're early," a young woman's voice told him. "Come right up."

He handed back the phone and gazed absentmindedly at the street. A chilling rain slanted angrily against a window unprotected by the canopy. The large drops clung to the glass before sliding down like dreams dying hard. He shivered and pulled at his hat again.

There was another camera in the elevator; two more watched the eighth-floor corridor. He showed his back to one and his profile to the other and went looking for apartment 805, finding it in an alcove hung with tarnished mirrors. He took off his hat and patted down his hair with the flat of his hand, pushed the bell below the number. A peephole opened. He glimpsed a dark brown eye as it snapped shut with the nasty click of a pocket guillotine. A dead bolt turned, a chain bounced against the panel, and the door inched back. A black woman wearing a red bandanna smiled and reached for his hat.

"Let me take your coat," she said. "Miss Rovere will be with you in a minute."

She ushered him inside the living room, led him to an immense beige couch. The cushions were so broad and deep that his feet dangled over the floor, and he felt more than a little uneasy, like a frightened child waiting to audition for a piano teacher; and, indeed, there was a concert Steinway beside the terrace doors. He edged forward until his toes brushed against the white shag and folded his hands in his lap.

Then he got up and gazed down on the city, and when he turned back, Alice Rovere was standing there, even better-looking than her picture. That's a first, he thought. She was short and square-shouldered in a tweed skirt and white ruffled blouse and double strand of pearls. The dowdy costume was at odds with her full-lipped smile, and he guessed that she had dressed that way to add a few years and some gravity to her appearance. Without the skirt and blouse she'd really look young. Without the skirt and blouse and everything else . . .

"Hello, Alice," he said, making sure to project enough shyness. He walked over to shake her hand. "This is a great place you have here. I was admiring the view."

"It is nice, isn't it? The building went up a year ago, and I was one of the original tenants. That's Cape Florida light out on the beach, and on a clear day you can see Crandon Park. Would you like a drink?"

"Bourbon, if you have any."

Dragging her left leg, she moved toward a glass cabinet near the piano. His eyes dropped below her knee and stopped at the withered muscle of her calf. When he looked up again, she was glaring at him. His face took on color.

"Straight up?"

"That's fine," he said.

She poured a double, brought it over, went back to the cabinet, and pulled the cork on a bottle of cognac. "What's your sign?"

"Huh?"

"You pass," she told him. There was an embarrassing silence that lasted until she said, "I'm rotten at making small talk. How about you?"

"I seem to have left my line in my other suit."

"Take your drink and come with me," she said. "There's something I want to show you."

Alice kept a red Mercedes-Benz sports convertible in the basement garage, parking in the center of the two spaces she paid for as added collision insurance. She wasn't as cautious on the road, weaving through heavy resort traffic and straddling the chatter strip on the Rickenbacker Causeway, which brought them downtown. West of the city she found the Tamiami Trail and followed it into the sawgrass heart of the Everglades. Norodny tightened his seat belt, berating himself for leaving the rest of the bourbon.

"I know you've already had a ride today," she said. "I hope you don't think I'm odd, taking you for a drive."

Norodny decided that Alice had a problem with her coordination. Whenever she opened her mouth, her eyes drifted from the yellow center stripe. He smiled nervously.

"Not at all. This is some of the most beautiful country I've seen, even under clouds."

"I felt so self-conscious at the apartment," Alice said. "I'd never placed an ad before, and you're the only one who responded I wanted to see."

"Were there many? You don't have to answer that." He laughed.

"Twenty-three. I got twenty-three replies. Most were collecting pensions, and the others sounded kinky. If you hadn't written, I would have asked for my money back from Rhoda Love. Why were *you* reading a magazine for lonely hearts?"

"For the same reason you were advertising in one. This is my first time too. I thought I'd feel foolish meeting someone this way, but now—"

"Maybe Rhoda Love knows what she's talking about, after all."

When it got dark, they stopped for hamburgers at a crossroads drive-in. Alice knew a dirt road that led down from the highway to a parking area at the tangled edge of a shallow canal. They ate without saying very much, and when they were done, she allowed him to kiss her and to touch her small, resilient breasts through her blouse. Then they exchanged seats, and he drove the red Mercedes back to Key Biscayne. Alice warned him to go slow, insisted on parking it herself. Her head was resting against his chest as the elevator brought them up to the eighth floor.

"It's a long way back to the Mar-A-Lago. Where are you spending the night?" She smiled.

He followed her inside the apartment and kissed her. "Here," he said.

"Uh-uh. Rhoda Love would never approve."

"To hell with Rhoda Love, then."

"That's not nice," she said. "We've done all right by her this evening. We don't want to let her down."

"You're kidding, aren't you?"

She let him kiss her again, then pressed her hands

firmly against his shoulders. "The King Orange on Indian Creek Road," she said. "If you stay out of their grill, you can't go wrong."

He went back to the bus stop and staked out a spot on the bench. The express to Miami Beach didn't leave until the hour. At five to, he put away his money and walked eight blocks to Indian Creek Road, guided by the illuminated sign on the roof of the King Orange Hotel. He borrowed a racing form from the bellhop and went upstairs to study. When he kicked open the door and flopped on the bed, the phone began ringing.

"What took you so long?" Alice asked.

"I was hungry. I stopped for another hamburger."

"You certainly made a meal of it."

"Yeah."

"Sid . . . we hardly know each other. Be patient."

"I've never gotten the hang of that."

"I'll start you off easy," she promised. "Will I see you tomorrow?"

He sailed the tout sheet into a wastebasket. "Trading shuts down at three. If I skip the paperwork, I can make it for cocktails."

"Take your time with it and I'll be ready for supper."

"Is there anyplace special to eat on Key Biscayne?" he asked.

"Uh-huh. My place."

When Alice showed him inside and he saw lighted candles on the table set for two, the tension that had been building all day melted in his stomach. Gone was the prim music teacher, banished by a girlish succubus in a low-cut black gown. She thanked him for the flowers with a lingering kiss and retreated into the kitchen. As she backed away he noticed that she was barefoot and that her limp was less pronounced.

"What's cookin'?"

"It's supposed to be a surprise" came the voice from the other room. "You're going to love it. I'm a great cook."

Alice wondered if this was still true. Many men had told her that it was, but lately she hadn't time for the kitchen. The housekeeper had fussed over the meal all afternoon, entrusting it to her minutes before her guest showed up. She came back to the living room juggling glasses, a corkscrew, and a bottle of white wine.

"I thought we'd start with this." She dug out the cork. "How was business today?"

"Terrific," he told her. "The commodities market is going bullish again, and my investors are redoubling their orders. I'm trying to push them into wheat. The Russians had another poor harvest, and they'll be buying in quantity again. Wheat's going to be big this spring."

"It sounds as though you've got to keep on top of everything going on in the world. It must be interesting work."

"Once I thought so too," he said. "But I'm getting tired of coaxing scared, greedy people with more dough than they know what to do with into letting me make them richer. And that's the fun part. Most of the time I'm trying to make sense of a gang of lunatic brokers with marbles in their mouths yelling at me over bad phone lines from the trading pits in Chicago. What's interesting is making money, so you can say it's been a fascinating year."

"You're doing well?"

"A lot better than that. Rhoda Love would want you to know."

"She's counting on me to find out."

"Alice, I'm surprised. I remember you saying in your letter that money doesn't matter."

"It doesn't, as long as you have it."

Candor was something he could do without. He put more muscle into his smile. "Are you always this subtle?" he asked.

"Why pretend? I could never be happy with a man who isn't well off."

"And if he feels the same way?"

"I expect him to," she said. "I don't think highly of the type who lets himself fall for the scullery maid."

"So you wouldn't marry for love?"

"I'd marry *only* for love. I just can't see loving someone who doesn't have money. Don't go away."

She went into the kitchen, looked in the oven, and came back with a silver tray busy with crackers and caviar. "My parents spoiled me rotten," she said, putting the tray on a glass table. "I've never been able to thank them enough."

"Did they leave you all this?" he asked.

"They gave it to me. They're still alive."

"You're on an allowance?"

"I support myself, if that's what you want to know."

"How?"

"By giving French and piano lessons."

"A new Mercedes, an apartment like this on—"

"And they chip in."

"Big chips?"

"Blue."

"They must love you very much."

"That's most of it," she said.

"And the rest?"

"Guilt."

"How did you manage that?" Before the words were out of his mouth, he was trying to take them back, but they were gone in the vacant space between them.

"My leg. My parents are Christian Scientists. They didn't believe in Salk shots. I was the last schoolchild in Connecticut to come down with polio."

"I didn't mean to pry."

"Don't let it bother you," she said. "It hardly bothers me anymore."

"What do you do when it does?"

"I spend. You've seen my car. Would you like to go through my closets?"

"I'd rather poke around your drawers." He searched for

a laugh and was glad to settle for a forgiving smile. "How about your jewelry box?"

"I'm supposed to be the mercenary one, remember?"

"I wouldn't want to lose your respect by not caring enough about money."

"Do you care about mine?" she asked.

"Not as much as I care about my own, or as much as you seem to care about it, but yes, Alice, I have to admit that I care."

"If we have that much in common, maybe we can be friends, after all."

"I assumed we were," he said.

"Good friends. I'll be right back."

She went to the kitchen again and turned down the oven. She picked up another bottle of wine and two more glasses and waited at the living-room entrance. Norodny got off the couch and reached for his glass. "Just the corkscrew," she said, showing the bottle.

He caught up to her inside the bedroom, a sensory-deprivation chamber of pale walls and carpeting. A signed lithograph of Dali's *Return of Ulysses* assaulted the monotony above a low bed. Against the other wall a blond dresser propped up a portable TV riding a lazy Susan. Alice put the glasses on the edge of the mattress and gave him the bottle.

"Supper's going to be late," she warned as she undid the knot on his tie.

They were awakened by news of a plane crash in Bolivia. Norodny groped for the button over the clock and silenced the radio.

"I've got a couple of ten-year-olds coming by in an hour to learn how to conjugate irregular French verbs," Alice said. "You'd better get going."

"I'm on my way. Checkout at the King Orange is at eleven."

"You're not going back to that dingy joint in Miami Beach?"

"I wasn't planning to," he told her. "I thought now that we'd, uh . . . broken the ice, I could stay here."

"I'd love that, but it's impossible. Key Biscayne is like a small town, Sid. What would my pupils' mammas say when they saw you? What would the maid say?"

"That's their problem."

Alice sat up. "It's mine. The scarlet lady isn't my favorite role."

"We could get married," he said. "I hear people do it all the time for sex."

"We could do it for sex and money. But isn't there something more immediate?"

He opened the blinds. In the sharp spring sun Alice looked as fresh as the night before. He wouldn't hold it against her. "Coming over, I saw a nice hotel on the beach at Virginia Key."

"The Royal Palm Club. No good. Everybody knows my car."

"We can take the bus."

"It's still too close. Besides, I'm tired of the beach."

He got back into bed. "You think of someplace."

Alice put her feet down on the other side. "Paris," she said.

"What's your second choice?"

"Do you know where I've always wanted to visit? Quebec City, Canada. I hear it's very French, that you'd almost think you were in—"

"Forget what you heard. You wouldn't like it there."

"My folks have a hunting lodge way out in the Everglades," she said. "When I was a kid, I thought it was the most romantic place on earth. I called it the honeymoon cottage. The front yard's thick with live oaks dripping Spanish moss, and out back there's a freshwater lagoon that empties into a mangrove swamp stretching all the way to Florida Bay. At night you can hear the panthers crying in the palmettos. I'd love to take you there."

"Sounds great." He reached down for his wineglass and drained the few drops on the bottom.

"It is. And if you'd like to meet my parents, I'm sure they'd be glad to have us."

"Why don't we just throw a suitcase in the car, fill up the tank, and go? We're bound to find something exciting."

"I can see you're no traveler," she said.

"What's that?"

"Never mind. I'm already packed."

10

With the top down and the air conditioner on high, the April sun jabbed harmlessly at the occupants of the red car. Alice, who wouldn't let him touch the wheel in heavy traffic, steered out of the city to Westbound Route 41, the Tamiami Trail. Often she said, "Soon, soon," and "Any minute now," but she didn't give up her seat until the sawgrass Everglades bled Miami from the mirror and only the Big Cypress Swamp and Gulf Coast lay ahead.

They cruised through Glades City and Laxahatchee Station without seeing a red light. In Ochopee a sudden cloudburst flooded the road and forced traffic to a single lane. At fifteen miles an hour they fell in line behind a road crew plumbing the gutter for plugged storm drains. Where the trucks turned off on the Chokoloskee Fork, Norodny touched the accelerator, and the car fishtailed in six inches of water and dived across the median. He fought the wheel to a draw, headlight-to-headlight with a stranded RV.

"Maybe Mercedes is trying to tell us something," Alice said above the hammering in her chest.

"Yeah, that she needs new shoes. And brakes. And a wheel alignment."

They traded seats again, and Alice drove back into town. A filmy moat guarded the driveway of the few open motels, and boys in khaki waders and tank tops were trying to sweep them clear. They rode along Main Street, U-turned and came down the other side, sized up the choices once more, and plowed through the water past a sign that read: KARVER'S KABINS.

"I got no airboats," Carver told them, "or swamp buggies, if that's what you come for. And there's gators got in the pond, so you swim at your own risk. There's fishing and varmint hunting, but only if you brought your own gear, and I can see you didn't think of that."

"What *do* you have here, Mr. Carver?" Alice asked.

Carver tilted a sweat-stained hat over his eyes and scratched the back of his head. He punched open the cash register and removed a drinking straw from the drawer, put one end between his lips, and maneuvered the other into the slender neck of a bottle of Mr. Pibb. "Privacy," he said after some time.

"We'll take it," Norodny told him.

"That's a nice car you're driving. Better leave it by the office and carry your bags to the cabin. You'll wet your wires for sure if you take it down the path."

Cabin 1 was down a marshy slope curling toward a gray, gritty beach. Norodny dropped the valise inside the door and quickly pulled it shut.

"That bad, huh?" Alice asked.

"Let's go down to the lake," he said.

"I feel damp all over. I have to change."

"Just for a minute. I want to look around before it gets dark."

He led her to the shore along a rickety walk of disassembled seesaws. A few rowboats, a canoe, a water slide, and a wooden raft on steel drum pontoons were piled, unpainted and splintering, on the coarse sand. They climbed into the raft and gazed across the pond at a cypress dome whose cadaverous limbs shooed away the last of the sun. Alice put her hands in his pockets and rubbed her face against his dry cheek.

"This is the guy who nearly wrecked your car, remember?"

"No damage done, so you're forgiven," she said. "Lucky too. We weren't wearing seat belts."

"You don't know *how* lucky," he said. "Assuming we didn't lose them in the crash, the repair shop would have demanded payment in arms and legs."

"Nick it or total it, all I pay is the first hundred dollars. Everything after that is covered by insurance."

"How much are we talking about here?"

"About thirty-seven thousand. Are you thinking of buying one?"

"Just curious," he said.

The rustic flavor of Karver's Kabins was half an inch deep, the thickness of the knotty-pine paneling losing its grip on the walls. There was a fine stone fireplace in the living room but no woodpile, and the chimney had been sealed against tropical downpours. The furniture was paunchy before its time. Norodny had seen better waiting for the trashman on the sidewalks of a dozen cities. The musty fragrance of mildew hung in the air like organic smog.

"On the other hand," he told Alice, rubbing a clear spot in the window, "the view stinks."

"To hell with the view. I'm soggy."

He pushed the thermostat to the right until he heard the assuring thump of the heater in the baseboard. The oven and all four burners added warmth. Alice wandered into the kitchen to stand near the stove and forage through the pantry.

"Damn it, not even a tea bag."

"You know I can't hear you when the water's running," Norodny called out.

Through the open bathroom door she saw him bent over the tub. "What are you doing?"

"As long as we're wet, we might as well relax and enjoy

it," he said. "We'll take a bath. By the time we're done, I guarantee the cabin will be dry."

"Don't be ridiculous. We have to find a place to eat soon. I don't want to go out looking like a drowned mink."

He looked up unhappily. "Whatever you say," he told her, and let the water out of the tub.

They forded Carver's driveway on a palm log and walked along Main Street. They went three blocks without passing a lighted window and then saw four of them huddled against the night beside the post office and town hall. One was a bingo parlor, religion's jangling reminder, and another was a pharmacy. They were more interested in a Hawaiian restaurant and a diner. After a spiritless debate they settled on Gus and Flo's.

Other than a handful of truck drivers at the counter, they were the only customers. They hung their raingear at a booth for six and sat down to study menus. A waitress with small teeth and frizzy hair caged in an opalescent net brought them water and withdrew inside a cloud of Tabu. Norodny held his glass to the light, sniffed, and sipped cautiously. "Taste," he commanded.

Alice dampened her lips. "Ugh," she said. "If that's what they thaw it from, I don't want to eat it."

Norodny slid out of the booth and reached for his jacket.

"I'm really not in the mood for a luau," Alice said.

"I'm going to grab some Alka-Seltzer before the drugstore closes. Order for me."

A tall, gawky youth, all wrist and Adam's apple, was shutting off the lights when Norodny came in. "We're closing," he said, assessing the stranger through narrow eyes.

"I'll be a minute. Do you have any sleeping pills that work?"

The boy nodded in the direction of a carousel display crammed with patent sleep aids.

"That it? Late show's got me by the balls."

"Let me see a prescription," the boy said blandly. When

Norodny didn't respond, he added, "They're showing two Bogart movies tonight."

"How about letting me have some Dilaudid?" Norodny asked.

"I'd be glad to, but the chicken croquettes at the workhouse give me the runs. Look, mister, if it's all right with you, I'd like to lock up and go home."

"Which of these is strongest?" Norodny asked, spinning the display.

"Take your pick. They're all the same."

Norodny examined a blue-and-red box of pills. "Can you get off on this crap?"

Quietly the boy passed judgment on him. He switched off the large display window, darkening the street to the curb. "Why didn't you say so in the first place?"

"What've you got?" Norodny asked.

"Thai sticks."

"Some other time, maybe. Pills?"

The boy looked out the window and laughed uneasily. "The strongest I can sell you are those Somizenes you have in your hand, and they won't do shit unless you wash them down with alcohol."

"What happens then?"

"You don't want to know."

"I think I do," Norodny said. "You'd better give me a package of Alka-Seltzer to go with them."

"But I hate *good* red wine. This stuff smells like carburetor cleaner."

"Try it," he said, clinking his glass against the greasy tumbler. "You'll like it."

Of the rest of the night Alice could be certain only that it hadn't been fun. When she woke up, her hands and eyes were out of synch and her tongue felt heavy in a pebbly mouth. Dizzying effort forced her head from the pillow as she tried to get a fix on the cabin walls.

"How did we get back here?"

"How do you feel? That's more important."

"Awful. Please bring me a glass of cold water."

With his help she hiked herself up on her elbows. She splashed some water against her eyes and forehead and guzzled what was left. Coming up for air, she asked, "What happened?"

"We're not sure. The doctor said you had some kind of seizure."

"What doctor?"

"You don't remember that, either?"

"I don't remember much of anything," she admitted, and handed back the empty glass.

He went into the kitchen and returned with more water. Alice grabbed it from him, dampening the sheets and the bodice of her nightgown.

"What do you remember?" he asked.

"Finishing that dreadful meal and that lousy glass of wine, trying to undo the damage with Alka-Seltzer. After that it felt like somebody did a tap dance on my skull. I must have blacked out."

"You did. Your feet went rubbery on the way to the door. I caught you and put you on the floor, and then you scared hell out of everyone by going into convulsions. I held your tongue against the roof of your mouth with a spoon while the waitress went for a doctor. After a minute or two you stopped thrashing and the owners were nice enough to drive us back."

"I can't believe it," Alice said. "Nothing like this ever happened before. What did the doctor say?"

"'Rest, rest, and more rest. And plenty of fluids.' He asked if you were epileptic, and I had to tell him I didn't know."

"I'm not."

"I mentioned your polio, and he said that wouldn't have anything to do with it."

"Of course not."

"And he suggested that you consult a neurologist as soon as possible."

She took another drink and sat up higher. "I still don't understand. I've never been sick. There's nothing the matter with me."

"It wouldn't hurt to see a specialist when we get back."

"I can't remember walking out of the diner," she said.

"We carried you."

"Jesus, how I hate it when people notice my leg and think they have to take care of me . . . and now something like this has to happen. Let's go home."

He nudged her against the pillow. "It's not like you got drunk and made a fool of yourself. No one's laughing behind your back. Besides, the doctor said it would be best if you hung around a few days before starting out on a trip."

"A few days *here*?"

"Until you're feeling more yourself," he said. "It won't be so bad."

"I'm better already. Let's pack."

"It's four in the morning, and right now we're not going anywhere. Let's sleep on it. We'll see how you feel later."

Muttered oaths, the sizzle of bacon, and the acrid scent of charred eggs and toast roused Alice from deep, dreamless sleep.

"I hope you washed those pans out well," she said. "They didn't look very clean."

"Don't worry, the heat'll kill the germs." Soon he appeared beside the bed with a breakfast tray. He darted back in the kitchen for a pot of coffee and some knives and forks.

"I don't know what I did to deserve this, but thanks just the same," Alice said. "I would have been mortified showing my face at the diner."

"Don't flatter yourself," he told her. "My stomach wouldn't let us go back."

"After we finish, let's throw the dishes in the sink and jump in the car. We can be in Miami in time for lunch."

"Alice, this *is* lunch. It's almost one o'clock."

"It can't be. I've never slept that late in my life."

"You never had a night like last night, either. The doctor knew what he was talking about when he said you needed to rest."

"We can still make it home for supper," she protested.

She hadn't touched her food. Norodny sat down next to her and dug in. "Maybe tomorrow."

"What in heaven's name are we going to do here all day?"

"Do you play pinochle?"

"No."

"You'll learn," he said. "I'll run over to the drugstore and buy a couple of decks."

"I hate cards. I want to go home."

And back to work—three dates confirmed for the weekend. She was feeling better already. Nothing worse than a bad hangover, though she couldn't remember ever being hung over or more than a little tight.

"I'll stop off at the post office too," he said. "Why don't you drop a line to your folks?"

"To tell them about the marvelous time I'm having? Why worry them?"

"They have a right to know you haven't been up to par."

"No."

"I think they do."

Alice put down her fork and pushed the tray aside. "I'm a big girl, Sid. I can take care of myself. If I'm sick, it's not their problem."

"I'm trying to make it mine."

"Stop being so damn morbid."

"Hey, that's my heart you're stepping on," he said. "Didn't they teach you how to accept a proposal at those fancy schools you went to?"

"Proposal? I thought it was a pitch for medical insurance. I don't even know you very well. It's the most ridiculous thing I ever heard."

"You don't show any mercy, do you?"

"Maybe not ridiculous but awfully abrupt. We've been together only a few days."

"How much time do you need?"

"Longer than an overnighter in the country," she said. "Enough to find out if you brush your teeth with paste or powder, what you're like when the TV breaks, when the Dolphins don't win, how you look with a tan."

A star sapphire rode Alice's pinky. She slid it off and forced it on the third finger of her left hand. It went as far as the second joint. "That's all there is to making it legal," she said. "Anyway, I hate to stand on ceremony."

She put the tray down next to the bed and brushed the crumbs onto the floor. Slipping out of her nightgown, she made room for him between the soft, warm sheets.

A low-pressure front from the Gulf spilled an inch of rain on Carver's driveway and the rest of the Everglades, and toward midnight he conceded that Alice was becoming a fair pinochle player. They slept late again; when he carried the bag to the car, it was noon. Alice twisted the key in the ignition. The solenoid clicked, but the starter whirred lugubriously and died.

"It's the battery," he said. "I don't see Carver's truck. We'll have to call a garage and wait for someone to come out and give us a boost."

"Tomorrow morning," Alice said. "Another day in the cabin isn't going to kill me."

That night she beat him three games out of five.

As they lay in each other's arms in the limpid silver of the moon off still water, Alice sat up suddenly and hung her feet over the side of the bed. "What are you going to do when we get back?" she asked.

"After the wedding?"

"You know what I mean."

"My work will keep me around for a while, and then I'll go on the road again. I like Miami but not enough to cool my heels in a hotel waiting for you to favor me with a date."

"Take me along," she said.

"You don't need that. What you want is to get married and teach 'Chopsticks' to your own kids."

"Don't tell me what I want," she snapped. "I can help with business."

"You don't know the first thing about commodities."

"Come off it, Sid, you're as much a commodities trader as I am." She swung around to face him, tucking her ankles beneath her. "You're a flimflam artist working *Rhoda Love's Bulletin*, and God knows what else, for suckers." Before he could answer, she said, "I know what I'm talking about. You're not that hard to see through."

"Alice—" If there was one thing he hated more than a dumb woman, it was a smart one. Why didn't she get off his case?

"It's no use," she said softly. "I've had experience with your type before."

Only he liked this one. He liked her a lot. The look, the way she tried to put him in his place like a schoolkid, whatever, was making what he wanted to do—no, *had* to do—that much harder. No hurry, though. He'd wait till she forced his hand.

"All right," he told her, "as absurd as it is, let's pretend for a minute, just pretend, that what you're saying is true. Why would you want to get involved? If I were you, I'd run like hell."

"I'm not that fast on my feet. Besides, you're right about Miami. It's boring."

"You don't have to live the way you do. You're a great-looking woman. Go out and find a guy who'll give you everything you want."

"He bores me too," she said. "I want you."

"Then marry me."

Alice's face lost all expression. "Not on your life. Especially not on mine. I may love you. I definitely don't trust you, not after you almost poisoned me."

"What's this now?"

"I tried to get away. The first morning I would have crawled back to Miami, but you never let me from your sight. I sneaked out when you went to the store and tried to start the car. The plugs, the wires, everything was soaked. That's when I found out why I hadn't lost you and the Mercedes. I tried so hard, I ran down the battery. And after that . . . I didn't want to go."

"Weren't you taking a terrible risk?" he asked humorlessly.

"Probably. But the way you treated me after making me sick . . . No one ever took such pleasure in babying me, no one who didn't pity me. It was almost worth feeling so lousy for that."

"Was it?"

Alice gestured with upturned palms. "I'm still trying to make up my mind. Who are you?" she asked. "Really, I mean."

He put a hand on her knee and spun her aside, climbed out of bed, and began gathering his clothes from the furniture. What the hell, it was only a car.

"What do you think you're doing?" she asked. "It's the middle of the night."

"You're too weird. I'll thumb a ride."

"Wait, Sid, you haven't heard me out. I know how hard it is playing a lonely-hearts scam. I can help."

"I don't want to hear any more of this."

"You're going to," she warned, following him around the cabin. "First of all, it's plain from your approach that establishing confidence is the hardest part of the score. I give you an *A*, *A* plus for looks, but you trade too heavily on them. You don't make the extra effort to inspire real trust."

"A charm-school critique. Something I've always wanted."

"Don't interrupt. The way you proposed . . . frankly, it was embarrassing. You part with compliments like they were platinum ingots. You think you can get away with murder with those bedroom eyes and that hairy chest, but those won't work with every woman. If I'm falling for you, it's because I have superficial values. Even features are nice to be around. So is some excitement."

"I thought you had your fill the other night."

"You don't frighten me anymore." She laughed. "You're a pussycat, more thumbs than claws. It comes with the territory."

"What makes you an expert?"

"You're looking in a mirror, Sid. We're playing both sides of the same game. If you can't see that, you do need help."

He turned around to confront her knowing smile. But she *didn't* know, he decided. It was just one of those million-to-one shots where your fantasies turn out to be real. Next she'd want him to pull a stocking over his face and play rape. "*One* of us does."

"We can both do with some. I've worked this con so long, the fun's gone out of it, and it's starting to show. Last year I scarcely cleared expenses. As for you, it's a mystery how you survive. Together, though, we'd clean up. If you were traveling with your sister, your sweet, lame, loving sister, there's not a woman in this world who'd hesitate to give you everything she had."

"Think so?"

"I know women. I know this racket."

"Tell me more," he said. "Tell me about you."

"There's not much you don't already know. I come from a good family, I'm well educated, I like money. Maybe too much. My folks encouraged me to—and then lost theirs. When I got started in this, I swore I'd quit at twenty-five with a nest egg a hammer couldn't crack. I've had to push the deadline back to thirty. This time I'm sticking to it."

"Fascinating. Do you have a record?"

"The only court I've seen the inside of," she said proudly, "is divorce court. I doubt you can make the same claim."

"I've never been divorced."

Alice looked wounded. "You'd have to pay for the privilege. With me it's the other way around."

"No," he told her, "I prefer to avoid entanglements. They rarely work out well. I've always lived alone, worked alone when I could. A lady once accused me of loving alone. She said there was a hollowness at the heart of me I'd never stop tapping because I liked the sound. Often that sound is all I hear. I doubt you'd change that."

"I wouldn't try. What I'm proposing is a temporary arrangement, a trial marriage. A trial marriage of convenience."

"Sure." He plucked his undershirt from the dresser and tugged it over his head.

"God damn you, you're not going anywhere without me." She snatched his pants from the back of a chair. With surprising quickness she dashed into the bathroom and slammed the door. She was letting the water run in the basin when he came in after her. "If you really don't want to stay, I can't keep you," she said, dunking the seat. "But these look damp."

He smoothed the pants against the side of the valise and hung them to dry over the heater. He tossed the curtain out of the tub and opened the taps. "Let's take a bath."

"Let's go to bed. We still haven't talked things out."

"We can talk in the tub," he said, scooping her into the water before she could back away.

The tub was short and deep, mottled with age and chipped on the bottom and along the sides. There was barely enough room for Alice to stretch out comfortably. Norodny made space at his end by holding her feet against his hip. When they had been sitting that way for several minutes, trying without luck to outstare each other, he flicked on the shower and a needle spray tattooed a pink circle in the soft flesh of her shoulder.

She endured it without complaining, then pressed the lever. The shower lost force as the water gushed out of the faucet and onto their legs.

"You've had your revenge," she told him. "Can we go to bed now?"

"I'm not finished with you yet."

She flinched as he lunged to pour kisses on her face and breasts. He eased her back until her head was resting on the edge of the tub and brushed his mouth against her stomach down to the tuft of wiry hair. She regarded him through heavily lidded eyes; he thought he heard her make a purring sound deep in her throat. He ran his hands along her thighs to her calves, touched the withered muscle. She stiffened, and he saw her looking at him with worry and shame and a little of what he recognized as hate. She tried to wrench free, but the leg wasn't strong, and he locked it in his fists.

"Please don't," she begged.

He kneaded the pale flesh with soap-smooth hands, ignoring her protests. She kicked feebly and then lay still as he dug his fingers into the small knot of tissue behind the tibia and massaged vigorously, brought up the leg so sharply that she had to grab the tub to keep her head above water. When she stopped squirming, he pressed his cheek against the leg. Softly he touched it to his lips. No, he thought, not this one. Not now.

"Do you ever feel there's nothing real to hold on to, that you could forget who you are because it's so easy to stop being that person?"

Alice told him, "It's an occupational hazard. I never let it go that far."

"It's more than that. I have to fight it all the time."

"Tell me who you are and there'll always be someone to remember."

"It would be a gun to our heads," he said.

"You're so melodramatic."

"No, you're too important to me to waste the truth on."

"But there's so much of myself that I see in you. I want to know everything about you."

"All you have to know is that there was a time I thought I could divide women into two categories, the ones you chased for fun and the ones you chased for money, the ones that didn't count. Somewhere along the line the distinction got blurred and I need you now to help me sort it out again."

"I still don't know your real name," she said.

"Norodny," he blurted. "Francis A., of Newton, Massachusetts, and Bar Harbor, Maine, and Ithaca, New York, and Montreal and Miami, and points north and south, east and west. Biography on request. Call me Frank."

"No," Alice said, "now that it's a matter of record, I'll stick with Sid."

11

As advertised, the catalog came in a plain wrapper, the return address a post office box in El Paso. Norodny tore the brown paper and thumbed through a rotogravure of prospective brides in black leather and case-hardened steel.

"Some of these look like men," he said. "Or like they used to be."

"Turn the page."

"'Oriental cuties'?"

"Keep going," Alice ordered.

"'Guatemalan gals want guys'?"

"I'm on all the sucker lists," she boasted. "I receive tons of junk mail."

"This isn't getting us anywhere."

"Why won't you try *Rhoda Love's Bulletin*? She helped you find me."

"What's that done for my bank balance?" he asked.

"Where else do you look for well-heeled single ladies?"

"In the obits. *The Miami Herald* obituaries are the Who's Who of the recent dead, the blue book of wealthy Southern widows. Let them mourn for six months, and most of them can't wait to start spending again."

From an attaché case on the floor he removed a sheaf of microfilm prints and spread them over the bed. "I had these made up yesterday at the library," he said.

Alice lowered a goosenecked lamp over the white-on-black pages. "This one's out of the question," she said immediately. "He was only thirty-one, and look how cute. I can guess what his widow looks like."

"What about *him*?"

"How much could a French chef have put away with a second wife and seven children to feed? What about the police chief's widow?"

"Very funny."

"Astronaut . . . Episcopal bishop? Here's a possibility," she said. "A Chicago Bear."

"He retired in 1951," Norodny told her. "He couldn't have made ten thousand in his best year."

"I really like this one," Alice said. "Used Car Baron of Birmingham, Hiram Porter, is dead at eighty-one. Survived by brother and widow, no kids. You do like older women?"

"I hate them."

"I'll get her number from information. It's time you earned your keep."

Norodny pressed her hand against the phone and held it there. "On second thought," he said, "who knows what bargains Rhoda Love is shopping around this month?"

When Norodny saw the puddle on the Mercedes's narrow rear seat, he thought he'd strangle Sam. He parked in the breakdown lane and attacked the mess with rags and newspaper. Jessie repeated the clucking sound, which made him want to wring her neck, too, and brought Sam onto the front seat.

She said, "I don't understand it. He never got carsick before."

"Maybe it was the chocolate. I hear it gives them worms."

"Don't be silly. Sam loves chocolate." She buried her nose in the white ruff and hugged the terrier to her heart. "Don't you, Sammy?"

"It must be the backseat," she went on. "He's not used to riding there. From now on he sits on my lap."

"No, he—" Norodny took a deep breath and let it out slowly as he carried the damp rags and paper to a trash barrel. A short walk in the woods restored his blood pressure to normal. They were still a good half hour from Key Biscayne.

"I'm glad you got me into pork bellies," Jessie said. She was a bulky woman sweating heavily inside a full-length mink coat and, Norodny decided, not very generous with her chocolate. As Sam whined hungrily, she peeled the gold foil from three truffles and popped them in her mouth. The terrier had to settle for a cherry cordial, which he spit up, half chewed, in her lap.

"It seemed like a natural for you," he said, not taking his eyes off the road, "but I still think you should have gone in deeper. Prices may never come down this low again."

"After we're married. After we're married I'll turn over all my investments and you can corner the market for us." She leaned across the console and kissed him on the ear.

"Please, Jessie," he told her, "not while I'm driving. You know what that does to me."

"You're cute," Jessie said. "A real cutie pie."

Unconsciously he brushed his shoulder against his ear.

Approaching Miami, a road sign announced the last service area on the turnpike.

"You'd better pull over," Jessie said.

"Sam looks fine to me."

"It's for me, silly."

"But you just—"

"I know, dear, but how many times do I have to remind you, I have a very small bladder."

"Can't you wait? We're almost there."

"I can see that you don't know much about women, Sidney. A girl has to freshen up every now and then. I can't have your sister thinking I'm some road rat you found at a truck stop."

"You don't have a lot to worry about on that score, Jessie, but if you insist . . ."

He downshifted so suddenly that Sam fell under the dash. The car cut across three lanes of traffic and rolled to a stop in the vast lot behind the gas pumps. While he waited for Jessie he went over the backseat with more clean rags. If Alice found out about Sam's "accident," he'd never hear the end of it.

"What do you think?" Jessie asked when she came out of the restaurant.

He attempted a wolf whistle but couldn't keep his lips from curling. "Not bad," he finally said. "Are you trying to impress my sister or make her jealous?"

Alice was impressed. When Jessie went into the bathroom to freshen up again, she took Norodny in the kitchen and said, "From the way she talks, she must be worth a million."

"We'll find out. Her first husband owned a Cadillac dealership in Charleston, and number two got lucky in the stock market. That's the problem. He taught her so damn much about investments, it's all I can do to stay ahead of her. She won't part with the big bucks till we're married."

"Don't be gross," Alice scolded, and threw herself against him. Norodny squeezed her until she moaned.

"Later for that," he said, eyeing the bathroom door.

Alice bit him gently on the lip. "Oh, Sid, I missed you so much. It's been the longest month of my life. When can we be alone?"

Norodny said nothing.

"Maybe we'll send her off in the morning to see the lighthouse?" she tried.

"Maybe."

The toilet flushed, and they went back to the living room. Norodny took a chocolate-covered marshmallow out of the heart-shaped box and tossed it in the air. "Watch this," he said. Sam caught it on the fly and chewed it, but then spit it on the white rug.

"Sam!" Jessie called from the foyer. "Have you been a bad dog again? I'm sorry, Alice. I'll clean it right up."

"Forget it," Alice said, walking to the kitchen. "It's no bother."

"I love her," Jessie whispered to Norodny. "If I had a daughter, I'd be delighted if she turned out like Alice."

Alice came back to the living room and went to work on the stain with a damp sponge and liquid soap. "What are your plans?" she asked.

"We'll stay here till the end of the week, then drive down for a few days in the Keys," Norodny answered.

"And if everything goes accordingly," Jessie said, "I'll be Mrs. Sidney Waldorf by the time we leave Key West."

"My brother is really something, isn't he, Jessie? All his life he worked so hard, he had no time for women, and now he can't wait to be married."

"I'm afraid *I've* been the aggressor," Jessie said. "I'll be fifty-four next month and don't know how many good years I have left to give a man. We could set up light housekeeping, but I wouldn't have done that when I was a girl, and I don't think it's proper now. I know what people say, a middle-aged woman hot for your handsome young brother. My friends told me I was a fool to get involved. I couldn't care less. Sid's been great to me, and I want to be around him all the time."

"That's terrific," Alice said.

"And I already have the perfect wedding present picked out. For our honeymoon I'm taking us on an around-the-world cruise. We'll be gone four glorious months, make port on five continents, visit thirty-two major—"

Alice turned her face away and got up off her knees. "Excuse me," she said, and hurried out of the room.

"Is something the matter?" Jessie asked Norodny. "Her eyes looked watery."

"She didn't want me to say anything, but she's allergic to dogs."

"I feel terrible. You should have told me."

"It's a minor irritation," he said. "She'll get over it."

Two commercials into the late news, Jessie yawned and behind her open palm said, "Pardon me!"

Alice asked, "Would you like to go to sleep now?"

"I think it's time we went back to the hotel. It's been a long day."

"Please stay," Alice said. "The weather service is predicting a bad storm, and it's already starting to blow. There's a cot in the hall closet. I'll move it into the living room. Sid can take the couch."

"I can't impose on you like that."

"You're not imposing. Sid and I shared a room whenever our folks had houseguests. We're used to sleeping together. It'll be fun."

"Alice, I won't hear of it. I'm not chasing you out of your bedroom or making Sid sleep on the couch. That's a very wide bed, and I'm a quiet sleeper. We can share it, and Sid can have the cot and some privacy here in the living room."

"Really, Jessie, it's no trouble," Norodny said. "I can't count the times I had to sleep on the floor after late parties."

"Sid's right," Alice said. "You won't be putting us out at all."

But she did—with an expert touch. She negotiated the bed assignments like Metternich carving up Europe and then fell asleep beside Alice while Norodny stretched out on creaky springs in the living room. For company he had Sam, who curled up on the couch.

A soft, moist, femininely fragrant buzzing in his ear woke Norodny. Groggily he rolled onto his back and felt the warmth of veiled breasts against his chest.

"Alice?"

The fine hand came down across his mouth and clamped his lips shut. "Shhh, who'd you think it was?"

"Are you crazy? If Jessie finds us like this, she'll—"

"I'm just being sisterly. Jessie will understand."

She pressed her weight on his body, and the cot shuddered beneath them. Sam cocked open an eye and shut it, beating his tail against the cushion.

Alice's nightgown was around her arms as she fumbled with his pajama bottoms. She yanked them down till they hung from his leg and thrust herself on him. Norodny set the rhythm of their lovemaking, controlled her lithe body with his hands. She floated over him on bent knees, her spastic breathing in time with the accelerating pounding behind her breast.

Sam yawned and jumped off the couch. He eyed the rolling bodies playfully and tried to climb on. A benign kick sent him sprawling, and when he found his legs again, he stayed away from the big feet. He trotted around the cot, saw painted toes, tasted some. This time he made a clean escape and he barked twice in triumph.

"Shut up, damn you," Norodny muttered.

Sam yipped exultantly.

"Alice," Norodny whispered, "Alice!" He slid his hands under her shoulders and tried to push her away. The manicured nails dug deeper in the muscles of his back. "Alice, you've got to get back to bed."

But the words were lost in the nasal sobs wracking her body and in a spluttering wail of horror at the entrance to the living room. Jessie, wild-eyed and out of control, charged inside in Japanese slippers and a kimono, picked up a candlestick, and brought it down blindly with all her might. A corner of the heavy base smashed into Alice's kidneys, and she groaned and stiffened. Norodny shoved her out of the way as the silver shaft came down again and found the soft center between his ribs.

"Fun," Jessie shrieked, hovering over the cot like a menacing fairy godmother. "It'll be fun. Here, have some more fun."

"For God's sake, stop," Alice pleaded. "I can explain."

"Fun! Fun!"

Jessie raised the candlestick over her head and whipped

it at her tormentors. Norodny's arm deflected the blow, which caught Alice across the shoulders. Her back jerked, and she twisted onto her side, gasping convulsively. Norodny rolled off the cot. He ducked under the swinging arm, quickly got back to his feet, and swiped at the candlestick. He missed, and it crashed into Alice's bad leg. He saw droplets of blood widening on the pale sheet, tears in both women's eyes.

"Sid, she's killing me," Alice cried.

He dodged another wild roundhouse and slipped easily behind Jessie, pinioning her arms in a full nelson. As he forced the candlestick from her hand Sam jumped on the cot with a sullen growl and snapped at the pajamas, tearing them to the knee. Suddenly the apartment reverberated with an angry clatter from the radiator in the bedroom.

"What's that?" he yelled at Alice.

"The neighbors are banging up. We're waking the whole building."

An empty voice she hadn't heard before told her, "Go in the bathroom and fill the tub."

"Why?"

"Just do it."

She had never seen him seize command of a situation and found it frightening that it required so little effort. What had attracted her to him was the nervous energy he seemed incapable of harnessing, so that it was asking too much of him to sit still for more than a few minutes. Defying him now was out of the question. If he told her to fly around the room, she would perch on the windowsill and flap her arms.

"You're out of your minds," Jessie howled, "and I'm twice as crazy for letting myself get mixed up with you. Wait till I see my lawyer. He'll have you thrown in jail for breach of contract, for incest. He'll get back all my money and clean you out."

Again the radiator clanged.

At the sound of running water Norodny pushed Jessie inside the bathroom. Alice was standing at the tub, rubbing an ugly welt on her shoulder.

"Get out of here," he told her.

He kicked the door shut and wrestled Jessie toward the tub. She moved clumsily, locking her knees and clinging to the basin with her fingers. In the medicine-cabinet mirror he saw his pallid features, hidden behind the mask of her rage. He shifted his hands to the back of her head and bent her over the water.

Jessie wrenched free with a wooden heel to Norodny's instep. Blinking in pain, he climbed on her back and she slammed into the tub, breaking her nose against the bottom and coloring the water. He was studying a gash on his arm when the tension went out of her body.

Alice went to the refrigerator for some ice to hold against her swollen leg. She called into the bathroom and, when there was no answer, nudged open the door. Norodny hauled Jessie onto the tiles and examined the burst capillaries in her eyes, the tongue lolling thickly against her palate. Pink foam dribbled from her nostrils and snarled in the hair on his chest. Then he stood over the tub, grappling with fistfuls of white fluff as Sam beat curtains of spray across the room. Damp paw prints ran along the wall. Sam fouled the water and stopped struggling, and Norodny flipped him beside Jessie and reached for a towel. Noticing Alice, he dropped the towel over Jessie's face.

"Are you all right?" he asked, grabbing her shoulders.

Alice slapped his hands away. She backed off shakily, stumbling over Jessie's legs. She steadied herself against the washstand, brought her head down over the basin, and threw up.

He dressed quickly. When Alice came out, he had folded the cot and was wheeling it into the closet. She walked past him without saying anything and closed the bedroom door. He thought he heard her talking to herself and then realized that she was gulping back sobs.

He switched on a floor lamp, got down on his knees to hunt for the candlestick. He noticed spots of blood in the carpeting and traced them to a gummy trickle on his bare right foot. Rolling up his pants, he saw teeth marks in the stringy flesh behind the ankle, confirmed by the first sensation of pain. He smeared Mercurochrome on the wound, then went back to the living room and sponged the stains before they could set. He didn't stop rubbing until Alice left the bedroom in her rain jacket and boots.

"Where are you going?"

"Out."

"Do you think it's a good idea?"

She shrugged, continuing toward the door. He headed her off in the foyer and brought her back to the couch. She sat down obediently, hunched forward with her chin on her chest, her hands clenching and opening in her lap. He draped an arm around her shoulders and pulled her to him as she dissolved in tears.

"I'm sorry," she cried. "She would have killed me, wouldn't she? I know you had to do it. I know it, *I know it*. I don't hate you. It's the dog I couldn't—" The rest caught in her throat.

"Let me get you a drink."

"No," she said sharply, and tried to wriggle away. "I have to clear my head. The police will be here soon."

He took her painfully by the arm. "*You didn't call them*?"

"Not yet. We have to decide what we're going to say."

"Anything we say, it's a ticket to the electric chair. Two tickets," he reminded her.

"I'm scared, Sid. I didn't bargain for anything like this."

Soon the tears began again. He went to the liquor cabinet and poured two fingers of bourbon. She pawed at his hand, but he got most of the drink down her throat. She took a second glass hungrily. When she sprawled out on the couch with her head in his lap, he unbuttoned her jacket.

While she dozed, he rummaged through her closets. He found what he was looking for in a louvered wardrobe beside the dressing alcove. The old-fashioned trunk, ornate hinges splotchy with patina, was embellished with the stickers of half a dozen steamship lines that used to make the North Atlantic crossing. He emptied it of a collection of children's clothing, twenty years out of style, and lugged it into the bathroom. It was heavy enough with nothing inside.

A sour, gut-rolling stench had gathered in the sealed room. He tore open the window and sucked fresh air till the green went out of his skin. He looked down at the torture frozen on Jessie's face, wondering why even good poets confused death with sleep.

He made a second trip to the wardrobe and came back with Jessie's coat, admiring the flawless weave of pelts that were blue in their richness. Too bad Alice couldn't be allowed to have it. In Florida, where furs of any kind never fail to turn heads, a mink like that would be a magnet for trouble. He'd make it up to her.

He cleaned out the pockets. He took apart a safety razor and used the blade to slice away the designer label. Then he stripped Jessie's body and shrouded it in mink.

Sam went in the trunk first. He took Jessie under the shoulders and straightened her body, knotted the kimono sash around her hands. He slipped his right arm under the knees, the left around her back, and let the slack out of his muscles. As he stiffened his legs he squeezed his arms together, and she jacknifed at the waist. He dropped her in on her side, nearly toppling in after her, catching himself on the edge of the trunk. By bending her knees under her chin he was able to move her face out of the way of the lid. Still it refused to shut. He considered the puzzle quickly and rearranged the arms, then slammed the lid—and wedged the body tighter. He leaned his weight on it, sat on it, stood on it, stamped his feet on it. It wouldn't close all the way.

He kicked the trunk over and dragged Jessie onto the floor, yanked Sam out by a foreleg. He felt the tingle of cold metal against his wrist and found a collar with the animal's tags in the dripping fur. He unbuckled it and tossed it in the basin. Then he set the trunk upright again. This time he started off with Jessie, and she fit with room to spare. Sam filled it nicely.

Careful not to wake Alice, he began hunting for Jessie's things. He spotted a leather handle under the bed and pulled out her valise. He ransacked it of bankbooks, an address book, and an envelope containing insurance policies, a will, and other personal documents. Underneath some lingerie was a japanned box in which he found bracelets, silver chokers, a watch, and diamond earrings. He was reminded of something he'd overlooked before and went back to the trunk and stripped the body of two jeweled rings.

Gentle pressure on her elbow, which wouldn't go away, opened Alice's eyes. She got up slowly and made a hissing sound between her teeth as she touched her shoulder with her fingertips. In a little girl's voice she said, "It hurts."

"I know, but we have things to do."

Alice tested her legs on the floor. She went to the window and looked out at a city electroplated in the aluminum sheen of chain lightning. In the foyer she saw Jessie's valise and her own steamer trunk behind the arc of the door. "It looks like someone's taking a trip," she said.

"Someone is. . . . How do you feel?"

"Everything's sore. Other than that, I want to die."

"I need your help for an hour," he said. "Then we'll come back and you can stay in bed as long as you like."

She rubbed some of the pain from her shoulder. "We have to talk first."

"What is it?" he asked impatiently.

"If anything like this . . . if anyone's going to be harmed again, you can leave. Do you understand?"

He nodded. "She was going crazy," he said. "She didn't give me any choice."

"You didn't have to kill her."

"All I wanted was to slow her down, keep her from going for us again. She was more than I could handle. You're not the only one who's shaking."

In the spasms of bleached light he looked washed out and exhausted. "No, I guess not," she said, wanting to believe him, knowing that she had to. "What do you want me to do?"

"Ring for the elevator. I'll slide the trunk out when it comes."

Alice stepped gingerly around the luggage as Norodny waited at the door. When he heard the elevator gate open, he raised an edge of the trunk over the sill and pushed it into the corridor. The scruffed nap of the runner grabbed at it and released it grudgingly.

In the time it took to wear himself out, the trunk went barely fifteen feet. Alice jammed the valise in the gate and hurried back to take a corner. The trunk moved faster but not much.

As they inched past the other elevator a circle of light shined down suddenly, and Norodny bolted upright. Alice froze, still bent over. The gate slid open, and a man in the comic-opera livery of a Ponce de Leon doorman came into the corridor. "Good morning, Miss Rovere. What you got there?"

"Oh . . . hello, Mr. Winston," Alice said. "Uh . . . I don't believe you've met my brother. Sid, this is Mr. Winston, our night doorman. Sid's going on a Caribbean cruise, and his boat leaves Fort Lauderdale at nine A.M. We have to have his bags at the dock by seven."

"I saw you struggling with them over the TV in the lobby," Mr. Winston said. "Funny how handy it is for everything but what it's there for. There's been five burglaries since the first of the year, and I didn't see a single thief. Here, let me get at that."

"No!"

"We can handle it," Norodny said.

"Don't be difficult," Mr. Winston said, taking Alice's place at the corner. "It's what they pay me for."

While Alice held the gate Mr. Winston helped Norodny push the trunk into the elevator.

"Whew, what you got in there?"

Alice looked anxiously at Norodny, and then both of them stared at the doorman, who smiled but didn't say anything. Alice hit the button, which brought them down to the garage. The trunk moved easily on the concrete floor, but Mr. Winston seemed troubled. He stopped pushing and said, "You don't want to tear up the bottom. Let's carry it over."

"It's too heavy," Norodny told him.

"We're a couple of strong guys," the doorman said, curling his fingers underneath his corner. "Let's go."

Alice ran ahead and opened the Mercedes's luggage compartment. The valise fit nicely over the spare tire.

"What do we do with the trunk?" Mr. Winston asked.

"There's room in the backseat," Norodny said. "Put down the top, Sis."

As the cloth roof retreated, the men brought the trunk down over the rear of the car. It balanced precariously on an edge, propped against the back of the driver's seat.

"That doesn't look too solid," Mr. Winston said.

"I'll ride back here with it while Alice drives," Norodny told him. He offered his hand. There was a five-dollar bill in the palm. "Thank you, Mr. Winston. You don't know how much we appreciate your help."

"Don't mention it," the doorman said. "It goes with the job."

Groping for the highway entrance down vapor-lit streets, Alice scarcely budged the speedometer. Wind-whipped rivulets eddied about the gutter, overwhelming her new all-weather tires. A block in advance, she braked for amber lights as well as red, and drifted toward intersections on locked wheels and white knuckles.

"Can't we go any faster?" Norodny called to her. "It'll be getting light in less than an hour."

"The water is hitting the undercarriage. I'm all over the road."

When they came off the ramp, she was able to shift into third. There were few cars on the highway; none from the west where the storm was centered over the Everglades. In the mirror she saw him with a hand on the trunk and the other clutching his collar to his throat. His face was livid where the rain thrashed against it. She reached for the heater, then remembered that she had set it on high.

She went along the route they had taken on their first drive in the country. She pulled off the highway and found the dirt road to the canal, almost impassable between billowing palms. Moving at a crawl, the Mercedes etched finely cleated tracks in the muck. Alice used the low beams to guide them into the desolate parking area. Norodny warned her not to cut the engine.

He hauled himself stiffly out of the back. In the dim corner of light reflecting off the trees, she saw that he was shivering. He had her switch on her brights and head the car toward the water. She backed up a couple of yards, swinging the wheel to the left. In the harsh glare they picked out a gap in the vegetation, which seemed to lead to the canal.

"Let me go down for a look," he said hoarsely.

She watched him disappear, listening to the gale. She blew inside her driving gloves and zipped her hood around her head, scrubbed the fogged glass with a tissue for want of something to do. And then he was standing beside her door, bleeding from the forehead where he'd walked into a low branch.

"Do you need help with it?" she asked.

"Help me? How can you, when I'm so damn stupid, I can't help myself?" He climbed into the car and sat down in water. "Let's get out of here."

"With the trunk?" In the mirror she saw him nod and shield his face with his open hands. "I don't get it."

He laughed, a sardonic wail sucked dry and blown apart by the wind. "The canal is silted up. It's maybe two feet deep."

"Can't we just leave it here?"

He blinked the rain from his eyes and shook his head. She fed the engine gas and let it rev until his laughter was all used up.

It was Alice's idea. South of the Tamiami Trail the canal had been widened and deepened to provide refuge for the Everglades' dwindling wildlife during the dry winter season. The Audubon Society had contributed to the effort by purchasing some of the surrounding land and dredging a maze of interlocking waterways into the channel. Easy access was restricted by the gates of a chemical plant that discharged protein-rich effluent into the water every day of the year. She had read somewhere that the plumpest catfish in south Florida congregated around the outlet, along with a cane-pole equipped army of fishermen. Although she was unfamiliar with the area, she was certain that they would find another road to the shore.

Slivers of tinny light wedged into the eastern sky as the Mercedes struggled back up to the highway. In the few minutes they spent at the canal the storm had obliterated their tracks. At the top of the grade the rear wheels lost traction, and Norodny hung on to the trunk with both hands as the car swerved wildly. Alice called out, "Sorry," but was sure he didn't hear.

There was no traffic in the eastbound lane. Alice hugged the shoulder and trained her high beams on the row of reflectors. Homing in on the strobe lights over the chemical plant's giant smokestack, some of the hurt went out of her bruised muscles. The outlet was less than a mile away.

At the first paved turnoff she touched the brakes, and they drifted off the highway. The crossroad branched into a net of gritty industrial streets purified by the rain. She came to three dead ends before finding a two-lane loop, which followed a feeder canal and then headed back to the main road. At that hour there were few lights on at the plant, but a beachhead of cars in the flooded lot told her that the storm wouldn't keep the morning shift from work.

"This ought to do it," she said.

"It better. I can't hold on much longer."

They drove around the tottering skeleton of a burned-out powerhouse into a straightaway that mimicked the shore. Fifteen feet away an aluminum dinghy was aground in shallow water. Alice mouthed the words *My fault* but was too drained to supply sound.

Behind her, Norodny whooped for joy. "We've got it made."

"What's that?"

"See that boat? The canal's overflowed its banks. It must be ten feet deep in the channel."

As Alice headed for the shoulder she heard him yell, "Keep going, keep going." Probing a curve up ahead was the focused glow of approaching headlights. A rusted Chevrolet with two men in the front seat and two others in back materialized, hydroplaned over a dark puddle, and hurtled past. In their wake miniature combers rolled along the pavement and crashed against the curb.

The Mercedes continued around the bend and lost the road, finding it again in a fury of brown spray. Alice took a sharp left into an open space on the far shoulder and attempted a broken U-turn. But when she threw the car in reverse, the wheels spun resentfully in deep mud. Norodny jumped out for a look, talking to himself.

"I don't believe any of this," he said. He set his feet in the ruts, and Alice shifted into first. As she stepped on the accelerator he leaned all his weight against the car—and watched the wheels carve graves for both of them.

"Put it in reverse. Try rocking it out."

When he was out of the way, she popped the clutch, and the right rear wheel whined in protest, grinding ribbons of muck into the air. The other clawed at the mud and gradually dragged the car back. She quickly shifted into first, and the Mercedes inched toward the lip of the rut before starting to slide. She held it there with the brake as a blue Chrysler came around the curve and slowed.

Norodny waved the driver off. "We can manage, thank you." Then to Alice, "Back up again and you're home free."

He hurried around to the front and leaned against the bumper. Alice pushed the stick forward and gave the car some gas. It fell to the bottom of the rut, hesitated, and then crashed out, sending Norodny sprawling in the mud. When he picked himself up, the car was straddling the shoulder with the rear wheels on the edge of the pavement. Beside it was the open trunk. A few feet away lay Jessie and Sam.

He dug Jessie out of the dirt and put his arms around her. There was a stiffness he hadn't felt before, and he couldn't tell if it was the onset of rigor mortis, or if his own muscles had nothing left. As he adjusted his grip he heard heavy tires plodding along the shoulder. He looked up to see a jeep with a whip antenna idling beside the Mercedes.

"What happened here?" a man called out.

"There's been a terrible accident," Alice cried. "This poor woman's been dragged by a car and has to be taken to a hospital, and there are three others lying hurt up the road. Can you go for them?"

"No problem. We'll call ahead for an ambulance and the police."

Norodny waited until the jeep was out of sight before he dropped Jessie in the canal. She landed facedown, drifting toward a dam of yellow palm debris. He leapt into water up to his armpits, waded after her, put her on her back, and watched as the mink took on water like a paper towel and dragged her down. As she disappeared below the surface he staggered up the bank and heaved Sam after her.

He caught up with the Mercedes as it rolled along the side of the road and vaulted into the passenger's seat. Alice raced to the end of the loop, to a concrete bridge joining the Tamiami Trail. A sheriff's deputy beside a fallen power line waved them across with his flashlight. In the windswept dawn the highway was filling with cars.

12

In the waning months of World War II, convinced that vast deposits of petroleum lay hidden beneath the limestone bedrock called Miami oolite, a consortium of oil companies hacked a seven-mile canal south from the Tamiami Trail into the heart of the Everglades. The canal was being broadened, the project moving ahead of schedule when government geologists determined that the reservoir was not commercially significant. Without wasting another dollar, the drillers pulled out and abandoned the site.

The Everglades, its reputation as a particularly nasty swamp notwithstanding, is actually a slow-moving river six inches deep and eighty miles wide. The fragile ecology heals slowly, and the seven-mile scar remained as the drillers left it. In the late 1950s, giving up on the notion that they would see oil derricks there, the Laxahatchee County fathers erected a seventy-five-foot wildlife observation tower at the end of the canal. To encourage pedestrian and bicycle traffic they constructed a blacktop lane from the highway to the tower paralleling the waterway, which they named the Ahningha Valley Slough.

Summer is the wet season in south Florida, when the entire Ahningha Valley is flooded. The tropical showers taper off with the start of autumn, and by Thanksgiving the lane usually is passable. As the Everglades dry out, the alligators and wading birds dependent on a watery environment migrate back to the slough.

Inevitably, so do the tourists.

Very early on a humid spring morning, a rental car with a couple of ten-speed bicycles mounted on the trunk pulled into the parking lot at the head of the lane. The man and small boy joking on the front seat were deeply tanned. For enduring a week on the beach at one of the glitziest hotels on the Gold Coast, the man had promised his son a visit to Disney World. The child, having had his fill of unreality, suggested a fishing expedition instead.

With one fist wrapped around the handlebars and the other clutching their tackle box and poles, the man led the way along the blacktop. The sun had been up an hour, and small alligators could be seen in the slough, motionless except for eyes scanning the water for gar.

Three miles from the tower they parked in the striped shade of a Paurotis palm, and the man baited his son's hook. After looking to see that there were no large alligators nearby, he let him have the rod. The boy, who was about ten, ran to the bank, checked for reptiles on his own, and dropped a line into the green water. His father was skewering a crayfish when he heard him cry, "Dad, Dad, come here!"

"What's the matter, son?" the man called, alarmed that they both had missed an alligator.

"Come quick," the boy insisted. "It's a dummy."

"A what?"

He leaned his pole carefully against the tree, ran to the boy, and sighted along his outstretched arm in the direction of the tower. Sailing toward them on the breeze was the pale form of what surely was a department-store mannequin. It was an unearthly shade of white, trailing long, flowing hair. He had never seen a mannequin with hair like that, and it troubled him. It wasn't until he saw the other hair, the dark patch at the crotch, that he understood why.

"Give me your rod and go back to the bikes," he told the boy. "I'll catch up."

Forgetting about alligators, he stepped onto some flat rocks and snagged the floating object. It was the body of a woman—about fifty, he guessed. He didn't care to look at it closely. Something had nibbled at the arms and legs, and the torso was bloated and distended. He tried to nudge it to shore but barely moved it. Then he noticed a dark mass clinging to what was left of an arm just below the surface. He poked at it with the rod, and the body submerged and bobbed ponderously.

The boy had a hard time keeping up as they pedaled back to the parking area. There was a pay phone on the side of the small comfort station, which ate their change without giving a dial tone. Leaving their bikes, they got into the car and sped to the highway. A road map led them to a town a few miles west of the slough. It was a Miccosukee Indian settlement, a grocery, a greasy-spoon café and souvenir shop, a floating dock tied to a dozen airboats, and an open arena where the only contest was alligator wrestling. They found a phone that worked in the grocery.

Their call sent Ma Rutledge racing from the substation at Big Cypress to the slough. He was met in the parking area by a crowd of fishermen and birders from which the man and his boy emerged without relish. They slid into his cruiser, careful not to disturb the shotgun standing upright against the dash. With blue lights flashing, they moved down the lane. Behind them, on bicycles and on foot, followed most of the others.

They found the body on the rocks where the man said they would. It had dried quickly in the Everglades sun, and the extremities were starting to turn black. The man told his son to wait in the car and walked to the water with the deputy. As they came near, he was hit by the smell and thought he was going to be sick.

By the time the crowd caught up, Rutledge was back at

the cruiser radioing headquarters. Then he reached into the rear for a length of rope and some paper signs that read: LAXAHATCHEE SHERIFF ■ CRIME SCENE. DO NOT CROSS.

He threaded the rope through the signs and strung it across the lane fifty feet from the body. He didn't take it down, and then for only a few seconds, until the arrival of a second car.

A tall blond woman and a black man with a feather in his white cowboy hat stepped smartly outside. Rutledge introduced them to the man from the Gold Coast as his boss, Sheriff White, and the pathologist, Dr. Riley.

"It's a floater," the deputy told them, "and she doesn't appear to be in top-notch shape. Near as I can make out, she hasn't been shot or stabbed. But she went under wearing a fur coat, and I expect we can rule out natural causes."

Dr. Riley gave out cigars. She lit one, herself, as they walked to the slough.

"I don't smoke," said the man from the Gold Coast.

"Don't care for it, myself," she told him. "It's a vile habit. But if you puff hard enough, you won't have to smell her."

Rutledge went back to his car for a portable video camera. He shot the corpse from all angles and then focused on the surrounding area. At the end of the tape he included the man and his boy. "She's all yours now," he said to Dr. Riley. "Not my type, anyway."

The medical examiner sucked deeply on her cigar as she bent over the dead woman. When she was done, Rutledge and White carried the body up to the lane and laid it out on a rubber sheet. Back at the water they found Dr. Riley examining a sodden fur coat.

"What've you got there, Daisy?" White asked.

"Ranch mink. And it's a beaut. She was using it for a bathing suit. I know better. Hang it out to dry and I'll show you."

Reluctantly she handed over the coat. White felt inside

the pockets and patted down the lining. "Cleaned out and the label's been cut," he said.

"You might have some luck showing it around Collins Avenue," Dr. Riley told him. "Miami Beach is the only place around where those run wild."

She drew on her cigar and exhaled toward the body. "We won't learn too much from her till the postmortem, and even then I'm not promising a lot. Her face is about gone and so is one arm."

"How long has she been in the water?"

"Five or six days, four at the very least. Whoever she was, mink wasn't the only luxury in her life. Her hand is smooth, not a callus on it, and I wish I had nails like hers. Not your likely candidate for a swimming lesson with a fur anchor."

"Bet you find her system's lousy with dope," Rutledge volunteered. "ODs are stacking up like cordwood in the city, crack freaks and freebasers included. Hell, coke and mink go together like ham and eggs."

"I doubt that's it," White said. "There's lots easier ways of ditching a body than bringing it all the way out here. Only a killer would go to all this trouble. Only an amateur would screw it up so bad."

"Don't be quick to blame," Dr. Riley said. "When she went in the water, it was a reasonable assumption that the world had seen the last of her. What someone didn't take into account is that as a body decomposes, gas collects in the abdomen. After a while a rotting corpse becomes as buoyant as a beach ball. Not everybody would think of slitting open her stomach to give the gas a chance to escape."

"Did the alligators chew her up like that?" the man from the Gold Coast asked.

"Uh-uh," she said. "They don't have much appetite for carrion. It was snappers, wouldn't you say so, Buck?"

"Turtles'd do it," he agreed. "And I'm not sure she

wasn't ground up by an outboard motor. But don't blame gators."

He knelt beside the body and looked into the disintegrating features. All that remained intact was the hairline, razor-sharp around a pulpy forehead. What he would remember most were the highly arched creases still visible in the loose flesh, as if they'd been frozen in horror. When he had seen enough, he stubbed out his cigar against a rock, and carefully put it in his shirt.

A few minutes before ten o'clock, two more sheriff's cars reached the scene, and the department's three-man Criminal Investigation Bureau got a look at the body. They were followed by Minicam crews from the local television station and reporters and photographers from the *Miami Herald* and the *Miami News*. It was noon when a meat wagon arrived and the dead woman was placed in back for the drive to the morgue. Dr. Riley rode up front with the driver and broadcast a hold for a refrigerator to house the corpse until the autopsy, which she would perform herself.

The others remained at the slough. When a search of the immediate area turned up nothing of greater interest than an Everglades kite, a rare hawk, they split into two groups. Rutledge and one of the CIB men, Detective Paul I. Sturges, a thirty-two-year-old former high school wrestling coach, combed the shoreline all the way to the parking lot while the rest of the men moved toward the tower. Three quarters of a mile from where the body was found, White spotted a cloth bundle in the weeds. Wrapped inside a cottony shift were panties, a bra, a girdle, sandals, and a straw handbag. He turned the bag upside down and dumped out a package of breath mints and some rags balled up inside three crumpled pages of the *Herald* of Tuesday, May 27, exactly a week earlier. Russet stains were caked on the newsprint.

They continued up the loop but found nothing that didn't belong there. Wilting in the midday heat, they trekked back to the cars. Rutledge was waiting for them in the shade.

"Come up with anything?" White asked.

The deputy spit brown tobacco juice into the bushes. "Waste of time. How'd you make out?"

White laid the evidence on the hood of his car. "We picked this up less than a mile from here. Bag it and we'll send it to Tallahassee. I want those bloodstains typed and referenced against specimens from the floater. Meantime I'd like to go through the swamps and hunt up some witnesses. Know where we can lay our hands on an airboat?"

"Miccosukees down the road might let you have one. They charge the tourists thirty dollars an hour. We can work out a deal."

Bernard Osceola, the chief of the Laxahatchee band, was reluctant to part with a boat unless his thirteen-year-old son went along to pilot it. Money was no problem, but it wasn't until White gave his word that the county would make good on any damage that he agreed to keep the boy at home.

Much of the Everglades is covered with sawgrass, a wiry sedge whose serrated blades choke the shallow waterways and foul the propellers of conventional motorboats. Flat-bottomed airboats, drawing speed from a giant fan over the stern, skim over the morass at upward of fifty miles an hour. Bernard Osceola gassed up *Sister Seminole,* a twelve-seater. White climbed into the pilot's chair in the scaffolding holding the fan, and the detectives crouched on the tourists' benches. The Indian started up the engine, and as the fan churned a beacon of ripples through the lagoon, the blunt nose of the boat lifted out of the water. White steered cautiously into the channel and leaned back on the throttle.

Blue herons and ahninghas, water turkeys, took flight and scattered, leaving webbed trails on the glassy surface. The great green log of a bull alligator submerged as the boat skittered by and then rose stoically in its wake. White threaded a maze of hardwood hammocks festooned with mahogany and gumbo-limbo, searching the small islands for signs of habitation. In the Everglades, where an inch of elevation means the difference between wet feet and dry land, the hammocks are known as Florida mountains. On a kidney-shaped tuft of marl west of the spot where the body washed up, they found what they were looking for.

Screened behind a cluster of dwarf cypresses was a chickee, a palm-thatched Miccosukee hut. White circled around the hammock, eased up on the gas, and guided the airboat to a wooden dock. A short, dark-skinned man, almost as dark as he, shaded his eyes against the sun and watched the officers get out of the boat.

His name was Mike Osceola, and by day he pecked a subsistence from the thin hammock soil. Darkness he spent poaching alligators, drifting silently through the glades in an unpainted skiff with a lantern in one hand and a bang stick in the other, hunting for two amber pinpoints in the swampy night and detonating a .44-caliber bullet in the soft reptilian forehead between them.

"Like a word with you, Mike," Rutledge said.

"Got no business with me, Deputy. Been a regular Uncle Tommyhawk since you let me out of your jail. Don't pay to 'jack gator, anyways, not since they made huntin' legal in Louisiana."

"It's not about gators this time. This here's Sheriff White. He wants to talk to you about a woman's body we found in the slough this morning."

"I'm always interested in a woman's body," Mike Osceola said.

"This woman was dead," White said, unsmiling. "We want to know if you were by the slough when she went in and saw who she was with."

"I ain't been off my island in more 'n a week. Honest injun."

"You stand by that, you'll have to do it in my lockup,"

White told him. "Listen good. You tell me what I want to hear, and the next time my men catch you out with your jacklight and your bang stick, they'll know to look the other way. Now when was the last time you were in the valley?"

Mike Osceola shifted his weight uneasily. "You ain't interested in that time. Tell me when this woman died."

"About a week ago, can't say which day. She turned up in the slough wrapped around a fur coat. We found her clothes in a bundle a couple of miles from the wildlife tower."

"I don't know nothin' 'bout no woman, but the night of the big blow, I was out tendin' to some business when I seen headlights in that dirt lot down by the Tamiami Canal. I figured it was one of your deputies, so I backed off and let the current take my boat. When I come back again, there was a fella heavin' somethin' in the water. I couldn't make out what it was, but he was damn serious 'bout gettin' rid of it, out there in the rain the way he was.

" 'Course, the water ain't but knee-deep there," Mike Osceola added. "Soon's he was gone, I come by and fished it up."

"What was it?" White asked.

"A grip," the Indian said. "A red one full of a whole lot of crap I couldn't use, fat lady's. I gave it to my brother, and he took it up to Devil's Garden day before yesterday. I chucked the rest of the stuff back where I found it. Recycled it, ain't that the word?"

"Did you get a good look at him?"

"There wasn't no moon," Mike Osceola said. "But when he come in front of the car lights, you could see he was a white man, about six feet tall, no whiskers, dark hair. And he wasn't local."

"How can you be sure?"

"He was a pale face. No tan."

"What was he wearing?"

Mike Osceola scratched his scraggly jaw. "City clothes is all I remember. A hat, a jacket. Everythin' soakin' wet."

"What about his car?"

"It was pretty well hid behind the trees. But it was a small foreign job, I'm sure of that."

"Why?"

"Didn't hardly throw no light, not like a Chevy."

"Anything else you remember about that night?" Rutledge asked.

"Comin' home with my boat full of gator. Now the county owes me another one for services rendered."

"First you get that valise back from your brother and you haul ass over to the office with it," White said. "Then there's some pictures of cars we want to show you."

White and his men scoured the Miccosukee hammocks till dusk but found no one else who had seen anything or was willing to talk about it. They spent the evening at headquarters, leafing through a stack of missing-person bulletins collected across seventeen counties in the south Florida area over the past three months.

"Nothing," Rutledge said as he tossed the last of them in a file drawer. "There's not supposed to be anyone looks like that missing around here."

"No telling where she's from," White said. "I'll have the DLE send reports on every female gone in the state since the start of the year.

The sheriff and his deputy sacked out in empty cells in the basement jail. They were back upstairs by seven o'clock, in plenty of time for Dr. Riley's call from the morgue.

The postmortem indicated that the dead woman was between fifty and fifty-five years of age, five feet, six and one half inches tall, 149 pounds, with blue eyes, dark brown hair recently hennaed, and a full set of excellently cared for teeth. The sole noteworthy identifying mark was an abdominal scar from a childhood appendectomy. It was the ME's opinion that death occurred six days before the body was found.

"What killed her?" White asked.

"Drowning."

"Come on, Daisy, she didn't jump in the canal with a mink on her back."

"I didn't say she had. There were traces of soap in the water we found in her lungs. She must have died indoors and been dumped in the slough later. Your guess is better than mine. The only hint of trauma was a subdural hematoma on the back of her head, like she slipped and banged it. The swelling was minimal. She must have stopped breathing right after it happened."

"What else do we know about her?"

"That she wasn't stoned on drugs. There was some alcohol in her blood but not enough to call her drunk. I'd say she tippled."

"And you can't narrow down the time of death?"

"Sorry, Buck, a little less than a week is the closest I can come."

"What about fingerprints?"

"A messy job. She'd been in the water so long, her fingertips had shriveled. What I had to do was amputate her fingers at the first joint and peel the outermost layer of skin. One by one I stretched them over my index finger, dipped them in ink, and rolled prints. I'll send them over by messenger later this morning. If I screwed up, you can have one of your boys come by and do the job, himself. I saved the fingers for you."

"You put those with the rest of the body, y'hear? Those prints are going to be just fine."

They were better than that. They were flawless.

He made copies for his department's use and sent others to Tallahassee and to the Federal Bureau of Investigation in Washington D.C. While they were being run through the files he went over a fresh batch of bulletins with Rutledge. No fewer than 717 women had been reported missing in

Florida over the previous five months, and only half could be eliminated from consideration on the basis of race and age. For the next two weeks Laxahatchee investigators worked exclusively on the case, speaking with police in the fifty-six of the state's sixty-seven counties from which women had disappeared. It was dull, time-consuming, and, above all else, unrewarding work.

An attempt at tracing the woman's clothing brought them to another dead end. There were no laundry marks on her dress. Her underwear was of a brand sold by the millions in department stores all over the country. They had no more success with the shoes and handbag, or the scuffed valise Mike Osceola unexpectedly showed up with at headquarters. Because they'd dealt with him before, there was no letdown when he claimed amnesia about the car from which it came. That occurred two days later, when the FBI and DLE reported no match for the prints.

But the well wasn't dry. The Ahningha Valley Slough floater had become something of a celebrity among Florida newspapermen, and her story traveled the Associated Press wire from Key West to Jacksonville. A short item even found its way into a Crimestoppers column in Pensacola. Rarely did a day go by without a call from the palmetto jungles and palm forests, the seaside condos and retirement villages promising the hot lead that would break the case, word of a recalcitrant wife or daughter or vanished neighbor. Although they learned to spot most as duds before the would-be informants finished talking, CIB investigators were under orders to run each one down.

Three weeks went by before a news item on the investigation in Laxahatchee County prompted a call from a hostess at a Fort Lauderdale restaurant. It was Rutledge's turn to take the mink for a drive. He arrived hot and sweaty and generally out of sorts at the end of another frustrating day. He began feeling better when he met the witness. Claire Pauley was a trim ash blonde in her late thirties. She brought him a cold Heineken without asking and pushed his money back across the table. "How could *anyone* forget a coat like that?" she asked. "I remembered it as soon as I read about the poor woman."

"Why'd you wait so long to call?"

"My former husband was in a bad car crash in Savannah over Memorial Day weekend, and I went up and stayed with him till he was back on his feet. I didn't get a look at a paper till I came home yesterday."

"When did you see the coat?"

"It must have been a Thursday, because it was two days before the accident. A tallish, heavyset woman with nice posture was wearing it when she came in for lunch. She was with a good-looking guy a few years younger, quite a few. All I had was a four in the corner, so I steered them to it. I watched him help her out of the mink and drape it over the chair. Vicarious pleasure, you understand. After they finished eating, they went away without it. Just drove off and left it behind."

She took a mint from a bowl on the next table and smoothed the foil wrapper around a finger. It was, Rutledge decided, a very stylish finger. "I have to confess, I tried it on. Fit like it was tailor-made. I guess I'm too honest for my own good. I checked the pockets for some identification, but all I could find was a matchbook from a restaurant—in St. Augustine, I think it was. I checked the label too. I thought that if the coat had been purchased around here, the store would remember who laid out all that money. But it was from some fancy shop in New York."

"Recall which one?" Rutledge asked.

"It was one of those Fifth Avenue designers with branches in London and Paris and Beverly Hills. An Italian name. I didn't know what to do with the coat. I couldn't hang it in the lost and found, because help is hard to find. So I locked it in the office. About five-thirty they came back, and the man asked if they'd left a coat. He said they were in Miami Beach before they realized they didn't have it. Can you beat that? I don't believe they even said thanks."

Although she was certain about the coat, she had little to add to what she had told the deputy about the couple. Nor had she gotten a look at their car.

"Did you notice if she was wearing a wedding ring?" Rutledge asked.

"I didn't, but I assumed that they were married."

"Why do you say that?"

"The man seemed very attentive. I was thinking I wished my ex had paid that much attention to me."

Rutledge put his notebook away. "Blue eyes?" he asked.

"I didn't notice her eyes. Or do you mean his?"

"I meant yours."

"They're hazel, actually. Why?"

"They're beautiful," he said.

"Thank you, but I don't see—"

"About your former husband . . ."

"What's *he* got to do with this?"

"He's feeling better?"

"Much better, thank you."

"Will you be going back to see him?"

"No, I don't think so," she said. "Do you want me to stay in town? Will you have more questions for me?"

"Yes," he said. "I have one now."

"What's that?"

"What are you doing for dinner tonight?"

"What I do every night," Claire Pauley said, furrowing her very stylish brow at the filling room. "Serving it."

When the body had gone unclaimed for sixty days, the medical examiner's office ordered it released for burial in the potter's field in Big Cypress. With time running short, White asked Dr. Riley to draw up a dental chart, which he saw as his last chance at having the woman identified. Sitting on his desk on the morning of interment was a full set of X rays plus a three-page report in which the ME took note of a number of unusual dental conformations. She also pointed out that the teeth were in superb condition and the quality of care first-rate. Obviously, the victim had been well off; such work would be unavailable to anyone without financial means.

Acting on her own, she had built plaster casts of the upper teeth and jaw. These were photographed and written about in detail on flyers that went out to police agencies throughout Florida, Georgia, Alabama, and Mississippi, and also received distribution among Southern dental societies. The problems involved in identifying the woman became the topic of a seminar at the Florida Dental Association's August convention in Pompano Beach, where White and Dr. Riley were guest speakers. Photos of the models also were sent to the editorial offices of the *Journal of the American Dental Association.* It was September when they ran alongside a short piece in the *JADA* newsletter, the last day of the month before the sheriff's office was contacted by Dr. Casper McNeil of Charleston, South Carolina, who thought he recognized his distinctive style of dentistry in the victim's teeth.

"You might say that for me each filling, every crown and inlay, is as unique as a fingerprint is to you," he told White over the phone. "I never forget a mouth in which I've placed my work. Would de Kooning forget a museum where he'd hung a painting?"

White let the question slide. "Whose mouth was it?" he asked.

"I can't say yet. I've been going through my charts for a week and haven't found the right one. But rest assured that I worked on that woman and that I'll get back to you when I find her."

A day later White received a second call from Charleston.

"Her name was Mrs. Jessie Rae Reynolds," Dr. McNeil said, "and three years ago next month I did bonded resin restorations of the proximal surfaces of teeth seven and eight, the front incisors. According to the *JADA* article, that's the most recent work in her mouth."

"What else do you know about her?"

"Not a lot besides her complete dental history, which you're welcome to. My records say that she was fifty-one years old when she was my patient and lived at 437 East Military Way here in Charleston. The only other thing I can tell you is that she was employed as a secretary for the A. B. Carswell Company. They're a big defense contractor."

White thanked him for his help, pressed the cradle, released it, and dialed South Carolina information. Soon he was relaying the particulars of his case to the Charleston homicide squad. When a Detective Sergeant Raymond Robey offered to send some men to East Military Way, White gave him his home phone number and told him not to be shy about calling late. Robey said he wasn't—and proved it shortly after midnight.

As White groped for a pad and pencil Robey told him that interviews with acquaintances of Jessie Rae Reynolds showed that the woman had left her job early in May after suddenly announcing that she was going to be married.

"The neighbors told us that they were surprised. Shocked is more like it. They said Mrs. Reynolds was twice-widowed, a quiet woman who hardly ever dated. In fact, she didn't appear to have close friends of either sex. She shared her apartment with a small dog, a gift from her second husband, and had grown increasingly withdrawn since his death. Her landlord said she had lived there four and a half years and one morning up and told her that she'd met a man and was moving away. She gave a month's notice, and then a van came and cleared out all her things."

"Can you find out who the movers were?" White asked.

"We're on top of that too. They were a North Charleston outfit. They told us she wanted the stuff put in storage in the city. We checked at the warehouse and learned that she rented space for a full year. It was real fine stuff. Nothing's been touched since."

"You fellows don't miss a beat."

"Hold the compliments, Sheriff. We weren't through yet. We also paid a visit to the Carswell Company and spoke to her boss, one of the vice-presidents. He couldn't believe it when Mrs. Reynolds told him that she was quitting to get married. She'd been his secretary five years, and he never knew her to have a boyfriend. We asked if he'd met her intended, and he said he hadn't. We didn't know where to go from there. We can't spend time on a Florida investigation, but I did ask if he knew of any kin we could contact. He gave me the name of an aunt in Murfreesboro, Tennessee, Mrs. Reynolds's hometown."

White switched on the light to copy his notes in a legible hand and saw the boys at the door. They ran into the bedroom in their pajamas and jumped on the bed like they had the keys to a private playground.

"Big trouble?" Buck, Jr., asked.

"No," White said. "It was just routine."

"Know what routine is?" Franklin asked his brother.

"Uh-huh," Buck, Jr., answered. "What Pa don't want to tell us about."

"Go back to bed, boys. I don't want to hear that you were dozing off in class. And Franklin," he said, letting the weight of his arm fall on the boy's spindly shoulders, "you're a heck of a lot smarter than an eleven-year-old has the right to be. Too smart for your own damn good."

The older boy smiled impishly. "Thanks Pa. It's a big case? That why they called?"

"Spies?" asked Buck, Jr.

"No," their father said, and got off the bed to shoo them away.

"The Mafia?" Franklin asked.

"Come on, boys, back to your room."

"Tell us," Buck, Jr., demanded. "Your stories are almost as good as TV."

"My stories are better than TV," White said with feigned indignation, "because they're true and because you know how much sweat goes into every case. TV is tame stuff next to my stories. I'm probably the only parent in the state who *likes* his kids watching TV. Bet you didn't know how lucky you are having me for your old man."

"We know," Franklin said. "Is it a bank robbery?"

"Some more dope smugglers?" asked Buck, Jr. "Like the time you got your picture in the newspaper with the airplane that crashed?"

"No," White said, raising his hands to try to quiet them, knowing what would come next.

"Like what happened to Mom?" asked Franklin.

" 'Cause if it is," said Buck, Jr., "I want you to shoot him dead when you catch him."

"Something like that," White admitted. "Now go on back to bed."

White got little sleep the rest of the night. At seven-thirty he was in the office, chewing impatiently on the unlit butt of one of Dr. Riley's cigars. As he waited for an operator to come on the line, it occurred to him that Murfreesboro was on central time and that it was too early to call. He dropped the cigar in a wastebasket and went out for coffee. Two cups later he dialed Tennessee. "I'm sorry if I woke you," he said after introducing himself.

"Not at all," Jessie Rae Reynolds's aunt said. "I have to be getting up, anyway."

Because he was afraid of alarming the woman, whose telephone voice sounded elderly and frail, he didn't explain why it was necessary for him to contact her niece.

"That's going to take some doing, Sheriff. She's been married for some time and living in Europe with her husband."

"Can you tell me where in Europe? If I could write her or get off a wire, it might save my men a lot of trouble."

"I . . . I don't have her address. To be honest, I don't

know the country. She left in May, and in all that time she never came back for a visit. She hasn't even written."

"I hate to have to say this," he began slowly, "but my office has reason to believe that your niece may be dead." Briefly he told her about the body in the slough and about the news from Charleston. "Don't you have any idea where she went?"

"Sheriff," the woman said, "I've been worried so about my niece. Not to call or write or come home to see me, that's not Jessie Rae. I've been debating for the longest time whether to go to the police, but I don't know what to tell them. I'd be hard-pressed to prove that she's over there in Europe, or that she ain't."

"What about this fellow she married? Have you tried getting in touch with his family?"

"His family? I don't know where he's from, much less if he has folks. I never met him. One day last spring I got a telegram saying there'd been a wedding and that Jessie was moving to Europe. It hurt me that I hadn't been invited and letting me know in such an impersonal way. I called Charleston right off. But she'd already left her place."

"What did you do then?"

"Well, I give it a lot of thought and decided, What do I know? Jessie was always a responsible girl with a fine head on her shoulders. If all of a sudden she wanted to change the way she was living, who's anyone to tell her what to do? Maybe it was time for her to kick up her heels, what with another birthday sneaking up on her. She never did have much of a childhood. And then losing two husbands before she turned fifty . . ."

"That might be the case," White said unconvincingly.

"I miss her something terrible," the woman went on. "She's my only kin that's left, my brother Bill's little girl. First thing I come home from the store, I look in the mailbox for a letter."

"Would it be asking too much for a snapshot of your niece? It could be important."

"I'll put one in the mail," the woman said.

At the end of the week a thin envelope with a Murfreesboro postmark arrived at the sheriff's office. Inside was a snapshot of a stout woman about to blow out candles on a cake. Tortoiseshell frames lent symmetry to a round face unaccustomed to makeup. She was neither pretty nor unattractive. A magnifying glass brought out the lines in her forehead, White's only point of reference. They appeared so perfectly straight that they could have been drawn with a ruler, as if rarely called upon to register emotion.

He had blowups printed and saw to it that each member of the department was supplied with at least two. Dr. Riley requested transparencies for comparison against the Ahningha Valley case file. Others went to Dr. McNeil, who confirmed that the woman was the one he had treated, and to Claire Pauley, who had reservations about making a positive identification.

"There's a difference," she told Rutledge at the restaurant. "It's hard to put a finger on it, but it's there." She brushed back a calico curtain and tilted the photo toward a window looking out on the sea-grape forest of Hugh Taylor Birch State Park "This isn't an older sister?"

"What makes you ask?"

"She seemed years younger when I saw her."

In the soft, natural light Rutledge noticed that Claire Pauley, too, was looking younger. "I don't see how," he said. "It's not a recent picture."

"An awful lot happier, at least. That'll knock years off any woman's age."

"Good enough," the deputy said, taking back the photo. He reached for his hat but made no move to leave. And how many years would *you* like to knock off tonight? he wanted to ask.

And kicked himself for days over an unprecedented failure of nerve.

13

White had a name to go with the body but only the sketchiest notion of who the woman was. What he needed was a detailed picture of Jessie Rae Reynolds's whereabouts and activities in the days leading up to her disappearance, what she was saying and to whom, her thoughts if possible, the concluding links in a chain of circumstances stretching to Laxahatchee County all the way from South Carolina. Again he turned to her aunt in Murfreesboro.

"We can't be sure," he told her. "If there's something more you can give us about the way your niece looked, how she dressed?"

"Jessie was neat and clean about her personal self," the elderly woman said, "but she didn't fuss over her appearance. She never wore her jewelry or bought fancy clothes, and Lord knows she could afford anything she wanted. The only reason she'd gone back to work, you know, was to get herself out of the house and be with people again. But a few years back the Carswell Company handed out generous Christmas bonuses to their employees, and she treated herself to a new fur."

"What kind was it?"

"The most beautiful, full-length ranch mink coat you ever saw. Jessie never looked lovelier than when she modeled it for me. It was the last time she showed any interest in pretty things. I couldn't tell you if she ever put it on again. She hardly had occasion to wear it."

In the afternoon Rutledge was told to start packing his bags. Inside a borrowed suitcase he folded a torn summer dress, women's underwear, and a mink coat. Pajamas and a clean shirt fit in a leather traveling kit. Because the sheriff's department was operating under budget constraints mandated by voter rejection of a county bond issue, he wasn't due to leave Florida until the first discount flight became available at eight P.M.

"I didn't ask for this," he told Pooler as he dropped the luggage in the trunk of the fat man's car, an oversize Chrysler equipped with hand controls and red-and-blue Florida disabled motorist tags. "There's a big-mouth bass derby in Frostproof dishing out seventy-five thousand dollars in prizes, and they'll be vacuuming the lunkers into the boats."

"You'll love Charleston," Pooler said.

"I'm already spoken for. Throwing my bass boat in the water and reeling in some of that cash, there's my one true love. . . . What does Buck expect me to find up there, anyway?"

"Some of his lost pride," Pooler said, putting the Chrysler on the airport road. "Ever watch him in the records room? He takes the unsolveds as a personal affront to his intelligence. The man's a perfectionist."

"A fanatic's what you mean," Rutledge said. "Solving South Carolina murders isn't his job. Working speed traps is, and making highway safety talks. And running for reelection, which is the most important part of it. What's he want to go playing Sherlock Holmes for? Black man has no business with games like that."

Pooler clenched the hand brake and slowed the car to seventy. "You Northern racists are the worst," he said.

"A what?" Rutledge sputtered. "I love the guy. He's pulled my ass out of the fire more times than I can count.

But that doesn't change the fact that if the county hadn't incorporated Lincolnville, where he's guaranteed about a hundred and ten percent of the black vote, he'd still be on patrol. He's good at that, running down DWIs, breaking up bar fights. The best I ever saw. Why doesn't he forget about all this gumshoe crap and let us concentrate on the basics—such as my fishing."

"You'll love Charleston," Pooler said.

He saw all he wanted of Murfreesboro on the ride from the airport, bean fields ravaged by "starter" home developments, cookie-cutter ranchettes. Surrounded by new construction in a muddy farm plot was a three-room cabin of hand-hewn ash. It was weathering badly, as was the woman who came to the door. She let him inside a sparsely furnished living room. She moved slowly, with the aid of an aluminum walker. Rutledge avoided her eyes as he unpacked the suitcase and showed her the garments from the slough. She failed to respond at first, then wept softly.

He was back in the air within the hour, over South Carolina before he could freshen his drink. Though everyone agreed that Charleston was his kind of town, in the rainy darkness he reserved judgment. A stewardess he met in the airport lounge offered a less unyielding mystery, and he ignored two wake-up calls attempting to solve it. Sandy-eyed and with a gentle buzzing in his ears, he arrived late that morning at the executive headquarters of the A. B. Carswell Company to speak with everyone there who had known Jessie Rae Reynolds.

The story never varied. He was told about an unusually reliable employee with few interests outside the job she had returned to after the deaths of her two husbands; a reserved introverted woman who lived by herself and showed little interest in men.

"Then that Sidney Waldorf came along last spring and changed all that quicker 'n quicksilver," the switchboard operator said.

Rutledge found a spiral notebook in his jacket and opened it to a clean page. "I don't know the name. Who is he?"

"A good question. Up until Jessie cashed in on her pension, I couldn't decide if he was man or rumor. I never saw him. I never heard any of the other girls say they did. If she introduced him to anybody, it would be to Henrietta Ryder. You might talk to her."

"I don't know that name, either."

"Jessie Rae's landlady. Far as I know, she still lives out on Military Way."

"He was a salesman," Henrietta Ryder said, "although I don't recall that he carried a sample case." She was a pink woman tenting inside a yellow housecoat, and she spoke with Rutledge on the porch of the two-family home where Jessie Rae Reynolds had been her tenant and closest friend for almost five years.

"What was it he sold?" Rutledge asked.

"Stocks and bonds, I think it was," she said. "No, it was commodities. That's it. Jessie told me he was a dealer in precious metals, and I asked if she'd seen any, and she laughed and said he didn't tote 'em around. She said he sold 'em by the ton."

"Do you know where Mrs. Reynolds met Mr. Waldorf?"

"I do," the woman said. "Would you like to come inside and have a cup of coffee?"

"No thank you, ma'am." Dying for one but unwilling to interrupt.

"You're sure? Well, I could hardly believe it, myself, but several months before she moved out, Jessie began subscribing to a lonely-hearts book. It was full of ads and photos from folks looking to mate up with someone and too bashful to pick 'em up on their own. I asked Jessie, I said, 'How can you be answering ads like that when you don't know the kind of person that's placing 'em?' You see, Jessie was a very refined lady, not bad-looking, either, but shy, and she had a hard time meeting men that came up to her standards. And she told me, she said, 'Henny, I'm fifty-four years old and I haven't been with a man but twice in five years, and I'll be damned if I'm gonna keep on depriving myself.' That's how she said it, Sheriff."

"Deputy," Rutledge said. "Did you ever see a picture of Sidney Waldorf?"

"Jessie pointed out his ad, and it was the only one on the page without a photo alongside. That raised my suspicions. I told her not to answer it, that he was some ugly whose map would frighten the girls away."

"I suppose he was."

"Hell, no, he wasn't," Henrietta Ryder said severely. "He was a fine-looking man with a strong profile and his own hair and lots of it. And he was young too. A nice few years younger than Jessie."

"That the way Mrs. Reynolds described him?"

"That's the way he looked," she said. "I should know. He became a regular fixture around the house in the weeks till he and Jessie eloped."

"*Eloped*?" Rutledge asked, and was answered by Henrietta Ryder's chilly stare. "How'd it come to that?"

"Sidney said he was coming to Charleston to sell his commodities and that he planned on leaving after he was done. He was from up north somewhere—Philadelphia I believe—but that wasn't where he was taking Jessie. He told her he was making so much money, he'd never have to work again, and they could spend their whole lives in Europe. I told her, I said, 'Jessie, this is the most outlandish thing I ever heard, marrying this fellow you don't hardly know and running off to some foreign countries with him.' And she told me, she said, 'You're darn right it is, Henny. That's why I'm going for it. A chance like this don't come along twice. Not for me it don't.'

"Once Jessie said she'd marry him, you couldn't keep that man from her door. Anyways, I couldn't. Don't be sure there weren't mornings I caught him slinking down the stairs on his tiptoes with his shoes in his hand. I didn't say nothing to Jessie, of course, but you couldn't avoid the change that came over her. She told me she never suspected she could care so much about anyone and that they'd be leaving Charleston and getting married just as quick as he wrapped up his business here."

"Do you know which brokerage house he worked for?"

"I don't believe he was connected with any of 'em," Henrietta Ryder said. "I remember Jessie telling me he was self-employed. When she took all that money from the bank and let him have it to invest, she said he was smarter than any of those big outfits like Merrill-Lynch and what's-their-names."

"Hold on," Rutledge said. "What's this about giving money to Waldorf?"

"Jessie wasn't one for high living, Sheriff, and over the years, what with leaving most of her pay in the bank and having Mr. Russell look after what her late husbands left, she must have saved up a pile. Sidney told her he could turn even a few thousand into a small fortune, if she had any faith in him. And even if he lost it, it didn't matter, 'cause he had so much that they could live high on the hog off that for three lifetimes. Jessie didn't bother for my advice. She couldn't wait to put some of it in his hands. 'Bait money,' she called it."

"Where did Mrs. Reynolds keep her funds?"

"The First Bank of Charleston on Congress Street. You'll want to see the president, Mr. Harvey Russell."

"Certainly we did everything to dissuade her, but she'd made up her mind. At first she wanted five thousand dollars. Then she insisted on withdrawing a much larger sum and turning it over to her fiancé, along with a substantial portfolio of stocks and bonds. If you'd like, I'll be glad to show you our records."

"In a minute," Rutledge said. "How was it going to be reinvested?"

"I don't think she had an inkling," said Harvey Russell, erect and distinguished in a pin-striped suit on the far shore of a sea-green desk blotter. When he turned his head, Rutledge noticed a hearing aid and moved his chair closer. They were still eight feet apart. "She was convinced that her fiancé was a brilliant speculator who could read trends in the commodities market weeks in advance. And that was one of his lesser miracles. There was no reasoning with the woman."

"About her fellow . . . did you meet him?"

"I asked her on more than one occasion to bring him by. I wanted to size up the man, satisfy myself that I wasn't turning over her savings to an out-and-out swindler. He never seemed to have the time. I got tired of waiting and made some calls around the state. No one at any of the more reputable brokerage houses had heard of a commodities trader by the name of Sidney Waldorf."

Rutledge asked, "What about the others?"

"True, there's always the chance that he was part of a boiler room operation," Russell answered. "Every now and again a bunch of slick talkers, sometimes just one working alone, will rent office space in Charleston or Columbia and do a land-office business for a couple of months or so, until the area is tapped out. A few are on the up-and-up, but most deal in naked options. Put a phone in their hand and they're all pretty ruthless, though."

"Naked options . . . ? I don't know what you mean."

"The way these traders work, our Mr. Waldorf solicits clients to purchase options, which are the rights to contracts on the delivery of commodities, such as gold or wheat or pork bellies, falling due in several months. Say an option costs five thousand dollars. Waldorf has the client send fifty-five hundred, which covers his ten percent commission, and if he isn't too greedy, he keeps the five hundred and buys the option with the rest. Then he sends the ticket, or receipt, to the client.

"The commodities market is highly speculative, and few investors see a profit. Most amateurs take a terrific beating, and it becomes Waldorf's job to call with the news that the value of the option has dropped and the entire investment is lost. If the client has any doubts, he can check the financial pages."

"I see," Rutledge said. "Least I think I do."

"On the other hand," Russell went on, "traders who write naked options are convinced from the start that the investment is going to be wiped out, so they pocket the whole fifty-five hundred and mail a phony ticket. When the client sees in the newspaper that the option has fallen in value, he tears up the receipt and throws it away."

"If there's no way of winning, why would anyone invest?"

"Oh, there's a chance of making a profit," Russell said, smiling faintly. "When the economy is booming, the value of commodities generally increases. At the time a contract falls due and the client sees he's, let's say, tripled his investment, he calls Waldorf to ask where his check is. If Waldorf is at all honest, or a shrewd crook, he'll reach inside his own pocket to make good. But you can be sure that if his check arrives Monday, by Tuesday he's pitching another investment. Nine times out of ten the client is so impressed with his quick return, he sends back all the money and then some. Later, when the market declines, as periodically it must, he loses everything."

"So Waldorf wins either way."

"Not so fast. Sometimes the market doesn't go down for a long, long time, and as his client's profits mount, there's no way for him to pay back all he owes. The only thing he can do then is pick up and run."

"Ever hear of one taking the client with him?" Rutledge asked.

"He'll take her," Russell said. "He'll take her any way he can."

"What I still don't understand," White said above the long-distance clutter, "is why he didn't skin her like the others, if that was his game, and just skip town. Once he had her money, why'd he bother with her anymore?"

"I don't think she'd have parted with a dime if he hadn't romanced her," Rutledge said. "And when he began showering her with attention, she got to liking it. He must have figured the best way to get her off his back was to keep her on her own."

"But why in our front yard? Say, Ma, you have plans for the weekend?"

"Do I? If I can get my crank bait working in Frostproof by tomorrow, there's some big fish that's gonna make me a rich man."

A tapping sound at White's end of the line was his answer.

"Buck, did you hear . . . ?"

"Listen, Ma, there must be some trouble with the connection, 'cause I can't understand a word you're trying to say. Let me make this quick, and then I won't waste any of your time. Take a few more days at county expense and see what else you dig up on those lovebirds. Come home when you have something good. Enjoy yourself, Ma. You'll love Charleston."

In the morning he was back at the two-family house on East Military Way.

"Miss Ryder," he said, "I've been in South Carolina close to two days, and you're the only intimate of Mrs. Reynolds I've found. I can't believe a woman as decent as the one you told me about didn't have other friends."

"Jessie Rae was a warm, wonderful human being, Sheriff, but she didn't feel comfortable around most folks. Still, you might want to look up Agnes Jeppison. She's the librarian at the Magazine Street branch. There were times

Jessie practically lived in that library. I'll call and let her know you're stopping by."

Agnes Jeppison was a leggy blonde in her early thirties who hadn't heard that miniskirts were twenty years out of style, or else didn't care. Rutledge's first instinct was to direct the questioning to what she was doing after work. His second, upon noticing a small diamond on her left hand, was not to jeopardize his professional dignity. After introductions, she brought him into the children's room, where they traded loud whispers.

The litany of questions began along tried lines. "When was the last time you saw her?"

"It wasn't long before Memorial Day," the librarian said. "Jessie Rae had quit her job, and she dropped by to tell me she was getting married and leaving Charleston. She was so happy, she was absolutely radiant."

"Did she say where she was going?"

"They were planning on settling in Europe. They were going to drive down to Miami for the wedding and take a honeymoon cruise from there. I'm still jealous."

"Have you heard from her since?"

Agnes Jeppison put a finger to her lips. "Lower your voice, please," she breathed. "About a week after they left, I got a card from a hotel in Florida. Jessie Rae wrote that she expected to be married soon and didn't know when she'd be getting back to Charleston, and she wanted me to know how much she'd miss our little chats. She promised to write again. I thought she'd send another card from one of her ports of call, or maybe Europe, but it must be close to six months and I haven't heard a thing."

Rutledge leaned close, almost into her ear. "Do you remember the name of the hotel?"

"I'm afraid I don't."

"What about the city?"

"I'm sorry. I didn't know it would be important. I just

read the note, took a look at the picture, and threw the card away."

"What was it a picture of?" Rutledge asked offhandedly, "the flamingos at Hialeah, an alligator?"

"Now that you mention it, I had a good laugh at that picture. It showed a whole mess of turtles, must have been a million of them. And it said something about this being the turtle corrals. *Turtle corrals*! Whoever heard of such a thing, keeping turtles in corrals like they were cattle?"

"*I have,*" Rutledge said, nearly deafening her. "Thank you, Mrs. Jeppison, you don't know what a help you've been."

Van Vliet's Turtle Kraal behind the Haulover Pier is the most neglected tourist attraction in Miami Beach. For fifty cents, half for children under twelve, the curious are invited to climb a wooden tower overlooking the dusty pens where Joost Van Vliet raises the giant sea turtles that go into his line of canned turtle soup and turtle steak. Van Vliet came to Florida from Holland in the late twenties, at the end of the big real estate boom. Searching for a tax write-off against his turtle profits, he sank a young fortune into a ramshackle hotel on a nearby lot and was as amazed as anyone when it became a south Florida landmark. After the war he tore it down and rebuilt it as Van Vliet's Leatherback Inn, a sixteen-story glass-and-glazed-brick testimonial to his turtles and himself. Later had come the Hawksbill at Fort Lauderdale and Ridley's in Key West.

When Rutledge got off the plane in Coral Gables, a waiting Laxahatchee cruiser flashed its lights and started toward him. White guided it through the airport's main gate and along Northwest Thirty-sixth Street to the MacArthur Causeway, which brought them over the yacht-clogged waters of Biscayne Bay into Miami Beach. They continued east to Collins Avenue, followed it into the Leatherback Inn parking lot. In the business office they learned that if Sidney Waldorf and Jessie Rae Reynolds had been guests, they failed to make any impression on the staff.

"A ranch mink coat?" the manager said, also unimpressed. "I had a dining room full for breakfast. As a rule, we fix the air conditioners in the lobby at fifty degrees to keep the ladies in furs from passing out."

"There's got to be a way to tell if they stayed here," White said. "We have to know."

"We store our billing records in the basement. We're supposed to clear everything out after four months, but there's papers from two and three years back."

"Can we get a look in there?"

"No problem," the manager said. "I should warn you, though, the stuff is thrown together according to room number, and there are more than two hundred rooms in the hotel. What month was it you said they were guests?"

The Leatherback Inn's May records filled ten corrugated paper boxes that once contained jars of gefilte fish. White gave Rutledge a folder three inches thick, held together with a frayed rubber band that snapped in his hand as he removed it. This was the file for room 101, and it took the deputy fifteen minutes to inspect while White worked on 102.

"If they stayed on the first floor," said White as he pulled the folder for room 103, "we can be out of here this afternoon. If we don't have that kind of luck, I'll call the Miami Police Academy. They don't know what to do with their probationary officers."

They were back in the basement the next day, and the day after that. Early on their third morning at the Leatherback Inn, the only woman among four rookie cops handed Rutledge a stack of papers from room 1003. The deputy examined the top two and blew her a kiss that went unreturned.

"We found it, Buck," he said.

The prize was a sheaf of thirty bills signed over a five-day period by Mr. and Mrs. Sidney Waldorf of East

Military Way, Charleston, South Carolina. According to the main invoice, they had paid for their stay with a credit card issued to Jessie Rae Reynolds of the same address. The line showing business affiliation had been left blank.

"So he married her, after all," Rutledge said.

"Maybe. Or maybe they just registered like that," White said. "Either way, the honeymoon wasn't over. Look at these chits: Thursday, May 22, dinner, $37.50, champagne $46.50; Friday, May 23, breakfast $9, lunch $16, dinner $41.75, champagne $46.50; Saturday, May 24, breakfast $18—"

"How do you run up an $18 breakfast tab?"

"Beats me," White said. "Lunch $15, dinner $35.50, champagne $46.50."

"This one's not theirs," Rutledge said, sliding the bill off the pile. "It must've gone in the folder by mistake."

"What mistake? It looks like all the others, right down to the champagne."

"The signature's wrong. A P. I. Campfield signed for this meal."

"Let me see that," White said, and held the paper to an overhead bulb. "It's made out to the guests in 1003 for May 24. And Waldorf and Mrs. Reynolds were still checked in on that date, because here's their chits for the 25th and 26th. You're right about the signature, though. Funny, if you look close enough, it's an awful lot like Waldorf's. It's even signed with the same pen he was using, the same light blue ink. That must've been vintage champagne if Waldorf forgot his own name."

"That other name mean anything to you?"

"Draws a blank for now. I'm going to give it to the feds, package it with Waldorf's, and let them run it through the NCIC computer. If there's a Campfield's ever been in trouble anywhere, we ought to know about it soon enough."

14

There was good news for White and bad news, too, and he was damned if he could figure out which was which. After a prolonged silence the National Crime Information Center had gotten back with word that the lone Campfield possessing a recent felony record had died in an inmate rebellion at the McNeil Island, Washington, penitentiary three years earlier. As for Sidney Waldorf, the computer counted three of them languishing behind bars on charges ranging from smuggling aliens into the country to air piracy. But two were in their fifties, and their namesake was twenty-three, and none had been walking the streets in more than a year.

Of greater interest was a DLE teletype announcing the arrest of still another Waldorf in Ellsworth County, on the Alabama border, for investigation of interstate transportation of a stolen motor vehicle. The brief physical description was as familiar to White as the one on his own driver's license and kept his optimism fueled when inquiries to the Ellsworth courthouse were shunted through a bagatelle of civil servants knowing little about the prisoner and caring less. A Glades City travel agent was more accommodating, booking him onto a morning flight to the Panhandle.

Although his family had lived there until the Great Depression, White had an abiding distaste for what he referred to collectively as "up north" and which meant, in practical terms, where waitresses brought lemon meringue instead of key lime pie with his coffee. His reasons had as much to do with the weather as with his stomach, however, because he couldn't stand the cold. And to Buck White cold was what caused Atlantans, for instance, to moderate the air conditioning. On the Tuesday his plane landed in Pensacola, and he was met by a driver from the Ellsworth police. The temperature in that part of up north stood at forty-one degrees.

He had bundled himself in his warmest things when he left for the airport, a thin cotton windbreaker, one of his three long-sleeved shirts, and his hat. Pooler, who was almost his size, had offered a quilted vest, and White regretted having turned it down. All the way to Ellsworth he fiddled with the car heater and was mad at the world by the time they pulled into the police parking lot on Jeff Davis Street.

The Ellsworth Public Safety Building was a three-story edifice that had been painted too red many years before and allowed to darken to its present charred appearance. The top floor was home to the long dormant Ellsworth Civil Defense unit and was used to store drums of 1962 vintage drinking water. The fire department took up the second story while the rest of the building belonged to the forty-two-member police force. Next door were the municipal and county courts.

His driver led White into a busy corridor where unshaded bulbs lent an ocher tinge to perpetual dusk. A rut in the linoleum pointed the way to a room reeking of yesterday's coffee and last week's cigars. Battered lockers, a cigarette-scarred table, straight-backed wooden chairs, and two rolltop desks, placed head to head, dulled the echoes of hunt-and-hit typing. The walls were painted two shades of green, lighter on top. White felt warm for the first time since leaving Miami. He stuck out his hand at a skinny, middle-aged man with jug-handle ears who looked up sourly from the larger of the desks.

"Lieutenant Kazmier," the driver said, "this is Sheriff White."

Barton Kazmier took back his hand as quickly as his visitor let him. He didn't like blacks and found dealing with them the hardest part of his job. He sized up White with hurt eyes. It was bad enough running to niggertown to settle their squabbles while dodging their knives, to haul them in by the carload every Saturday night. But this was asking too much. He motioned White into a chair and perched on the edge of his desk and looked down at him.

He would make it short. Sidney Waldorf had been arrested four days earlier after an off-duty officer noticed a silver Lincoln in apparent violation of the safety code idling at a red light on Boone Street. Kazmier didn't mention that the patrolman had assumed he'd find a young black behind the wheel of the high-powered car and was elated to discover that the light above the rear license plate had burned out. Curbing the Lincoln with his gun, he ordered the driver outside. When a white man emerged from behind the tinted glass, he was sorry he had bothered. But a crowd was starting to gather, and it was too late to let him go. He asked for a license and registration, and Waldorf produced both. The registration was issued to a Helen Neville of Theater Street, Mobile. Because he was unable to produce her as well, he was brought to headquarters as a matter of routine. The Lincoln was towed to the impoundment lot.

"This was not what you would call a high-priority case," said Kazmier, trying as best as he could to hide his disdain for the towering black man. "If your department is like ours, you give him a hard time for spoiling your day off and let him go with a warning to come back later with a certificate of title. But not this one, you don't, not when he shows Alabama tags and a Florida license. Not when he can't explain what he's doing in Ellsworth, which ain't exactly on the beaten track. And then there's the problem of what to do with the ten thousand dollars in cash and the bankbooks belonging to this Helen Neville we found in an attaché case under the front seat. Since we're so interested, he says, the money's his and the Neville woman's a relative. But he's shy on details, so we book him on suspicion of auto theft and put him in a cell downstairs. Judge Carson in Circuit Court sets bond at twenty-five hundred dollars. You'd think he'd try to post it right off, but he doesn't even use the phone calls we allow him. He's due in court tomorrow morning, and if we don't come up with something substantial, we have to give him back the money and the car."

"You sent his fingerprint classifications to Washington?"

"Yeah," Kazmier said, "but they tell us the computer's been out of action. We haven't heard a word." He squirmed off the desk and leaned a hip against it. "I've scratched your back. What have you got for me?"

White rattled the bare bones of his murder case and then went downstairs to the bullpen where he would interrogate the prisoner. A turnkey relieved him of his gun belt before letting him inside. He nudged two chairs into the center of the empty room, sat on one, and put his feet up on the other, pried the lid off a tin of snuff, and pinched some under his lip. He tamped it with his tongue as the bars clanged shut behind a dark-eyed man wearing chains around his waist and an empty expression on his bloodless mouth.

White studied him with a scowl of belligerent contempt made art by Sonny Liston. The pale features triggered dampness in his palms, dryness in his throat. He rose slowly and rolled the snuff against his gums, less concerned with sorting out his reactions than with hiding them.

The man glaring back at him showed little indication of discomfort, nothing worse than severe boredom. He was dressed in a bright orange jumpsuit three sizes too large with ELLSWORTH CITY JAIL stenciled across the shoulders. To prevent him from hanging himself, his shoes and socks had been taken away. He wore cheap rubber thongs that slapped against his feet when he walked and made it impossible to run. His eyes told White that he was determined to bottle up what little personality might show through the dreary uniform. He said, "It's been a while, hasn't it?" and shook his head when he was offered a chair.

"Can I have this man unshackled?" White asked the turnkey. "How's he supposed to act human trussed up like that?"

"He'll have to find a way. Lieutenant Kazmier's orders."

"It's no big deal," the prisoner said. "Read me my rights and let's get going."

"What's the hurry?" White asked, reaching inside a breast pocket for the laminated card he consulted whenever he was about to question a suspect. "You have plans for tonight?" He fingered the plastic but did not look at it; recited the Miranda warning from memory, returned it to his shirt, buttoned the flap over it. He adjusted his pinch again. "I don't believe I caught the name," he said.

"Waldorf," the chained man told him. "Sid Waldorf."

"I'll call you Novotny."

"Novotny's dead and buried, Sheriff. I put him out of his misery myself. After his girlfriend died, the man wasn't the same. He had no future."

"He tried to steal one," White said. "He made a grab for her estate."

"Novotny was an opportunist. A man like that doesn't deserve to live."

White spit his pinch on the floor and ground it beneath his heel. "I was thinking the same thing."

"You didn't come all the way here just to tell me that."

"It's something I want you to understand."

"You've covered the rules. What's the game?"

White put both hands on the man's shoulders and

pushed him into a chair. "It's no game," he said. "I want some information about Jessie Rae Reynolds."

The groundwork for a smile crinkled the prisoner's eyes. "Do you talk to Jessie? How's she doing?"

"You'd know better than me."

"I wish I did, Sheriff, but we haven't been in touch for a long time, since she gave me the heave for another man."

"From what I heard, she didn't seem the type."

"That was my guess too. But when they get to be Jessie's age . . . Tell me, why are you so interested in her?"

"She got herself murdered in my county," White said. He looked into the man's eyes again and saw them widen. His lips quivered. Why don't you drop your jaw for me too? Why don't you hang your head in your hands and start sobbing while you're at it? "We fished her out of a canal in the Everglades."

"I'm sorry to hear that. I really am. In the short time we had together I grew very attached to her. For a while we even considered marriage."

"The way you were considering it with Miss Belson?"

"I've been on the road a long time. What's wrong with wanting to settle down?"

"Your women have an awful high mortality rate."

"Everyone dies."

"They don't all drown."

"Nobody felt worse about Merry than I did. And now Jessie . . ." He lowered his head and then looked up ironically. "I know what you've been trained to think, but that isn't the way it is. I'm not the car thief Kazmier told you I am, let alone a killer."

"Nothing worse than a cheap swindler."

"I make plenty of money for my clients. Jessie was way ahead of the game when we broke up."

"Why you change your name as often as your socks."

"Character names are common in our industry. Many investors are reluctant to go with an ethnic broker, so those of us who need them take WASPy names. There's nothing unethical about it. Stage actors do it all the time. The difference is that with us, when a name stops working, we keep switching till we find one that does."

"Like Campfield?"

"You're not doing your homework, Sheriff. That one wasn't mine."

White put his foot up on a chair and rested a forearm on his knee. "Tell me about Campfield," he demanded.

"There's not much I know. I was staying with Jessie at the Leatherback Inn in Miami Beach, and he had a room down the hall. I could see that Jessie enjoyed his sense of humor, so I cultivated his friendship. He was traveling by himself and seemed lonely. Next thing I knew, he had all the company he could handle, and I had my walking papers."

"You don't sound upset."

"I was at the time. Like I said, it was a while ago."

"It won't wash," White said. "We know you're Campfield. We've got receipts from the Leatherback showing his signature for meals charged to your room."

The other man laughed. "If that's what brought you here, you made a long trip for nothing. I'm not Campfield any more than you are. And if he was buying her dinner, all it means is that they didn't wait till I was out of her life to start getting it on. They had plenty of opportunity. I was on business in Miami every day."

"I might buy that from Sid Waldorf. From Francis Norodny it doesn't mean shit."

"You *were* doing your homework. I'm touched."

"What you are is lucky. You turned up in my county, I'd nail your hide to the wall."

"I thought the South had changed. That would be a violation of my civil rights."

White grabbed the chain around the prisoner's midsection and jerked him to his feet. "Fuck you *and* your civil rights. Dead men don't need civil rights."

"You take your job too seriously. You'll end up with a heart attack."

"Worry about your own health," White said, feeling the heat of his anger spill across his face. "Watching you conduct electricity is going to make me twenty years younger."

"Peculiar sort of therapy. I could be innocent."

"You and Jack the Ripper," White said.

"That's pretty fast company."

"You were keeping up."

"I never got out of the gate. Listen why?"

White let go of the chain, and the prisoner stumbled back in the chair. "Amuse me."

"I met Jessie a few months after Merry died," he began. "I was working my ass to the bone trying to forget what had happened, and when I arrived in Charleston, I was given her number, I don't remember how. She invested five thousand dollars with me and saw a large return, a nice percentage coming back to her, so she decided to let it ride and try her luck again. The second time she wanted to put down a lot more, almost everything. I warned her about the risks, but she didn't seem concerned. The nature of our relationship had pretty much changed by then, and she had a lot of faith in me, maybe too much."

"She gave you all she had?"

"She was worth four hundred thousand dollars, but no more than half was liquid. Most was tied up in securities. I viewed her portfolio as a sound investment, and since I thought she was going to be my wife, naturally I wanted to keep it in the family. I proposed buying the stock myself."

"What was its value?"

"Close to two hundred thousand. I didn't have that kind of money with me, so I suggested a trip to Florida. I'd relocated after Merry's death, and Miami's where I keep the bulk of my assets. I sold off some bonds to raise the cash."

"There's a record of the transfer?"

"The lawyer's name was John Hanratty, and you can find him on Southwest Eighth Street. We were at his office a few days after Memorial Day. I gave Jessie a check for the full amount and reinvested it in silver futures and corn before trading closed that afternoon. We went back to Miami Beach, and you know the rest better than I."

"Do you still have the securities?"

"Uh-uh. The market turned bearish, and I had to get rid of them at a loss. I'm sorry I ever got involved."

"Didn't you try to reach Mrs. Reynolds again? What did you do when it was time to pay off on her investment?"

"Her time never came. She was wiped out."

White said, "You've got a bad attitude. That'll cost a man in your situation."

"Nothing personal."

"To me it is. My wife, my ex-wife, was killed by a man like you."

"Not like me, Sheriff, I—"

"No matter. Till I find the right bastard, you'll do."

White signaled the turnkey that the interview was over. At Kazmier's desk he placed a call to John Hanratty.

"I'm sorry," the operator told him after the sixth ring. "No one seems to answer."

"Thanks anyway." He looked at his watch and saw that it was five-thirty. "I'll try again in the morning."

A call to Glades City caught Pooler in the records room, where he was donating a vacation day to the county. "Say, Pools," White said, "you think you can find Francis Norodny's rap sheet without tearing the shelves off the wall?"

"Whose?"

"Norodny's. The Belson case."

"One sec," the fat man said, wheeling away with the receiver wedged between his shoulder and ear. "What are we looking for?"

"Check the AKAs and see if you find a Campfield anywhere."

"Peter I. Campfield," Pooler said without pause. "His favorite alias. Why?"

"It's a long story," White said. "Maybe with a happy end. Tell you about it when I get back. Meantime, you see Ma, have him keep his bags packed. I might be needing him to help transport a prisoner."

He went outside wondering where he was going to kill a dozen hours. A hand-painted shoat wallowing in a hickory haze suggested a start at Smokey's Real Pit Bar-B-Que. On the courthouse lawn a dull plaque stopped him, a rueful memento from the Daughters of the Confederacy that on the same spot for more than a century had stood the busiest Gulf Coast slave market east of New Orleans. Unmoved, he saw inside a lighted window a black porter trailing a mop down a linoleum canyon.

If the Old South's notion of fair play still kept his people fettered, Buck White understood better than most that its cruelties were not entirely selective. What the Confederate daughters would deem fitting for the highborn, twice-accused Norodny was a two-hour trial before a trash jury and soon after a ride home in a plain pine box, a sentence endearingly immune to appeal. "Try 'em and fry 'em," he said out loud. "Got the right idea about *that*."

He spent the night in Ellsworth's only hotel, a walk-up over a pool hall on Boone Street. The mangled cadenzas of breaking glass, of fists pounding against walls and unsuspecting faces kept him awake well past midnight. When he finally shut his eyes, he slept fitfully. It was nine-thirty when he woke up, tired and in no mood for breakfast. He tried the Miami law office again. A secretary put him on hold.

He waited five minutes before John Hanratty bellowed a good morning and reminded him that time was money—his. From his voice White judged him to be fifty, prosperous, and unprincipled, a storefront ambulance chaser gorging himself on the miseries of Little Havana. Although the names Sidney Waldorf and Jessie Rae Reynolds meant nothing to him, he offered to have his secretary check for any notation that he had done business with the couple. White heard papers rustling and muted protests in Spanish and English before Hanratty came back on the line.

"You're right," the attorney said. "They were in my office last May twenty-ninth, to arrange the transfer of some stock from Mrs. Reynolds to Mr. Waldorf."

"The *twenty-ninth*? That can't be. Look again."

"I have it in front of me in black and white. Why do you sound surprised?"

"Because Mrs. Reynolds disappeared from her hotel three or four days earlier, and her corpse turned up in my county with her purse stuffed with newspapers of the twenty-seventh."

"I don't see how that's possible," Hanratty said. "She was very much alive when she came to the office. I recall them quite clearly now. He was a handsome man in a winter suit who didn't smile or say a lot. She was a rather petite brunette in her early twenties, extremely attractive."

"Describe her again."

"Short, dark, about twenty-two or twenty-three, very serious, very demure, dressed for a literary tea. You know the type. She looked like she'd swallow poison sooner than take a little sun."

"You're certain?"

"Yes, I am. Once I saw my notes, I remembered the transaction. You don't often find girls so young with such large blocks of stock. My secretary remembers them too."

"I need details. How much was the stock worth?"

"Let me see," Hanratty said. "Exactly $167,400. They asked me to notarize the transfer, and I saw him hand her his personal check for the entire amount. Everything was perfectly legal."

White caught Lieutenant Kazmier as he was leaving the

office. "I can't talk," Kazmier said. "There's trouble at the jail."

"This will only take a minute. I think we can draw up new charges on Waldorf."

"I'm listening," Kazmier said, tapping his foot impatiently as White briefed him on his conversation with John Hanratty.

"On information like that I can get a magistrate in Laxahatchee County to sign an arrest warrant this afternoon," White added. "What I'd like you to do is line up a judge to handle arraignment."

"I don't have the time," Kazmier said, snarling, and pushed past him toward the door.

"Then make it," White said, blocking his way. "Or find someone who will."

"You're too late."

"What are you getting at, man?"

"Just this," Kazmier said, "That Mr. Waldorf, or whatever it is you call him, is no longer a guest of the city of Ellsworth."

"Jesus H. Christ, you didn't let him go?"

"No, *man*, we didn't let him go. He checked out on his own."

"How? You had him chained up like he was Scrooge's ghost."

"Damn it, I can't explain. I got to find the son of a bitch. Go downstairs and talk to the jailer. He'll tell you."

Burt Crosby was a stooped, shapeless bundle of despair whose razor kept a day or two behind the salt-and-pepper stubble on his colorless cheeks. He wore the bleached pallor of a man who had spent two thirds of his life in jail, even with the keys on his belt. He was fifty-four years old and obsessed with young women but didn't know any. On his best days he rarely made a favorable impression. This was one of the worst.

"It's been a bad year for me," he told White, "a real bad year. If it wasn't for they put civil service in the jail, I don't know the city would keep me on. He's the third one I lost since Fourth of July."

"How'd he get away?"

"Made it look easy," Burt Crosby said. "The others had to work at it. Not this one."

"How—?" White stuffed his hands deep in his pockets and hoped they wouldn't find their way around the faded man's neck.

"Well, last night we got a fresh load of prisoners. There was a ruckus over by the pool hall on Boone Street, and when the officer got there, he couldn't tell who the wise guys was, so he run everybody in. We're used to that, and we always let the drunks go in the morning, after they sleep it off."

"I still don't see—"

"That's what we done this time. We arrested six boys last night and we released six boys this morning. Only, when I looked in the holding cell at the courthouse, there was still one in there and he was wearing a jumpsuit like the serious offenders. He was out like a light, but a pitcher of ice water in the face done him fine. He said he didn't know what happened, said they let him out of the tank and put him in the holding cell with the others, and next thing he knows, he's out cold. And there *was* a nasty bump upside his head."

Burt Crosby was starting to feel better, and he paused for dramatic effect. "And there wasn't no Sidney Waldorf. When Judge Carson called that boy's name in court, Waldorf must've answered for him. Judge makes it a rule to release all drunks on their own recognizance, and that's what he done with this boy. Only it was Waldorf. And now the whole police department's out looking for him. What'd you say you want him for, Sheriff?"

"Don't trouble yourself about it, Burt. But next time—"

"Yes, sir?"

"Try to be more careful."

"Yeah, but what about this time? What if the lieutenant don't find him?"

"You know these parts, Burt. Where would you be running if you were in his shoes?"

"In that one's?" Burt Crosby let some of the sag out of his shoulders. "I'd light out of the county, get as far away from Ellsworth as there is."

"And then what?"

"Don't look back," Burt Crosby said without hesitating.

"Make a beeline for home, that it?"

"Guess so."

"I think you've got something there," White said.

"No charge for the advice," Burt Crosby said modestly.

"Home's probably where he's headed."

"Shit, yeah. Where's that, Sheriff?"

"You tell me, Burt. He likes women, likes 'em almost as much as he likes money and easy living."

Burt Crosby started to say something but changed his mind. "So do I," he said sadly.

15

Both of them looked like money.

The younger one couldn't have been out of her teens. What he liked best about her was the way she walked, tilted the least bit forward with an elegant stiffness that somehow didn't look awkward. Her posture was superb, the figure restrained. Her face, while still retaining a hint of childish pertness, was worldly, the pale skin outlined by sculpted red hair. Alice would know what to say to her. He could see she was going to be one pain in the ass.

There was a seasoning of vanity in the older woman's makeup. She was dressed in the same long silk blazer and straight skirt as the girl and wore high heels to avenge a three-inch disadvantage in height. Her head did not stop turning, as though trying to confirm that a proper share of admiring stares were directed at her. But she did not make eye contact with strangers. What was it about forty-year-old women that made them torture themselves that way? The girl's mother wouldn't have felt threatened. He hoped there was no doting uncle or, worse, a brother-in-law waiting at the hotel.

He followed them through the galleries, keeping three or four paintings behind. They sat on a bench opposite a winter landscape by Cornelius Krieghof and leafed through pocket guides to the city. This was his cue.

Pressing the corners of his new mustache against his lip, he approached from the girl's side.

"You're Canadians, aren't you?" His eyes were on the older one. "I couldn't help overhearing."

"Overhearing what?" the girl asked pleasantly.

Score another point for her smile. "Your accents. Americans don't clip their vowels like that. They take their time with them. Even the Yankees."

"You're the ones with the accents, then," she said. "We speak perfectly well."

"I like to think I do too. I'm from Montreal."

The older one went back to her book. "Morrison," and a darkly ingratiating smile were all she noticed of his introduction.

"Is this your first time in Miami?"

"Yes," the girl answered. "We're also from Montreal, from Westmount."

"Miami's not really the States," he said. "You'll find that with such a large Latin and Caribbean population, the city can be quite foreign. I've lived here a couple of years and would consider it a privilege to show you—"

"*Al . . . Al . . . Oh, there you are*!"

The girl followed his gaze inside the museum shop. Coming off the cash register line and wearing a white poplin dress was a woman a few years older than herself. In her hand was a small paper bag, which she waved till she caught his eye. "I was beginning to think you'd left without me," she said as she moved toward them haltingly. "Look at these lovely earrings."

"They're beautiful," he told her, taking them in the palm of his hand. "Wear them well." To the others he said, "Excuse me, this is my sister, Alice. Alice, these are—"

The older one looked up from her book. "I'm Sybil Cornish, and this is my friend, Nancy Dietrich. It's a pleasure to meet you, Miss Morrison."

"The pleasure is mine," Alice said.

"Nancy and Sybil are Montrealers," he explained. "I was asking if I might escort them around the city."

"That's a wonderful idea," Alice said.

"It's very generous of you, Mr. Morrison," Sybil said. "But I'm afraid we're not going to be in Miami very long."

"Then we haven't any time to waste," Alice said, positioning herself between the women. "Nancy, have you been up in the Goodyear blimp yet? It's moored along the MacArthur Causeway. There's usually a long wait for a ride, but the pilot's an old friend. We go every month."

"I've never even seen a blimp," the girl said. "It sounds exciting."

"It is. You fly all the way down past Key West. On a clear day you can see Cuba. You'll never forget it."

"That's tomorrow," Norodny said to Sybil. "We can get better acquainted tonight at Asia de Cuba."

"We've already made engagements for dinner," Sybil informed him.

"Later, perhaps. For drinks."

"Well, I don't—"

"Oh, let's," Nancy said. "It will all be very proper, Sybil. I'll be your chaperone tonight. We're staying at the Boca Chica Club. Is ten o'clock okay?"

A quarter of an hour ahead of time he walked beneath the coral arch guarding the hotel. Nancy was waiting for him in the crowded lobby sunk in a leather armchair beneath a portrait of Tigertail, the legendary chief of the Tallahassees. She took a long drag on a Gitane and stubbed the butt against the Boca Chica Club's mansard roof, where it was etched in the glass bowl of an ashtray. "You're early," she said.

"So are you. Where's Sybil?"

"She's sorry, but she's tired and can't make it tonight."

He brought a hand to his face to keep it from falling. "Your dinner wore her out? Why don't we put it off a day? Alice is pooped too."

"Oh, we didn't do anything special for dinner. She just wanted some time to give me fifty reasons why we shouldn't see you."

"They weren't good reasons?"

"Some of them were excellent. Tonight I wasn't listening, I guess."

"It sounds to me like she has your welfare at heart."

"She'd better," Nancy said. "It's her job. She's my chaperone."

"I didn't think young women traveled with chaperones anymore."

"Young women don't. Young ladies, according to Sybil, never go anywhere without them."

"Or very far with them."

"I wouldn't know, I'm really not much of a lady."

"What are you, then?"

"An *artiste*." She laughed. "A dancer. I just completed an engagement with a touring company of Les Ballets Quebecois in Jacksonville, and I've been sent to Miami to soak up some culture as a reward. Then it's down to the Keys to commune with nature, minus the birds and the bees, of course, before I go back to school. Sybil's the company chaperone."

"You're kind of young to be dancing professionally, aren't you?"

"Kind of," the girl admitted, and squirmed out of the chair. In heels she was an inch or two taller than him. "But I've been studying ballet my whole life. I don't feel all that young."

"How old are you?" he asked.

"Nineteen. How old are you?"

"Old enough to know better," he said as she took his arm. "The bar's downstairs."

Three kirs and an occasional sip of his Jack Daniel's inspired an abridgement of Nancy's autobiography. Back home in Westmount, the Montreal suburb where she was born, she was considered something of a prodigy as a dancer and singer. When she was eight, her parents brought her to New York for a winter in the junior ballet of the Metropolitan Opera, and she had spent other seasons with the Denver Ballet and the Toronto Opera. At fourteen there were two months in Hollywood for a minor role in the film version of Verdi's *Falstaff*. The following year she was a featured performer with the Connecticut Ballet. By the time she was sixteen, she had banked enough money to put herself through her first year at the New England Conservatory of Music. That spring she had signed a contract to endorse a Canadian line of ballet slippers and leotards, enabling her to repay her parents for years of sacrifice and making her almost wealthy in her own right. Now she was debating whether to go back to Boston for her music degree, start all over again at a liberal arts college, or forget about school for a principal role with a small but prestigious ballet company in Vancouver, British Columbia.

He had an ear for such detail. He interrupted only to light her cigarettes and order fresh drinks and, when he saw that she had had enough, to bring her upstairs. He said good night with a chaste kiss and the promise that they would meet for dinner the next evening at the Stone Crab House in the marina, no matter what Sybil had to say.

The older woman was asleep when Nancy came back to the room and, in the morning, didn't grill her about her date. Nor was she perturbed to learn that Nancy would be seeing the stranger again. Although she knew nothing about Morrison, other than that his sparse mustache would flatter him more after it had been allowed to grow in, Sybil was convinced that there wasn't nearly enough time for him to sink his hooks into the girl. Under those circumstances she would allow him first call on Nancy's evenings, while hers would be her own. The arrangement couldn't have suited her better if the ballet master had put him on payroll. The cost became apparent when Nancy proclaimed that in a lifetime in Miami she couldn't get enough of him.

Sybil attacked frontally. "He's twice your age. At least."

"I like older men," the girl said sharply.

"Last week it was rhythm guitarists, wasn't it?"

"Well, I just found out."

"But what do you know about him?"

"That I love him. Isn't that enough?"

"Hardly," Sybil said. "Can you so much as give me a hint as to how he earns a living when he's with you every day?"

The girl assumed a pained expression, matching Sybil's. "No I can't," she admitted. "What does that have to do with it?"

"Everything."

"To you. All that matters to me is that he makes me happy. I've never known anyone like him."

"You're not supposed to," Sybil said. "That's why women like me are paid to keep their eyes on girls like you."

"Then where were you looking when I met him?"

"That was uncalled for," Sybil said.

"Oh, Sybil, I didn't mean it the way it sounded. It's just that I've never wanted anything or anyone so badly. I know it's your responsibility to break us up, and I can't blame you for trying. But please don't ask me to make it easy for you. He means too much to me."

"It's not my responsibility. Our travel plans will see to it. What I'm here for is to make sure you don't get hurt. It would be a mistake to become too involved when you'll be unable to see him after this week."

"That's why you have to let me be with him while I can. You will, Sybil, won't you . . . won't you?"

"I can't forbid you to do anything, Nancy. I can only advise."

Sybil did not relish playing the witch to Nancy's trusting ingenue. It was not so long ago that the sisters of

Sainte Dominique had been afraid to let *her* out of their sight. She saw little danger in such flirtation when the girl would be gone from Florida in days. But it was her duty to maintain Les Ballets' outmoded ideals of propriety, and she could not relax her vigil and keep her job.

"Our bus leaves first thing in the morning," she said on a fiery November day. "Will you pack now or when you return from your date?"

"Later, I suppose." Nancy sighed.

"It will be beautiful in the Keys this time of year."

"I know."

"You mustn't look unhappy."

The girl caught her breath. "He owns a country house . . . somewhere in the Everglades," she said hesitantly. "And he knows so much about the wildlife and the history of the place. He's invited us to stay there while he shows us around."

"He must be joking," Sybil said. "My job is chaperone, not procurer."

"You don't have to be melodramatic. Alice lives there too. With three women and one man, even my mother couldn't find anything to object to."

"That will never do," Sybil said. "Take his phone number and perhaps we'll be able to visit one afternoon. But staying there, it's out of the question."

Nancy sat at her dressing table and adjusted her makeup. The mirror was her most loyal friend. "Oh, Sybil, you treat me like such a child."

"I do, and sometimes I'm not proud of it, but you know it's for your own good. Now remember, we have an early bus to catch, so don't stay out till all hours."

"I'll be back by ten to pack. I promise."

Sybil had dinner on the bayfront and spent the rest of the evening at a Coconut Grove Playhouse production of *Our Town*. It was a few minutes before eleven o'clock when she returned to the Boca Chica Club. The room was still double-locked. None of the lights were on inside. Tucked beneath a corner of her pillow was a pink envelope in Nancy's fastidious script: ". . . Came back an hour early but you weren't here, so I thought I'd go for one last walk along the water. I'll be back no later than eleven."

A worrier by profession, Sybil began earning her pay. She had come to know Nancy as a conscientious girl, hardly the type to leave the hotel unescorted when she should be upstairs packing. And she hadn't even begun to gather her things. Sybil dropped the note in her bag and reached for her cigarettes, flicked on the television. When the late news chased her movie off the air, she began pacing the room. The cigarette burned down to the filter. She put it out and rang for the elevator.

She described Nancy to one of the night clerks. "Might she, by any chance, have come back and put a note in our box?"

The clerk was underweight with rheumy eyes, a skeletal hanger for a shiny suit. He said, "Let me see," and turned around to the pigeonholes behind the desk.

"No messages, but I do recall seeing the young woman in the lobby. She was with a dark-haired gentleman with the beginnings of a mustache. They mentioned having a drink in Miami Beach."

Sybil had seen it coming. Nancy was spending the night with Morrison and didn't give a damn what anyone thought. Her anger rushed by, and she felt strangely relieved. The girl would be home soon, and if she didn't turn up pregnant, where was the harm? About children, the clerk volunteered, one could never be certain.

It was cold in the room when she woke up with a frightening heaviness on the left side of her chest. Her hand went out automatically for a cigarette. The pack was empty. So was Nancy's bed.

Outside, the street lamps dimmed and glowed orange and died. Sybil raised the blinds and looked out over the six-lane washboard of Matecumbe Boulevard toward police headquarters. She went to the bathroom to splash cold water on her face, then picked up the phone and asked for an outside line.

The sergeant was a veteran of the robbery detail, relegated to desk duty by a burglar's .38 short lodged in his knee.

"A teenage girl gone less than twelve hours and you're calling out the troops? Have some patience, lady. Hormones don't know from the bus schedule. If it turns out he forced her, you might try pressing charges. All you can do now is hope she don't come down with something that eats penicillin for breakfast."

Never had Sybil felt so helpless and alone. There was no one in Miami to confide in without being laughed at as a crank. Les Ballets Quebecois was only a long-distance call away, but she still held to a vague hope of enduring the sorry affair without losing her job if word did not get back to Montreal. Over the next forty-eight hours she went downstairs only for cigarettes and coffee. She was paying for her stay out of her pocket now. The room was one of the Boca Chica's finest and left her little for meals. She had no taste for food, anyway. Her clothes felt big on her.

Lingering over a breakfast of black coffee and Marlboros, she heard her name called and gestured to a man moving through the restaurant with a small tray. "I'm Sybil Cornish," she said. "What is it?"

"A letter, ma'am."

She didn't notice the look of annoyance or the outstretched hand that slowly withdrew the tray. The letter, postmarked the day before, was written on familiar pink paper.

Dear Sybil,

Now I can let you in on all the good news. Yesterday I became Mrs. Nancy Morrison. We are honeymooning in our country house and will be flying to

Europe in a few short weeks. Would you be such a dear as to gather all my things and pack them for me? Please don't forget my jewelry and traveler's checks and the bankbooks and commercial contracts I left in the second drawer. I will be stopping by for everything and to say good-bye in person. I know you've already forgiven me for all the inconvenience I've caused.

She read it a second time, hurrying upstairs. In the clutter on the dresser she found the note left under her pillow the night Nancy disappeared. She brushed aside an overflowing ashtray and placed the messages side by side. Though each was from an unmistakably feminine hand, the penmanship did not appear the same. The script on the letter was cramped and rushed, and there were erasures. Many of the words were broken, as if the author had lifted her pen from the page, deciding where to put it next. Drawing up her own search warrant on such evidence, she opened a thin journal she had noticed among Nancy's possessions to examine the handwriting without prying into its meaning. What she saw convinced her that the letter was a forgery. She stuffed the proof into her purse and looked out the window again toward police headquarters.

As she marched along Matecumbe Boulevard, she went over a few remarks for the desk sergeant who had treated her so shabbily on the phone. She would be firm but not self-righteous, make him pay for his accusations without compromising her dignity. Her plan began to fall apart when she arrived. The sergeant was not on duty. She told her story to a bored civilian clerk who turned her over to an auxiliary officer, a woman with swollen hips corseted in blue uniform trousers. In a basement room, where the dead air pushed back hard against a ceiling fan, she was given three sets of forms to fill out. It was half an hour before she saw another face—deeply tanned, with slate-gray almond eyes and a V-shaped hairline pointing away from a silver tonsure. To the caricaturist these were Hector Alvorado, Chief of the Missing Persons Bureau, whose theories about Nancy's disappearance blew apart like wet tissue the arguments that would have rendered the deskman speechless.

"This is the letter you have been waiting for," he said, "and let me congratulate you on your young friend's good fortune. Many women in her position might find themselves, as you say, seduced and abandoned. Miss Dietrich seems to have found a man of outstanding character. What you must do is collect her things as she asks and ready them for her. I am certain she will be back at your hotel shortly and you will share an enjoyable reunion."

Sybil strained to understand him. Although his syntax wasn't bad, his pronunciation was victimized by a heavy accent. She guessed that he had learned his English from television. "You must be mad," she said. "Compare the writing in this letter with these others. Someone has kidnapped Nancy, and now they're after her valuables. This letter is a blatant hoax."

"It is?" Alvorado asked. "On whose part?"

"What are you implying?"

"Isn't it true that Miss Dietrich is a public figure in the advertisements? I am not yet convinced that she did not arrange this mystery herself. The story of her strange vanishment and subsequent return as Mrs. Morrison should sell many of the popular periodicals back home."

"Don't be asburd," Sybil said, incredulous at his thickheadedness.

"It is one of many ideas I have on this subject. The others are, I think, less flattering to Miss Dietrich, er . . . Mrs. Morrison. It is not an unserious offense to play games with the police."

Her days were built on black coffee and Valium, sugary food and little sleep, a vigil by the phone interrupted for short, agitated walks along the bay. Another seventy-two hours and she was desperate for a way out. Nancy's safe return or the dread call from Montreal—one was as good as the other. She gave up the idea one morning in the lobby when her pulse began racing as a clerk motioned her to the desk.

"There was a call for you. I think it may be the one you've been waiting for."

"What did she say?" Sybil asked anxiously.

"It was not a she but a gentleman. I . . . here, I wrote it down." He took a sheet of stationery from her box and squinted at the inscription through bifocal lenses. "He said he'll come to the hotel at nine tonight to pick up Miss Dietrich's bags."

"Did he mention anything about Nancy?"

"No," the clerk said, crumpling the note to the size of a golf ball and arcing it into the wastebasket. "Only that he wanted very much to talk with you."

"I'd like that, if you don't mind."

Gallantly he retrieved the paper and flattened it against the counter.

Although she had just eaten, she called room service for two hamburgers and a baked potato and a carafe of wine. While she waited for the cart she emptied Nancy's luggage on the bed and repacked everything. Then she turned on the television. Then she shut it off and looked at the note again, read it over and over. If everything was all right, the girl, herself, would have called and would be coming to see her. She found the number for police headquarters where she had left it under the phone.

Sybil's lunch, at room temperature, was all White had to eat that day. He poured her a glass of wine as she recounted the events surrounding Nancy's disappearance and drank what was left from the carafe. Wiping his fingers on the tablecloth, he asked to see the clerk's message, which he filed in a pocket.

"Don't be angry with Lieutenant Alvorado," he told her. "He sees so many missing person reports, he won't move on one unless it's the governor's granddaughter or someone like that. He gave me the squeal because my county takes in most of the Everglades. As I understand it, that's where she's supposed to be."

"Somewhere out there," Sybil said. "Will you find her?"

"The question is whether she needs finding. It'd be damn embarrassing if we cuffed the guy and he showed us a marriage license for ID."

"Why is it," Sybil asked, "that everyone with the power to do something believes Nancy ran off with him and is acting irresponsibly for the fun of it?"

" 'Cause that's what most of the girls we're asked to locate have done. Finding out which are the others. . . it's a neat trick."

"You don't believe anything I've told you."

"You're telling the truth as you see it," White said. "What the facts are may be another story."

"Then you won't help me, either?"

"I didn't say that."

"If you won't," Sybil said, "I'll catch him myself, him and that Alice, that gimpy sister of his, and make him talk. I'm serious about this, Sheriff White. Can you lend me a gun or show me where I can buy one?" When White shook his head, she asked, "What do I have to do to get you on my side?"

"Could be you already have."

"It doesn't seem like it."

"It will tonight," he said. "Even if he didn't snatch her, he's going to have to come up with a lot of answers—for both of us."

"What can we do till then?" Sybil asked. "Would you like to see the letter?"

"Hang on to it for now," White said, blotting his hands again. "If we grab Morrison tonight, the girl can have it for her scrapbook."

"What should I say to him? Should I insist on seeing Nancy before handing over her things?"

"No way you give him Miss Dietrich's valuables. Once he has them, he may have no use for her anymore. Pack the clothes, but that's all."

"I should let him have the bags?"

White nodded.

"And then what?"

"If he doesn't bring the girl, we'll put a tail on him. You have to understand that there's the chance he'll give us the slip, so it's important that he doesn't come away with the stuff he wants. The clothes he can keep." He tossed the napkin on the cart and got up. "And that's about it." He started toward the door, then came back.

"Did we overlook anything?" Sybil asked.

"No," White said. "Is Miss Dietrich a relative?"

"Let me think about it," Sybil said, and White almost caught a smile. "It seems like it now, but we became acquainted only last month. Why do you ask?"

"You've been suffering."

"I'm fond of Nancy," she admitted, "but it's more than that. I can't help feeling that this is so much my fault because it happened while she was under my care."

"If it helps," White told her, "that's the way we feel about what you've been going through."

Shortly before eight o'clock the operators of the Boca Chica Club's passenger elevators were relieved of their duties and told to take the night off. They were replaced by men whose poorly fitting uniforms barely concealed the small holster each wore inside his left shoulder. Other armed men moved into the room across the hall from Sybil. Downstairs, Alvorado turned away fares from a borrowed yellow cab. White was double-parked across the street in a Plymouth sedan with the engine running.

Neither one noticed as a battered Checker rolled up to the end of the hack line and a stubby black man in need of a shave and a clean shirt backed out of the driver's seat. He left greasy fingerprints on the revolving door and then shambled across the lobby to the desk. In a thick Creole accent he asked where he could find Madame Sybil Cornish.

The cabbie drew a wide berth in the elevator. *If this is what the Boca Chica is coming to,* thought the new operator, *I'd as soon spend the night in the park.* He pushed the handle all the way to the right and, with their stomachs still on the ground floor, stopped the car a foot and a half below the fourteenth story, then a foot above, then six inches below again. That was as close as he was going to come. He opened the gate, and his passenger climbed out, dragging a toe to measure the distance.

The cabbie walked past two doors, saw the numbers running the wrong way, and went back. Outside Sybil's room, he scratched his head and looked beneath his nails. From their vantage point across the hall, detectives monitored his grooming with disapproval. After checking his fly he knocked.

Sybil called out, "Yes," and opened the door. Her throat constricted when she saw the grubby stranger. "Yes?" she said again.

"Madame Cornish?"

"That's right. Who are you?"

"The Canadian *monsieur* told me to pick up some luggage. He said it would be waiting."

"But where is she?"

"*Excusez,* I do not understand."

"Where are the bags going?"

"I am sorry," the cabbie said, "but I cannot tell you this."

Sybil looked over her shoulder, though she had been instructed not to, and a very young officer whose name she didn't know nodded gravely. "*Un moment,*" she said. She brought out Nancy's valise, then went back for the other bag. The cabbie took one in each hand and carried them to the elevator. Sybil closed the door and watched him move out of the narrow circle of view circumscribed by the peephole. Across the hall, Detective Sturges radioed his description to the unmarked cars in front of the hotel.

Two cabs pulled out of the hack line a few seconds apart. Alvorado flashed his off-duty sign at a gaggle of conventioneers and followed the Checker under the arch and into the street. Framed in his mirror was a gray Plymouth, a constant three car lengths behind. At Dinner Key the Plymouth steered around him, and Alvorado eased up on the gas and dropped back.

A late evening shower had swept the streets clear of traffic, and White allowed the Checker to open a two-block lead. At McFarlane the cab turned without signaling, snapping the whip on them, multiplying its lead along the broad straightaway of Main Highway.

"Move up on him," Alvorado muttered. "We're letting him get too far ahead."

A sharp right and then a left put them on South Dixie Highway, U.S. 1, as the Checker ran an amber signal. White buried the accelerator and charged into the intersection, halving the gap when he was nearly broadsided by a bakery truck trying to beat the light. He kicked hard at the brakes, and the rear wheels locked, losing their hold on the damp pavement. He steered into the skid, touched the gas, and the car veered away from oncoming traffic. He tried his brakes again. The Plymouth slowed gently. Braced against the wheel, he listened to the scream of tires as Alvorado tried not to run up his tail.

Through rain-streaked glass he watched the Checker careen around a stalled Fiat two blocks away. At Kendall Drive the cabbie hung another right and was gone. White cursed and pressed a blue flasher against the roof and burst through the cross traffic with Alvorado glued to his bumper.

With his foot to the floor he wove the sedan through glistening nighttime streets. He turned blindly onto Kendall, where a yellow cab was stopped for pedestrians at the crosswalk. As he drew even, the lady driver winked at him, and he raced five blocks with his guts in knots before Alvorado spied the Checker wedged behind a garbage truck. Leapfrogging the Plymouth, he nosed alongside and pinned it. The cabbie rolled up his window and leaned on his horn. He didn't quit until White pulled in behind and drowned him out with the siren.

They moved on the cab behind drawn guns. The stubby man wiped his eyes and reached across the seat. At the flash of metal they felt for the cold comfort of taut triggers. White sighted along the barrel, then holstered his revolver. "Put that away," he demanded.

"You are the police, after all?"

White nodded.

"You scared the piss out of me," the cabbie said. He dropped the change maker in his lap. "What do you want?"

"A word with you."

"Was this necessary? My dispatcher can reach me by radio at any time. It is a lot easier that way."

"But not as much fun," Alvorado said. "This is serious. Where are you taking those bags?"

"It's no big deal. To the bus terminal in West Miami."

"Why?"

"Because that is where the customer wants them."

"What customer?"

"You will have to ask the dispatcher. I received the call not an hour ago: 'Go to the Boca Chica Club and pick up two pieces of luggage from a Madame Cornish in her room. Bring them to the terminal and give them to a man who will be waiting in front.' I have been asked to do worse things."

"You don't know his name?"

"I was told only to meet him there at nine-thirty and that I would recognize him by his car, a silver Cadillac."

White checked his watch. "Okay, you're gonna do us a

favor, and if you get it right, you'll see a tip you won't ever forget. Drive to the station like you were told and wait for the customer. We'll be right behind. And step on it. We've got less than seven minutes."

With the Plymouth bringing up the rear, they headed west along Kendall. It was 9:33 by the clock over the main concourse when they reached the terminal and the Checker found space at the hack stand. The curb was lined with cars, none of them silver, none Cadillacs. White parked across the street as Alvorado went in. They waited.

Ten minutes went by. Then a light gray limousine pulled into the loading area, and a man with a yellow rose pinned to his lapel got out and looked around. He went to the passenger's side and opened the door. Two little girls in identical green dresses jumped onto the sidewalk, kissed him, and ran into the terminal. He looked around some more and drove away. White waited another five minutes before calling off the stakeout and joining Alvorado inside.

A canvass of bus company employees turned up an off-duty driver who thought he'd seen a silver Coupe de Ville an hour ago but wasn't certain. The cabbie, keeping the meter running, brought White and Alvorado to his garage, where they questioned the dispatcher. She had little to add to what they already knew. The call for the Boca Chica Club had come in about eight-thirty. When the customer was asked his name, he had answered hesitantly, "Don Reagan," which, in retrospect, she decided was a phony. White scribbled the name in his pad and invited the witnesses to headquarters to make formal statements. Then he drove back to the hotel and returned the luggage to Sybil.

"You can't give up hope," he said. "He'll try to contact you again soon."

On his way out he stopped at the desk and arranged for a waitress from the bar to spend the night with her.

16

The phone was ringing when Sybil stepped off the elevator. She dropped her papers and sprinted down the corridor, jabbed keys at the door till one let her inside. A corner of the nightstand bruised her hip as she crushed the phone to her ear. "Hello?"

The woman's voice sounded vaguely familiar. It told her, "If you'd done what Nancy asked, you'd have her back this morning."

"Who is this?"

"There had better be no more tricks. Do I make myself clear? You'll deliver the bags personally. Rent a car."

"You're holding Nancy against her will. Is she all right?"

"Yes."

"Let me speak to her."

"Do everything I say and she'll be back at the hotel tonight. Talk all you want then."

"But I want to speak to her now," Sybil insisted.

"No. Listen closely, because I won't repeat myself. Leave the hotel at six and drive north along Brickell where it runs into Biscayne Boulevard. When you come to the Miamarina, park in the lot. Across the street you'll find a bar, The Pelican's Pouch. Go inside and sit at a window booth. We'll reach you there with further instructions."

"How do I know that you really—"

A harsh click, followed by the drone of the dial tone, was her answer.

Sybil went to her purse and dug beneath the tin of pills that was always close to the top. She counted barely enough money to get through the week. She had no credit cards. Digging deeper, she saw White's number and called him at home.

"This smells bad," he said. "I'll come right over."

"You can't," Sybil blurted. "They said no police."

"Then why'd you call? They're not running this investigation. We are. How are they going to find out?"

"I don't know. Maybe they're watching the hotel, or watching you or your men. Can't we meet somewhere else?"

"I understand your fears, Miss Cornish, but really, they're groundless."

"Even so, I won't see you here."

"Okay, do you know where the Planetarium is on South Bayshore?"

"I can find it."

"There's a coffee shop a few doors down," he said. "It's called Maurie's, and it's not a cop hangout. Meet me there in two hours."

The manager stopped her at the velvet rope. He pointed her to the back where she saw White with Rutledge and Alvorado at a table littered with dirty dishes.

"You're fifteen minutes late," Alvorado said unpleasantly.

"I know. I couldn't get a cab."

"Excuses don't do Miss Dietrich any good."

"I'm sorry," Sybil said, "I—"

"It's all right," White interrupted. "While we were waiting, we worked out what we think is a foolproof plan. All we need is your say-so."

"What kind of plan?" asked Sybil.

"Like a steel trap," Alvorado answered. "One with no way out for the kidnappers."

"You have to bait a trap," Sybil said warily. "I won't have you using Nancy."

Alvorado swung his chair around and patted the back of her hand. "We'll use sugar," he told her, when what he meant to say was saccharin.

Toward evening, when the dinner shift reported for work at The Pelican's Pouch, service at the blue-collar bar—never crisp—wilted like the lettuce in a lunch-bucket sandwich. To the Pelican's regulars, who enjoyed their beer in plastic cups decorated with their favorite Miami Dolphin, it made no difference that the bartender used a spoon for a swizzle stick, or that the waiters had the dropsies, or that the new cashier at the steam table was having trouble with the register. Only Sybil noticed. She was struck by the sameness of the hard-pressed help—heavyset, middle-aged men, thick-necked and close-cropped, wearing highly polished black shoes. Even the flower girl, who darted in and out every few minutes, looked beefy.

Sybil was the only woman in the place. She ordered a Manhattan, tried it, and sipped slowly. She had been sitting behind it for half an hour when a pair of day laborers in greasy seersucker shirts and straw hats came in and joined her at her booth.

"*Qué pasa?*" said the more personable of the strangers, flashing a smile that showed a couple of teeth gone. Jai alai players, Sybil said to herself as spasms of panic riffled her composure. "What're you drinking?" he asked with a nod toward her glass.

"I don't want another," she whispered. "Please, I'm very nervous."

"*Qué?*"

"I've brought the bags with me."

"*Qué?*"

"We're not good enough for her," the other one explained. A mouthful of teeth did nothing for his looks. "Here she is, a guest at our table, and she will not even drink with us." He slammed his fist on the table so that Sybil had to steady her glass. "These high-class bitches, they give me a pain in my—"

The nearest waiter hauled him out of his seat and escorted him to the door with an arm twisted behind his back. His friend got up after them, debating whether to throw a punch. Out on the sidewalk they were joined by another waiter, and the bartender and he decided against it. Sybil finished her drink and ordered another.

Her eyes never drifted far from the door. Alone and in garrulous clusters, drinkers wandered in off the street and froze like deer in the hard light of her gaze. A waiter came by twice, and she ordered more Manhattans, each an improvement over the ones she had tasted before. The bartender was learning his craft. But that was the evening's only achievement. No one made an attempt to contact her, and Nancy's luggage remained locked up in the lot across the street. At eleven o'clock the bartender threw off his apron and sat down at her booth.

"Relax," White said. "They're not coming tonight."

Sybil went into the bathroom to scrub the sleepless night from her face, and when that didn't work, to hide it under makeup. The sooner she returned to Montreal, the better it would be. Arrangements were being made for a car to bring her to the airport.

The early news featured two minutes on Nancy's disappearance. Sybil pulled the plug when the anchorwoman concurred with a reporter's assessment that the incident was nothing more than a shameful attempt at garnering headlines at the expense of Metro police. Sybil sat at the darkened screen until despair shut her eyes. She was awakened around seven A.M. by the phone.

"Go home now. She's dead."

Sleep-fogged, Sybil accepted it dispassionately, as though Nancy's were just another name in the news. As the meaning sank in, she went to the dresser and emptied all the drawers, laid her clothes out on the bed, and packed her bags again. From memory she dialed White's home number. "They called," she said.

"Who's this? You woke me. Give me a second to clear my head."

"Nancy's not coming back. Chase them, shoot them if you like. It makes no difference to me anymore."

"Miss Cornish?"

"She's dead."

"Who did you talk to?"

"The woman, the one who called before."

"What else did she say?"

"Nothing."

"It could have been a crank," he said.

"It was her."

"Damn their souls, *they're* dead."

Sybil didn't respond.

"Miss Cornish?"

"Take my number in Montreal. I'm going home."

"Not yet," White protested. "I need you here."

"There's nothing I can do."

"She needs you too."

"Not now."

"Did they say where we'd find the body?" he asked.

"No."

"We have no proof they killed her."

"I do. Their word is good enough for me."

"When they've never leveled with us? Not every kidnapping is for ransom," he said. "They may be keeping her for some reason."

"I don't think so."

"If the worst is true, do you think she'd want them to get away with it? At least let's hear what Lieutenant Alvorado has to say."

Some of the hollowness went out of Sybil's voice. "Why?" she asked. "He never had time for Nancy when she was alive."

"He's a good cop," White said. "But he's been under all sorts of pressure, catching flak about unsolved cases that aren't even his responsibility. He's been coming over to our side. He'll be there now."

"It's too late," Sybil said.

"I'm asking as a personal favor. I understand what you've been going through."

"Do you, Sheriff White?"

"My . . ." He paused, then started again slowly. "No," he said. "Not really."

"Good-bye."

The limo to the airport had four more stops to make, and a miracle was in order if she was going to catch her flight. As the car waited in the drive of the Coconut Grove Hotel, Sybil looked away from her watch and pushed her sunglasses against her forehead. Walking toward the lobby with his back to the street was a birdlike old man with a shiny black stick protruding from a gnarled hand. The other clutched the arm of a much younger woman moving with a stiff-kneed gait. Sybil started and then settled back in her seat. Such coincidence was the stuff of movies and cheap fiction. She lowered her sunglasses and lit a cigarette, checked her watch again.

17

Alvorado was willing to concede that Nancy's disappearance should have been a major investigation from the start. He was not an insensitive man, he told White over a beer at The Pelican's Pouch, but the victim of a grievous error in judgment. Though it might be too late to save the girl, he would make it up to her parents by finding whoever had stolen their daughter. But not right away. More pressing cases demanded his attention at the moment.

"Whose?" White asked.

"Morris Garvin, for one."

White shrugged. "Only chance I get to look at a Miami paper is my day off."

"Then you did not read about Garvin," Alvorado said. "The night he went missing, you were staked out at the Boca Chica Club."

"That's two of us who didn't make out so hot. What happened to him?"

"Nothing special. He went and got himself shot. What is happening to me because of it, *there* is a real crime."

"Details, Hector, I want details."

"Garvin was sixty-three, semiretired, recently arrived from Worcester, Mass. He made his home with a widowed daughter in a storefront near the Orange Bowl. When he wasn't going to the dogs, he drove a limo, if you call a seventy-nine Chrysler with eighty thousand miles on it a limousine. Eight hours after his daughter reported him gone a newsboy found the body in the roots of a banyan tree in the park behind the main library."

"Nasty place to be after dark," White said. "Let me tell you the MO. Pockets turned out, wallet and wristwatch missing."

"A nice try," Alvorado said. "But his billfold was on his hip and there was seventy-five dollars inside. He didn't wear a watch. He didn't die where he was found, either. Drag marks in the grass led all the way from the curb."

"What've you got to go on?"

"Next to nothing, not even the motive. The car is gone, but that was a crime of opportunity by the usual vultures, no doubt. The evidence consists of a single slug from the back of Garvin's head. Out of a nine-millimeter automatic, which we are still looking for. It singed the hair and left a hole crusted with powder. A regular coup de grace."

"Look for a Frenchman," White said.

Alvorado squeezed out a smile but lost it on the way to his lips.

"You're a wonderful raconteur, Hector, but why are you telling me all this?"

"Broad shoulders," Alvorado answered. "No one here has shoulders so wide."

White drained his glass and tilted the empty at a waiter. "I'm still listening."

"I don't have to tell you that it's a nothing case. But the papers that are now screaming for blood over the Dietrich affair have ganged up on me. If I had gone looking for Garvin before he disappeared, it would not have been soon enough for them."

"You know how to cover your ass," White said. "You've been a cop long enough."

"Maybe not much longer," Alvorado said glumly. "Not after this Sally Behagen went missing too."

"Who's she?"

"A realtor from Coconut Grove," Alvorado answered,

producing a snapshot of a lithe blonde on the cutting edge of thirty, looping a graphite racket at a yellow blur. "She is the real reason I asked to see you."

"It wasn't the shoulders?"

"It's more like this," Alvorado confessed. "I'm in plenty deep shit, and I need your help."

"Break it to me gentle," White said.

"The call came from Miss Behagen's realty partner, a Sam Sturdivant. Two days earlier the woman had gone to show a house out your way in Glades City. On Coacoochee Street. Know it? She planned to meet the prospective buyer at the train station and drive him to the property, then return to the office to sign papers or else place another listing in the *Herald.* She never came back, never called. I took personal charge.

"I need a win bad," he went on, the flesh beneath his eye working double time. "Only, they are breaking off curves and I'm swinging at air. You would be doing one big favor if you would go out to the house and have a look around."

White studied the photo, sipping from a fresh glass. "I could use a win too," he said finally. "Give me Sturdivant's number. I'll want to talk to him first."

Twenty years as a policeman had taught White that the chances of success in an investigation were inversely proportional to the amount of time he spent away from his desk. He went back to the office and dialed the number Alvorado had written on a napkin. Sam Sturdivant answered in a syrup-smooth voice, running vinegary with worry.

"Why'd you wait two days to report her missing?" White asked.

"I didn't think it was such a long time," Sturdivant said. "The house was listed in excess of three hundred thousand dollars, and it carried a hefty commission. I'd made Sally my partner only last month, and she was anxious to clinch a big sale. I thought it reasonable to expect that she would take the buyer out for a drink."

"For two days?"

"Sally was a lonely woman. If the buyer was a good-looking man, and she'd told me more than once that he sounded like a winner, I thought there might be a night on the town as well. Maybe two. Maybe the town was Freeport. Fault me for not calling when she didn't come back by morning. But at first I didn't want to embarrass her. Then I didn't want to face up to the likclihood that something had happened."

"You can make up for it," White told him. "Does your firm have an associate in Glades City?"

"George Zurkin on Bowlegs Avenue. Sally was going to stop there for the keys on her way out."

"Do you know if she did?"

"No," Sturdivant admitted. "I was so upset, I forgot to call."

"Do it now," White said. "And then get back to me."

The sap was rising in Sturdivant's voice when he returned the call inside of ten minutes. "She came by directly from the office," he said. "Zurkin assumed she went to the house, and when he didn't hear from her again, he figured she'd made the sale. He didn't even know she was missing. What will you do next?"

"Does Mr. Zurkin have another set of keys?"

"He should."

"I'll pick them up," White said. "Then I'll run down to Coacoochee Street and have a look around."

The house was an architectural battlefield with no winner, broad Caribbean verandas under a Spanish red tile roof. It stood on four acres of Sabal palmetto and live oak at the end of a rutted dirt road. White's car whisked the gray dust that lay all around like fingerprint powder on a giant crime scene. He parked beneath a blight-ravaged coconut palm and cranked down a window, took it all in. The only tire tracks ended beneath his rear wheels. There were no footprints or litter, nothing to indicate that the property had been visited in months.

He was wasting his time, his and what was left of Nancy Dietrich's, squandering his day off on someone else's investigation. Why was he surprised? Hadn't Rutledge been spreading it around that he was a fanatic? Hadn't he always been? He was reminded of the summer when, as a seventeen-year-old he was so obsessed with bodybuilding that between his morning and evening workouts, he took a job in a barbell manufacturer's stockroom, so that when he wasn't lifting weights, he was lifting weights. He got out of the car.

With the realty associate's spare key he let himself inside a dark anteroom. He hit a mercury switch with the back of his hand but got nothing for his effort. He pushed back chintz curtains from a living-room window, and shafts of smudged light pointed to three flights of stairs. At the top was an attic piled floor-to-ceiling with newspapers baled in brown twine, some broken cane chairs. He worked his way down through silent rooms of stolid furnishings cloaked with yellow sheets. If Sally Behagen had been there, again she had left no sign. He was preparing to lock up when he recalled George Zurkin telling him about a large recreation room in the cellar. A look downstairs might take another minute.

He discovered steps leading down from the kitchen and took them slowly in the near total darkness. On the bottom two, melting into the unpainted wood, were the remains of what in life had been an athletic woman with sun-streaked hair. It was warm in the cellar, so warm that little else was recognizable other than a small hole high on the back of the head. A pocketbook stripped of cash lay over her chest. Clutched in one hand was an unsigned copy of the sales agreement. He went upstairs and tore the sheet off a chest of drawers to spread over her.

Alvorado read from White's report as he broke the news to Sam Sturdivant the next day. Sensing tears, he hurried his questions. The realtor told him that on the day she vanished, Sally Behagen was carrying a large sum of cash, as much as three thousand dollars. His secretary suggested twice the amount.

"Was that wise?" Alvorado asked.

"Every one of us is aware of the danger in meeting strangers in out-of-the-way, vacant homes," Sturdivant pointed out. "But if we stop, we go out of business."

"It is a choice to consider," Alvorado said, mostly to himself. "But why so much money?" When Sturdivant couldn't answer, he said, "Can you tell me the name of the man Miss Behagen was to see?"

"Not offhand. He sent a card, but if he's responsible for this, what's the use—"

"I have to insist that you find it just the same."

In a moment the realtor came back to the phone. "If I make out this Gothic script, the name is Jorge Alfonsin," he said. "There are two addresses, Flagler Street in Miami and the King Philip Hotel in Miami Beach."

Alvorado broke the connection without saying good-bye as the buttons on his phone lit up like one-way windows on an untidy world. He punched one and heard his top investigator's ex-wife above the faint whir of the recorder. Another brought White onto the line sounding loud and effusive.

"We lucked out, Hector," he said.

"Does that mean good or bad?"

"What if I told you one of my men, an Officer O'Connell, was at the train station when Sally Behagen's buyer arrived?"

"I would ask where he has been keeping himself."

"Working a radar trap in West Laxahatchee," White answered. "He buzzed me after recognizing her picture in the paper. Said he was waiting for relatives when the buyer came off the train, and she picked him up in a yellow convertible."

"Did he get a good look?"

"So so. He puts him in his mid- to late thirties, six feet

tall, average build, a conservative dresser. Business suit and brown oxfords."

"What else?"

"They backed out of their space and stopped at a green light," White said, "and O'Connell nearly rear-ended them. He'd have forgotten all about it if they weren't smooching in the front seat. He honked them, and they took off."

"Does the name Jorge Alfonsin ring any bells?"

"Sure did for Sally Behagen, if it's the same fellow. I'll have my men start digging."

Alvorado assigned investigators of his own to hunt for Alfonsin. At the King Philip Hotel a clerk told them the man was not a permanent resident.

"If he had cards made up, he may have rented a suite during a trade exposition. He isn't one of our registered guests, or a frequent visitor. I'd know him if he was."

A rental agent on the three-thousand block of Flagler Street showed Alvorado a dreary apartment overlooking a factory parking lot where Jorge Alfonsin had lived for more than three years before moving out six days into the month.

"Did he say why?"

"He still hasn't," the rental agent said. "One day he just wasn't here anymore."

"Where did he go?"

"Search me."

"Well, where are you forwarding his mail?"

"No mail comes here," the rental agent said, smoothing a tear in the kitchen linoleum with his toe. "We're holding his deposit till he tells us where to send it."

"How well did you know him?"

"As well as anyone you see for five minutes on the first of each month. He was a pleasant man but not what you'd call expansive. All he ever talked about was the weather and the lack of hot water. And there wasn't a thing I could do about either. He took so many baths that he overtaxed the boiler. He said he needed them for his knees.

"Mr. Alfonsin has bad knees."

"At his age everything goes bad."

"I don't get you," Alvorado said.

The rental agent tightened the bulb in an unshaded floor lamp. "I thought you knew him," he said. "I should have asked before, but I'd like to see your badge.

"He was eighty if he was a day," the agent went on as Alvorado flashed his shield and ID. "His knees were the least of his worries. His back was so badly stooped, it was hard for him to look straight ahead. He walked with a cane with a silver handle like a horse's head. It was his prize possession."

With nothing new from White's end, Alvorado called homicide detectives into the Alfonsin case. Plans for a full-scale probe were scrubbed when an elderly gentleman leaning on an ironwood walking stick and wearing a custom-tailored suit that was the height of fifties fashion came into the squad room. "I believe you are looking for me," he announced in a tired, reedy voice.

Alvorado didn't wait for an introduction. He jumped up from his swivel chair and wheeled it behind the old man. "How do you do, Mr. Alfonsin? You are not the easiest person to find."

"I am if you know where to look for me. What are these rumors about my being murdered? As you can see, I am very much alive." He tapped his stick twice against the floor. "Ah, well, almost that much."

Alvorado briefed him on the investigation that had brought his name to police attention. Jorge Alfonsin took off his glasses and slouched in his seat. "I don't understand," he said. "How could my card have been left on that unfortunate woman's desk when I have never heard of her?"

"I hoped you could tell us that," Alvorado said.

"I don't know. I deal professionally in rare stamps and coins and am not stingy with my cards. They circulate freely. A few have gone to friends and some even to young ladies who might make interesting acquaintances. You will excuse my vanity if I am not ashamed to say that there have been a number of these. One must have found its way into her hands."

"Can you provide us with the phone numbers of everyone who has received a card in the past six months?" Alvorado asked.

"Not even in six weeks," Alfonsin boasted. "Not even the philatelists and numismatists."

"Try."

"It is impossible."

"It can't be. How do you run your business?"

"I deal mainly with colleagues of long standing who know where I can be reached. The others . . . they call too."

"But, you see, your help is all we have. And there are lives at stake."

Alvorado was out of the office when a teenager in a satin windbreaker, Jorge Alfonsin's nephew, left three pages of names and numbers with the night commander. "Uncle dug out his Rolodex, and I worked all afternoon on this," he said.

The following day, as detectives went to work on the *F*s, he showed up with another page and the promise of more to come. Alvorado sat him down at an empty desk and put a phone in his hand.

"I don't need new lists," he said. "We have more numbers than ten men can dial. What I need is your uncle. Tell him how badly."

The boy pushed away from the desk defensively. "He's . . . he's downstairs, waiting in my car," he stammered. "He doesn't like to climb the stairs. His knees—"

They went out through heavy steel doors to a midnight-blue Corvette rumbling beside a hydrant. Jorge Alfonsin turned down the radio and lowered his window.

"Mr. Alfonsin, we are getting nowhere this way," Alvorado said.

"What did I tell you?" the old man gloated.

"Please, sir, a little more of your time. Is there anyone with a card you may have overlooked? I don't necessarily mean a business associate."

"There is my nephew," Alfonsin said, gesturing with liver-spotted hands, "but he's a fine boy, as you can see for yourself. I am certain you are not interested in him."

"No one else? It's very important."

"Alice must have one. But she, too, is above suspicion."

Alvorado stepped back and drew himself to his full height. "Let us be the judge of that, Mr. Alfonsin. "Who is she?"

"A friend of mine."

"What is her full name?"

"Miss Alice Rovere."

"And you say she is your *friend*?"

"A very good one." The old man smiled. "We are almost engaged."

"Can we have her address?"

"She shares a small house in the Everglades, on national park land, with her brother. They are Northerners."

"And her age?" Alvorado asked.

"I do not know for sure."

"Try to guess."

"I would rather not. She is very young, no more than thirty, if that much. Still . . . it is love."

18

It was the kind of place that looks like it's been whipped together out of leftovers from a construction site, cinder blocks and rubber shingles, a stovepipe chimney, and it sat in front of a forested lot hemmed in by a high wooden fence. The expensive sports car in the garage might have been slumming. White left the cruiser in the driveway and walked up to the door. The bell chimed the first few notes of "Dixie." Bare feet slapping against the floor set an oddly irregular beat.

"Sheriff White," Alice said. "It's so good to see you again."

"Been a long time, hasn't it?" He took off his hat as he came inside. "And this is Deputy Rutledge."

They followed her into an undersize living room crowded with furniture that would have looked more comfortable on the lawn. An upright piano against the wall was probably worth as much as the rest of the stuff with the house and lot thrown in. She made room on the couch and sat facing them on the piano bench. "I'm still not sure I understand what brings you all the way out here," she said.

"A long and complicated investigation," White told her. "I won't trouble you with details. We have only a few questions to ask."

"What would you like to know?"

"I should warn that it may touch on personal matters."

"My relationship with Jorge? I have nothing to hide."

"Good. A business card of Mr. Alfonsin's was found at the scene of a particularly brutal murder in Glades City, and we're trying to run down all the cards he's given out. He says you may have one."

"That's right."

"Do you know where it is?"

"I . . . I'm sure I do." She padded out of the room and came back with a wallet, flipped through the clear windows till she found the one she was looking for. "No mystery about that."

"No mystery at all." He touched her lightly on the wrist. "Can I see this?" He pointed to a snapshot in the opposite window. "That's you on the fishing pier at Flamingo, am I right?"

"I was there last month."

"Have any luck?" Rutledge asked.

"I was out for scenery. I'm afraid I'm not much of a fisherman."

"Flamingo's a long way to go for scenery," White said.

"My brother is the angler. He caught a giant tarpon we're having mounted. If he hadn't wasted all the film on me, that wouldn't sound like such a fish story."

White showed the picture to Rutledge, who looked at it without comment. Then he folded the wallet and gave it back to her. "Your brother lives here with you?"

"For the time being, till he finds a place of his own in the city."

"I see."

"Too bad he missed you," she said. "He'll be disappointed."

"If he enjoys the water, tell him to look around South Beach. The fishing pier can't be beat, and it's one of the few places left where there's nice apartments at reasonable rents."

"Thanks, I'll do that."

"Thank *you,* Miss Rovere. It's time for us to go."

"But you haven't even begun. Surely you didn't drive out to ask one question."

"Just one," White said. "It's all we wanted to know."

White went around to the passenger's side and tossed the keys over the hood. "You drive," he said. As Rutledge backed out of the driveway he squinted into the garage and scribbled the Mercedes's license number on a clipboard.

"You're sure it's her," Rutledge asked.

"Not until I speak with Miss Cornish."

"She's not the only woman in the world who walks with a limp. Probably not the only Alice."

"Yeah, but how many of 'em live out here with their brother? Till I find some of the others, I want this place under surveillance."

"Nothing I like better than a nice, exciting stakeout." Rutledge yawned. "But I have to see a witness tonight."

"Who we talking about?"

"Claire Pauley."

"First I heard of it," White said. "What do you want from her?"

"Whatever she's putting out. I've been hounding her for a date for months. Finally broke her down."

"Sorry, Ma, but you're gonna have to wait a little longer. If it is Morrison, I want to take him tonight."

"There's the story of my life," Rutledge said, coming off the gas to ease the car through axle-deep ruts. "I settle in this miserable swamp for the hunting, and hunting season's when the hunters keep me from having a day off. I meet a woman, I have to put her on the back burner, the one that's already SRO. Why don't you ask Alvorado? The man has no private life, sleeps on a hook in the squad room."

White said, "He'll be there."

"I'm beginning to think there's not much difference between you."

"Don't rub it in. What with everything going down, it's getting harder to tear myself away."

"The cop disease," Rutledge said. "They ought to give shots."

"Wouldn't bother me so much if I was making collars. But the boys are growing up on their own while I sort crash photos for the drunk-driving exhibit at the high school."

"It's the job."

"Screw the job. It's not worth the grief. All these years in uniform, and now I have to prove myself again, to the boys, hell, to myself."

Rutledge studied him out of the corner of an eye. "No one's blaming you for anything."

"I do."

Rutledge looked back toward the road.

"You know, Ma, I'm starting to get excited about tonight. I hope we make headlines clear to Canada."

"You can have your ink," Rutledge said. "Mine too. I'd rather stay home and turn up the heat on that burner."

At precisely eight P.M. an unmarked car left the garage under police headquarters heading west out of the city. Where the Tamiami Trail entered the sawgrass Everglades, it stopped in a pull-off, and the driver cut his lights. As if on command, a Plymouth sedan wheeled out of the scrub and came alongside, and a man in the drab uniform of a Laxahatchee sheriff got out and exchanged cars. The driver flashed his high beams and followed the Plymouth back to the highway.

A raw wind off the Gulf had stacked storm clouds over the shimmering river of grass. The moon poked jagged holes in the heavy sky, then scudded into darkness as the cars whipped across the low country in unison, a night flyer drawn by an invisible locomotive. Not quite nine-thirty, the lights of Glades City spilled across the highway, and Rutledge turned the Plymouth south to probe unpaved roads to the borders of Everglades National Park.

They cruised past the house thirty seconds apart. A Florida Power and Light panel truck was parked in a cluster of live oaks with an unimpeded view of the property. Inside, three men shading tired eyes beneath hard blue hats fixed on the empty yard. Rutledge dimmed his lights as he went by.

In the second car Alvorado asked, "Friends of yours?"

"Colleagues," White answered.

They turned behind the Plymouth, which was stopped in the shadow of the fence. The panel truck came around the corner, and everyone piled in back.

"The gang's all here," Rutledge said.

"Soon," Alvorado told him. "The National Park police promised to join in our welcome for Morrison. They take very seriously what he is alleged to have done to Miss Dietrich on their land."

"Where are they?"

"They'll be here. Count on it."

One of the hard hats, Detective Sturges, passed around a thermos. Over cups of lukewarm coffee Alvorado reviewed the plan. While the others covered the house from all sides he would lead two men in through the front and place Morrison under arrest. It was as simple as that. If everyone knew what was expected of him, it would be over in seconds.

"You'd better tell them," Rutledge said from the passenger's seat. "The lights just went off in the main room."

"Even better. They are going to sleep," Alvorado said.

"At nine forty-five?" White asked. "More likely they're getting ready to go out. If we're going to take him, we'd better do it now. The feds can read about it over breakfast."

"No," Alvorado said. "I'm in charge here, and I say we wait."

"The lieutenant's got a point," someone said. "We're running short the way it stands."

"Then you wait with him," Rutledge said, opening his door. "Who made this case, anyhow?"

Alvorado rolled down a window as the light came on over the back porch. He splashed his coffee in the dirt and screwed the cup on the thermos. In a low voice empty of excitement he said, "Very well, let's get started. Edwin?"

A hard hat scrambled into the driver's seat. Another, Officer O'Connell, dropped outside, a 30.06 rifle clutched to his chest. As the truck moved around the corner he scaled the fence. Sturges went out the back at the next stop. Edwin took another right, and they were in front of the house.

"Dark as Maggie's muff," White said.

Edwin laughed and said, "This afternoon we came out with a real FP and L man and shut off all the streetlights. I nearly barbecued myself, but it was worth it. No one'll see you approach."

They went out the side door, all but Edwin, who clambered to the roof of the truck and surveyed the yard through an infrared scope. Bunched together, they ran to the fence and entered through the unlocked gate.

White tugged at his flak jacket where it chafed under the arms. He dipped into his holster. He had brought his heaviest gun, a .357 magnum, and the fresh oil on the barrel lent a metallic fragrance to the moist air. They marched across the yard and climbed the porch. Alvorado peered inside but made out only the vague form of the living-room furniture. Then they were listening to the familiar strain of "Dixie."

"Who is it?" a woman cried out. She sounded tired, languorous, in no mood to be disturbed.

"Maybe they *were* sleeping," White whispered.

"Florida Power and Light," Alvorado answered.

"Who?"

"Electric!"

"I didn't call an electrician. Go away. I'm in bed."

A man hollered, "Get lost."

"I'm sorry to have to bother you at this hour, but there's trouble on the line and we have to come inside."

"Okay, okay, give me a minute."

White and Rutledge flattened themselves against the house. Alvorado, in a borrowed hard hat, stood at the door, his thumb against the hammer of his .38. He leaned toward the window again. There was no light, no movement inside. He punched the door bell impatiently.

"I'm coming, I'm coming." The voice was closer and more alive.

They heard footsteps, faintly at first. The door moved open. The wind dislodged a cloud in front of the moon, and they were looking at a tangle of silken hair, bare legs. Alvorado lunged for the woman and dragged her out, tearing the buttons off her pajama top. He gave her to White, who clamped a hand over her mouth till she stopped struggling. "Police" was all he said as he brought her into the yard.

With Rutledge a step behind, Alvorado ran inside the house. In a foyer off the living room they paused to get their bearings, breathing silently through their mouths.

"Alice? Alice, who's there?"

They trailed the voice down a carpeted hallway that brought them to three doors.

"Alice, what's wrong?"

Alvorado pointed to the center door. A bed squeaked. They heard slippered feet on the floor. Alvorado touched his fingers to the knob, twisted it and froze, then rocked back and forth on his heels. The second time he came forward, he threw his shoulder against the wood and burst inside—almost into the tub. A dead bolt slid across the door on the wall to their left. Rutledge backed off and kicked at it. It didn't budge.

"Come out with your hands on top of your head," Alvorado ordered. "We have the house surrounded."

Behind the door a chair scraped along the floor. A drawer opened, then another.

"What's that?"

"You're covered on all sides. To try to escape is suicide."

"What is this, some kind of joke?"

"It's no joke."

"Who are you?"

"Lieutenant Alvorado, Miami police."

"Okay, Lieutenant, I like to know who I'm dealing with. You caught me with my pants down. Literally. Give me a chance to get dressed and I'm yours."

Rutledge felt pressure on his elbow and looked over his shoulder. Alvorado, shaking his head no, took two quick steps past the door and pressed himself into the wall.

"You have sixty seconds."

Rutledge planted his foot in the rug and catapulted into the door. The thin pine groaned, fighting back, then buckled and gave way, and he crashed into the room. Alvorado went in after him. A bullet tore into the jamb, spraying splinters across his scalp. Through a red haze he saw Rutledge stumble and pitch forward on the floor. Straddling the windowsill with an automatic aimed belly-high was a man wearing only pants and shoes. He fired and then dived outside as Alvorado threw himself across Rutledge's legs.

White was at the gate when a light came on in the bedroom window and Edwin blew out the glass. He dragged the woman back into the yard and drew his revolver. Barely thirty feet away, someone was running, head down, for the garage. White let go of her arm. He spread his feet and assumed the two-handed stance he had learned as an Army MP and only four times before had been forced to employ. He leveled the gun, steadied it, cried, "Halt," reluctantly put weight on the trigger. Alice kicked at the side of his knee, and a stab of pain tore his leg out from under him. He went down, the gun discharging into the air. With his free hand he dragged the woman to the ground and cuffed her across the mouth. Then he scrambled back to his feet. As he sighted his target again the moon punched another hole in the clouds, and light fell on Detective Sturges. White felt the blood drain out of his limbs. He lowered the gun. Behind him the woman was crying softly.

An untied shoelace was giving Sturges as much trouble as a broken foot. He ran across the yard in an awkward crouch with the tail of his shirt fluttering against his back. His heel caught on the edge of the drive, and sharp gravel poured inside his shoe. He shrugged off the pain, intent on the squat silhouette of the garage and the sound of someone moving around inside. As moonlight showered the low roof he came down stiffly in ankle-deep water. Wet sand sucked at the shoe, pulling it off his heel. He pocketed his Colt and bent down to tie the lace.

He heard the animal squeal of hard rubber on asphalt, a machine-gun burst of gravel against steel, and rolled out of the way of the red Mercedes tearing down the drive without lights. He fumbled for his gun and fired. The bullet thudded harmlessly against the soft bumper. The car ran out of the yard and turned onto the street past a Park Police van, which jumped the curb and backed into a U-turn, nearly pinning O'Connell to the fence.

White stuffed his gun in his waistband and helped the woman wipe the dirt off her face. He moistened his handkerchief with his tongue and dabbed around her eyes, searching for hardness underneath. Like newlyweds after their first spat, they walked in silence to the porch.

Alice went in ahead of him, touched a switch that put light in the foyer. In the bedroom they found Alvorado cradling Rutledge's head in his hands. A splotch of red marked the spot where the deputy's eye had been.

"He's dead," Alvorado said. "And when word of this reaches the press, we will be too. Don't waste your tears on him. His worries are at an end."

"You didn't know him," White said, forcing a grim smile. "They're only just beginning."

Then he went around to the back of the house and lost himself in darkness.

South of Long Pine Key, Norodny checked the mirror again and settled into overdrive. He clung to the center stripe for two miles more before flicking on his lights. If he hadn't lost his tail, he'd have had a five-minute lead. His pockets were empty, the tank about the same. The road wandered thirty miles through national park wilderness to Flamingo, where the continent fell into the sea.

A map hinted at a fire trail cutting east through the coastal prairie. It emerged on Manatee Bay and U.S. 1, where he could ditch the Mercedes in water and thumb a ride to Miami. He looked at the gauge again, taking comfort in the two gallons stashed beneath the *E*. He cut his lights as twin beams split the blackness overhead, felt for the turnoff until the whoosh of turborotors chased him off the pavement. He pulled beneath the canopy of a gumbo-limbo hammock and pounded his fists on the dash. Who in their right mind would send up a chopper on such a shitty night? Who besides that goddamn black sheriff.

He fished inside the console for his driving gloves and snapped them around his wrists. The soothing softness of the leather had taken on the scent of Alice's perfume, and he wondered how she was standing up to the police. Let her talk, for all the good it would do them. Not that she would, so long as they didn't tell her everything. He began to miss her. And surprised at how badly he did, was pleased.

He watched the lights float off behind a cypress dome. Another precious minute went by before he crept back to the road, craning his neck for the helicopter. At the next mile marker he spotted it, outlined above the flickering radiance of the Gunsight River ranger station. He turned onto the first solid ground he came to, little more than a game track into the mangroves. He stayed with it till it dead-ended on a muddy dike overlooking the Flamingo marina.

An aging Chrysler Newport had gotten there first. Fogged windows and a rhythmic bounce told him that he wouldn't be noticed. He backed into the shadow of some red mangroves and killed the engine. After a while he went out with his gun in his hand. His bare skin prickled in the cool night air.

The Chrysler was still bobbing, the brake lights flashing in not-so-secret code. He tried the passenger's door, but it was locked. The back door wasn't. He slithered onto the seat so quietly that the couple in front had to be told that he was there.

"Don't let me interrupt." To show that he didn't mean it, he put the gun against the man's ear.

"Anything you want," the man croaked, inhaling the last syllable.

Norodny poked the barrel into a pile of clothes on the seat. "Your shirt," he said, "and your undershirt and that jacket you don't need."

He pushed open the driver's door. The light came on above a man with long sideburns descending from a yellowing toupee. From what he could see of the woman she wasn't young. He pocketed the keys and shut the door.

"Go on with what you're doing," he said. "I don't want to spoil your night. I know how you feel."

He patted down the man's trousers for a wallet. He went outside and pulled on a rayon shirt and plaid waterproof jacket, rolled the sleeves up over his wrists.

"Because you've been so accommodating, I'm gonna trade my snazzy new sports car for this old heap and your clothes. Is it a deal?"

He yanked open the driver's door and dragged the man out. The woman backed from the other side, pressing a ball of underwear against her body. He tossed sandals and a yellow dress out the window and fitted a key in the steering column. The Chrysler came to life in a haze of oily smoke.

"You better wait in my car," he said. "It's too wet to be out, the way you're dressed. Beat it. I left it unlocked."

Then he released the emergency brake and rolled away from the dike. "Anyone you want me to call?" he hollered.

"No, I guess not." He didn't think it was funny.

He drove back to the road and went north toward Homestead. Far ahead he could see the lights from the helicopter raking the traffic. It was starting to rain. He twisted the wiper knob and it came off in his hand.

Franklin took a bounce pass from his brother and dribbled between the parked cars. He fed the ball back to the younger boy, who rattled the county seal over the jail door with a jump shot, then gathered in the rebound and followed him inside the strangely silent building.

They found their father at his desk, gazing out the window. He was wearing his new dress uniform, the one he kept in mothballs. His hat was on his desk with a black band around the crown.

"Hi, Dad."

"What're you doin' here?"

"School let out early 'cause tomorrow's Thanksgiving," Franklin said.

"You should be home studying."

"Got all weekend," Buck, Jr., said. "Four whole days." He couldn't take his eyes off the hat. "You been at the graveyard?"

"Just got back."

"Was it sad?"

" 'Cause if it was," Franklin said, "we can stay here with you."

"Yeah," his brother said. "You need us, we don't got to be nowhere."

White looked sternly at his boys. "Get out of here, both of you. Go shoot hoops or something."

He wandered down the hall to Records. Pooler was also in his best uniform, a strip of black crepe across the badge.

"How you doing, Buck?"

"You too?"

The fat man turned away, then looked back at him in a sardonic double take. "Did I say something?"

"Everybody's being too damn nice, and I don't like it. A minute ago the *boys* came by to pat me on the head. First time there's been trouble and they're not hounding me when am I gonna find who done it, blow his brains out."

"They're growing up," Pooler said.

"The hell they are. They feel sorry for me."

"Have a drink," Pooler said, opening his desk for the office bottle. "It's how everybody's getting through the day."

White put out a hand, palm up. "Makes me too full of myself, 'specially when I can't stand my own company."

Pooler tilted the bottle at a paper cup. "You're not looking to get crocked with the rest of us, why not call Daisy? She'd be glad to trade a sober ear."

White went to the door, then stopped. "We have her number? She wouldn't be at the lab."

He tried both phones for half an hour before reaching her at her house. "Where you been?" he asked.

"I needed a drink after the services," she said. "Then I needed a couple more. Then I thought I'd better stay put a while, if I was going to drive home."

"I don't see why," he said bitterly. "There's no one around to cite you."

"What's on your mind?" she asked.

"Do I have to spell it out?"

"Isn't that why you called?" Before he could apologize, she said, "I'm glad you did, Buck. Someone has to spell things out for me."

"I'll be here till seven, if you want."

"Tell you the truth, I'm in no mood for men in uniform today."

"Where, then?"

"How about your place?" she asked. "I think it's time I saw it."

"You sure? You know what's gonna get around, anyone sees us together away from the office?"

"Your neighbors gossip, do they?"

"Uh-huh."

"Not to mine. I'll be right over."

The house was smaller then she'd expected, but crisper-looking, with fresh paint on the clapboard siding and shiny gutters on the roof. Next door a woman with an umbrella over a broken porch chair kept an eye on her as she parked behind the cruiser and went in without knocking.

She walked past a cool, dark living room into a small kitchen missing the smell of food. The refrigerator door was decorated with school papers, *A*s from Franklin, *B*s and *B* pluses from Buck, Jr. Their father was sitting at a Formica table stirring something in a fruit jar. He was wearing chino pants and a white shirt open at the neck, and it occurred to her that this was only the second time she'd seen him out of uniform.

"Want a drink?" he asked.

"What is it?"

"Kool-Aid."

She said, "Yecch," and immediately wished she hadn't.

"I'm addicted to the stuff," he told her. "When I was a kid, it was that or tap water, couldn't afford pop. Gets in your system. The boys, they won't touch it."

"What flavor?" she asked.

"Red raspberry."

"Pour."

He put some in a green tumbler he'd gotten with ten gallons of gas. She tasted it and said, "Not too bad." He filled the glass to the top.

She took another drink, watching him over the rim. "It's

not like the end of the world, not yours," she said. "It'll pass."

"Don't want it to," he said without looking at her. "I want to carry it with me, remind me what a lousy cop I am."

"Don't be ridiculous."

"Daisy," he said, "I'm sick and tired of everyone stroking me. I know my strengths as a policeman. I'm methodical, I pay attention to detail, and I go by the book most of the time and forget about it when I need to. But the bottom line is making arrests, and that's where I come up short."

"You're too hard on yourself."

"Not when it's open season on the people I'm closest to. First Irene, now this. . . . If I can't keep *them* safe, or at least bring in the responsible parties, what can the citizens expect?"

"How about the Jessie Reynolds case? You tracked down her killer when no one knew where to start looking."

"And came back without him. No," he said, "even the boys see it. If you can't be a hero to your own sons . . ."

She touched his face but took her hand away when he didn't seem to notice that it was there.

"I want you to hear this from me," he said. He sounded unsure of himself, not even the second time she'd heard him like that. "They've been interviewing for a new assistant head of security for the Lawson Department Stores around Daytona Beach, and the job's mine if I want it."

"I can't believe you'd just quit. What will you tell Pools, the boys?"

"My term ends in March. I'll announce I'm not running again and back out gracefully. It's as simple as that."

"Nothing's simple," she said.

"Why shouldn't I?" he demanded. "What am I accomplishing here? Any rookie can handle domestic complaints, patrol the roads. Laxahatchee needs a sheriff with real training, someone who made his way up through the ranks of a big-city department, like Alvorado."

"Heaven forbid."

He smiled but had nothing more to say, and she had no answer for his silence. He set down his glass and knotted his fingers in hers, folded his hands together as the door flew open and the boys came in with three other children.

"Hello, Alvin," she said to a sweaty ten-year-old in shorts and a torn polo shirt. "How's your sister?"

"Fine, Dr. Riley."

"Where do you know Alvin from?" White asked.

"I work two nights a week at the Everglades Dispensary. Alvin's an old friend."

He saw the boy watching them curiously. "Maybe you'd better go."

"If you think so . . ." She went to the sink and rinsed out her glass. "I like this place, Buck. It's comfortable."

"Yes," he said, "it is fairly comfortable."

"I think it's time you see where I live."

He didn't know what to say to that, either.

"It's comfortable too," she told him. "You'd feel at home."

"Would I?"

She kissed him quickly and walked out to her car.

19

Alvorado considered his options and, seeing that he had none, squeezed the trigger. The windshield absorbed the slug over the steering wheel, exploding into a spiderweb of splintered glass. The second bullet cut down the mirror and embedded itself in the headrest. It made a small hole that looked more impressive after he widened it with his thumb. A third shot left a jagged gash slanting across the seat. Alvorado examined the Mercedes with the attention to detail of a painter surveying a work in progress. He walked around to the driver's side, emptied the cylinder into the door, and went upstairs. A matron told him that Alice was talking to a lawyer and couldn't be disturbed.

He was waiting when they brought her back to the bullpen. In a shapeless jailhouse shift she seemed tired and unhealthy. Purplish circles traced the orbits of her eyes. Her nostrils were rubbed raw. She smelled of disinfectant.

"I have something to show you," he said, and slipped the cuffs off her wrists. She went listlessly to the elevator. The muscles in her jaw twitched when she saw the car.

"There is no reason for you to remain silent any longer."

"No!"

"I am sorry. We learned of it just this morning. A tow

truck brought your car from Flamingo. The body is still in the Laxahatchee morgue.

He walked off and leaned against the wall, letting her alone with her thoughts. She stared at the car for a long time and brushed some broken glass off the dash. When she looked away, the resistance had gone out of her. He saw her nod.

"Upstairs," he said. "We will do it right—in front of White and a stenographer."

Alice knew little more than they did about the killing in Glades City. Her part had been limited to supplying Alfonsin's business card and playing his secretary over the phone. When Alvorado asked why Sally Behagen had left the office carrying so much cash, she clammed up and asked to go to her cell. It wasn't until White took over the questioning that she admitted that Morrison had been sleeping with the realtor in vacant homes all over the county. He had told her that Sally was looking forward to a summer wedding and insisted that he oversee her investments right away.

"It was not so different from the game you were playing with Mr. Alfonsin," Alvorado said.

"It wasn't anything like that," she said, seething. "I never let him near me."

"Only because he demanded so little for his money."

White saw that they were losing her again. "It doesn't matter," he said. "Give us the rest of it. That's what we want to hear."

"You mean, about the limo driver?"

White was puzzled. That wasn't what he had meant at all. "Yes," he said.

"We needed his car. Mine sticks out everywhere. And we had to move easily around the city that night if we were going to pick up the money."

"What money?"

"The ransom. Didn't you make the connect—"

"Go on."

"You didn't even know about him, did you? Yes, he was ours also."

"Tell us," Alvorado said. "Tell us about all of them."

"Not without my lawyer."

"Tell us or I'll break your neck."

Alice said nothing.

The DA put his foot down. She would have to do time. A few years on accessory charges followed by closely supervised parole. The judge would be made to understand that she was virtually his prisoner, that her life had been in real danger. It was the best he was going to offer.

"I shot the Dietrich girl. I did it the night she disappeared. After they said good-bye he went back to the hotel and asked her to go for a last ride in the country. He told her he loved her and didn't know what he would do without her. She was a stupid twit who believed everything he said. He brought her home and sat her down in the kitchen and poured her a glass of milk. He gave me the gun, and I went in and shot her. We tried shaking down the other one, but something always went wrong. All we got out of it were some traveler's checks."

"He made you?"

Alice lowered her head.

"Where is the body?"

"Under the house, wrapped in a green blanket. I helped dig the grave."

They stopped at the medical center to talk to Dr. Riley. She called for an ambulance and followed them to the cellar in a soiled gown reeking of formaldehyde. The dust and cool dampness aggravated a lingering cold. She lit a cigar and supervised the excavation with the enthusiasm of a tomb robber in the Valley of the Kings.

They went to work with sledgehammers on a dark patch in the center of the floor. The cement was less than an inch thick. In the layer of sand underneath they found a pickax, a shovel, and rubber boots crusted with dried mud. Alice watched from a corner, drenched in sweat despite the chill.

White scraped at the sand till he came to moist earth, which yielded tan-and-white pumps and a beaded bag. Inside were some bent snapshots of Sybil and a tall, red-haired girl. He gave them to Alvorado and grabbed a hand trowel, clawed out a long silk blazer and mother-of-pearl opera glasses. Dr. Riley ordered him from the hole. She pushed away more dirt and uncovered a swatch of coarse fabric—green wool.

The body lay on its side, the hands pressed over the heart in frozen prayer. White went back down with Detective Sturges and hoisted it onto the floor. Dr. Riley unwrapped the heavy shroud beneath powerful arc lights.

"This girl's dead less than two weeks," she said. "And no way was she shot. See for yourself, there are no bullet wounds."

"What was the cause of death?" White asked.

"It's too soon to say, but if you pressed me, I'd have to guess strangulation. Notice the froth on her lips? If this was a med school exam, I'd say she drowned."

Alvorado called White to the edge of the grave, where he had been spreading out the evidence as it was exhumed. "Look at these," he said.

White shined his flashlight at a gunmetal-gray steel box, at two six-inch stacks of legal documents and bankbooks. Dropping to one knee, he sorted through the papers, copies of wills and records of financial dealings involving women in four Southern states. The passbooks had been picked clean and voided. On the bottom were four from Charleston, South Carolina. Beneath the ten-digit identification number was the name J. R. Reynolds.

White snapped off the light. There was a tremor in his hands as he unstrapped his gun belt and draped it over Alvorado's shoulder.

"What are you doing?"

"You'd better hold on to this."

He yanked the woman out of the corner and shoved her ahead of him. Her feet tangled in his, and she stumbled. He dragged her to the grave and flashed the light in the box, then at her face. He grunted at what he saw and changed it with the flat of his hand. Alvorado tried to step between them. White pushed him away. "I want it from the beginning," he said. "And I want all of it."

Alice smoothed a tissue between her palms and clamped it over a scraped knee. White opened his hand again and reddened the other cheek. "Now," he said.

"He had to."

"What? Say what you mean."

"I don't understand, either. He cared about me, I think. But that's not why—"

"Make sense, damn it," White said, tightening his hands into fists.

"That's enough," Alvorado said, and muscled him out of the way. "Can't you see that she's terrified of you?"

"If she's scared now, let her be there when I bring in her boyfriend."

Alvorado blocked White, pushing him into the wall, and turned around. Alice's face showed nothing. She was touching her lips, feeling for the start of swelling. "What do you want from him now?" she asked bitterly. "Let all the dead rest."

"Wishful thinking."

"Why are you saying that?" Her cheeks drained of color except where he'd slapped her, the outline of his hand livid on her skin. "You said he'd been killed," she screamed at Alvorado. "The car was all shot up."

"You don't need a car anymore," Alvorado said. "Anyway, a good body man can repair all the damage. Speak to your lawyer about indemnification. We had to make you talk." He relaxed as White stopped battling him and stood quietly against the wall. "Be more concerned about Morrison."

"You shot my car." She started to laugh and stopped just as quickly. Then she began to cry.

She retreated into her corner. She was laughing again, laughing and sobbing in short fits she couldn't control. On the ride to Miami she sat handcuffed between them, dry-washing her wrists. As they brought her into headquarters she told White, "If you see him, tell him not to write."

20

When Norodny found her, Marlene Calle was waiting tables in the cocktail lounge of the Santiago Hotel across from Domino Park in Little Havana. At twenty-nine, it was five years since she danced off the runway of a drafty Belle Glade strip joint for the last time, stuffing damp fivers in her G-string, hustling the truckers and braceros for ginger ale at champagne prices. She was short and full-breasted with narrow hips and thin lips rouged to petulance. Norodny couldn't keep his eyes off her legs. He explored them through the black fishnet stockings that were his favorite part of her waitress's uniform, if he didn't count the tooled leather pouch she wore on her hip.

In the week he had been in Miami he'd left the Santiago once, to buy clothes and to pick up a *Herald*. The front page was hung with one of his old mug shots. Beside it were identikit pictures of how he would look with a mustache and a full beard. A four-column headline capped a story about a dragnet involving police agencies throughout the Southeast. Since then, he had taken his meals at odd hours in the coffee shop, and his entertainment, such as it was, at the dimly lit bar. His photo had been pushed back to the second section; in a few days it would stop being news. He told Marlene that he was a safecracker, and since it was a nice hotel and he wore a nice suit and took no for an answer with a nice smile, she believed him.

Marlene had a secret too. She confessed it after work early one morning in bed beside the open window in his room.

"I am married."

"Congratulations."

"You are not surprised?"

"I seem to run into a lot of broad-minded people," he said. "Your husband one of them too?"

"He doesn't mind."

"That kind of arrangement wouldn't work for me."

"Nor for me," she said. "It is not what I had in mind when I married Derek. He was possessive then, and I enjoyed it. But things did not work out as we expected, and we take our consolation with whom we wish."

"Why don't you leave him?"

"It is not so easy anymore to be alone."

"You'd find somebody in no time."

She brushed his ear with her mouth and rested her cheek on the pillow. Her fingertips found his lips. "I have."

He pulled away. "Uh-uh. Man in my profession could never make you happy."

"How do you know this?"

"I'm married to my work. And you want plenty of attention. Most of the time I don't have it to give."

"It would be an experience being with you," she said. "Take me with you."

"Am I going somewhere?"

"Surely you don't plan to spend the remainder of your life in this hotel."

"I'm not looking forward to it. But I may have to. I'm hot everywhere, Marlene, and the only ID I have is for a short, fat redneck old enough to be my father."

"What if I could provide you with the passport of a man your own age and size?"

"Where are you going to get something like that?"

"Derek has no use for his." When Norodny didn't answer, she asked. "What are you thinking of?"

"London."

Marlene crouched at the side of the tub and watched him spin the taps. When she felt the diaphragm in place, she waded into the water. She slid down the cold porcelain until only her head and the high arc of her breasts showed above the surface. "You must make a good safecracker," she told him.

"Why do you say that?"

"You adjust the water with such precision, as if you were feeling for a combination."

She pressed his hand between her breasts. He came closer, and she wrapped an arm around his neck and guided his lips over her body. He helped her to her feet. She let him turn her around, surrendered her damp cheek to his. He crossed his arms around her shoulders and pressed himself against her. She tugged at the shower control. Fine spray lashed their shoulders, poured down their hips, their legs. He buried his face in the wild knot of fragrant hair. Neither of them heard the door.

When Derek saw the empty bed, he tiptoed back to the hall and read the number over the bell: 418. That was what he had written on his palm. Then what were they doing in the john? He poked around the room till he spotted the green passport beside Marlene's traveling bag. Instinctively he whisked his hand against his pocket, measuring the comforting mass of the nickle-plated .22. If he was making a mistake, he'd probably have to use it, anyway. He went inside the bathroom and tore open the shower curtain. His cheeks flushed as the gun came out and fixed on them.

"Derek!"

He moved the gun to the other hand and pulled her from

the tub. A towel came off the rack between his fingers, and he flung it at her. "Cover yourself," he said.

Norodny reached for the tap.

"Keep your hands where they are."

"What are you afraid of?" Norodny asked. He shut off the water. "Give me a towel."

"Shut up," Derek said, showing the revolver's delicate silver muzzle.

"I thought you had an understanding about these things, Marlene."

"Derek must have changed the rules without consulting me. Ask him."

"Shut up or I'll kill you both right now."

She stepped back shakily and began drying herself. "Why *does* it bother you so much this time?"

"I didn't mind your sleeping around, Marlene. But going into my drawer and stealing my money and my passport, taking off on me . . . that wasn't part of the deal."

"I love him."

"That wasn't part of it, either."

"It happened," she said, and gave Norodny the towel. "I want to be with him now, always."

Derek thumbed the hammer. "I can arrange that very easily."

"This is ridiculous," Marlene cried. "We have done nothing to you. And you cannot kill us and expect to get away with it."

"We'll see."

"The police will not have to be brilliant to know who to look for when they find my body like this next to his. What satisfaction will you take in spending your life in prison?"

"She's got a point," Norodny said.

"You keep out of this."

"Under the circumstances I don't see how I can."

"Listen to him," Marlene pleaded.

"I wouldn't be thrilled, either, knowing my wife was

fooling around with another man," Norodny said. "But I can make it up to you so none of us will have to suffer. I'll buy your passport."

"And my wife?"

"Just the passport."

"It's not for sale. But you'll pay," Derek said. "Let me see his money, Marlene."

She hurried into her underwear and went to the other room. "I can't find his wallet," she called out. "It's not in his jacket or his pants."

"Where is it?"

Norodny put a foot out of the tub. "In the bed. I'll get it for you."

"Stay where you are," Derek said, pushing the gun in front of him. "Tell Marlene where to look. She'll find it."

"What if she doesn't."

"Pray she does."

Norodny stepped onto the bath mat with both feet.

"Watch it," Derek warned.

"It's under the mattress, Marlene. You can never be too careful about being robbed."

Marlene wriggled into her skirt. She raised a corner of the mattress and swept her hand underneath. "There's nothing here," she said.

"It's on the other side, near the wall," Norodny told her. "I'll show you." He moved past Derek toward the door.

"That's far enough."

"It is," Norodny said, and whipped the towel at Derek's eyes.

The revolver jerked back, and a bullet passed through his arm above the biceps. He hit Derek low, bulling him into the wall, drove a shoulder into the tight midsection and heard the wind rush out of him, felt him sag. He spun him around and wrapped the towel across his Adam's apple. With a snap of his wrists he tightened it.

Derek clawed at the garrote, bloodying his throat. A dull

ache filled his chest. He gulped air through his mouth but couldn't swallow it. He angled the gun upward. Norodny let go of the towel and slapped the gun to the floor. Derek filled his lungs and dived for it, had it in his hands when a knee to the small of the back sent him crashing into the tub.

Norodny grabbed the back of Derek's head and forced him down to where a few inches of cloudy water stood above the clogged drain. He wedged his foot against the toilet and stood up, summoning all his strength into his hands. He watched with occasional interest, like a fight fan at a hockey brawl, as Derek brought his arms under his chest and tried to push off, then gave up to flail uselessly at the air. Behind him the medicine cabinet creaked open, and white-hot pain traveled the length of his spine.

Derek went limp suddenly and Norodny shoved him away and whirled around. Marlene swiped at Norodny's face, bloody razor blades between her knuckles, nicking him under the eye. "Bitch-bastard," she cried, and lunged at him again. He tripped her up with a foot between the ankles and wrestled her into the tub. She landed on her back with a soft moan that once had delighted him.

He squeezed her face below the surface. Her hands came up and raked his chest, the lacquered nails slicing jagged red streamers. She squirmed away and he saw the gun. He scooped it up on the second grab and cracked her over the ear. Then he went back to Derek, reaching under his shirt for a heartbeat, finding nothing. He opened the taps, and a foot of water surged into the tub. He kept his hand over Marlene's mouth until she ran out of bubbles.

He gathered Marlene around his good shoulder and carried her from the tub. Her foot slapped against his rump, death's jockey booting home another winner. He put her in the closet and then went back for Derek, dragging him in beside her and covering them with the spare blanket. He lowered the venetian blinds and set the air conditioner on super cool. The room was paid for till the end of the week. Barring a power failure, they wouldn't be noticed for days.

He went to work on his face with a dry towel and toilet paper. His back felt as though it had been split open and his insides were spilling out. Only a little blood was flowing from his arm, and he pinched off what there was between his fingers. The slug had gone through muscle, missing the bone and veins, sterilizing the wound with its heat. But he was asking for trouble if he didn't have it dressed. Already it was starting to throb.

He washed and put on clean underwear. Dark crimson spread across his T-shirt. When it stopped, he daintily got into his shirt and suit, careful not to break the clots. He went through his pockets and counted less than forty dollars.

He found eighty dollars in Derek's wallet, and ID to back up the passport. There was another fifty-five dollars in Marlene's purse. He stirred thirty dollars in change inside the leather pouch and dumped it in her traveling bag with his clothes. He tore up the redneck's papers over the toilet, shut off the light, hung out the DO NOT DISTURB sign. No one was in the hall. Derek's gun and his own went down a laundry chute sealed with a decade's grime.

He caught a cruising Checker at the corner and followed his bag onto the rear seat. "Airport," he told the driver.

"You want that on the meter or off?"

He peered into the mirror through the grilled partition. Under the visor of a Mets cap, pouched eyes stared back, blue where they weren't red. The cabbie looked over his shoulder, flashing bulldog features humanized by a peeling, bleachers-burned nose. "Suit yourself," Norodny said.

The off-duty sign came on, and they raced into traffic. Norodny fell back against the seat and was jolted forward as the ribbed upholstery sliced across his shoulders. He felt moisture seeping down his sides. It crept beneath his arms, and a red Rorschach blot answered its own question on the front of his shirt. He began to shiver.

"Damn it," he said, "I left my attaché case. Forget about the airport. I have to go home."

The eyes in the mirror narrowed. "Where's that?"

"I . . . uh, keep going. I'll tell you where to turn."

He went into his pocket but was stopped by the pain. He reached behind his back with the good arm and fished out the wallet, flipped it open. "4632 South Bayshore," he read. "And make it snappy. I still have a plane to catch."

The address was hidden behind a bougainvillaea-and-palm stockade, three floors of terraced apartments around a swimming pool the size of a Third World postage stamp. The complex resembled nothing so much as an economy motel—transient architecture for a city in flux. Norodny dismissed the cabbie with a twenty-dollar bill and carried his bag inside. The directory showed no Derek or Calle. He checked the wallet and saw 3D beside the street number. The name above the buzzer was Stevens. The key from Marlene's purse opened it just the same.

He tossed the bag on a Naugahyde couch and sat on the edge of the tub, sliced the sleeve off his shirt with cuticle scissors from the medicine cabinet. His fingers evened the torn skin at both ends of the hole. In a way he'd been lucky. If he hadn't been in the shower, the arm would be contaminated with shredded cloth.

There were some sterile pads in the cabinet and a roll of gauze. He painted the arm with iodine and patched the exit and entry wounds, wrapped them. He crawled into bed and swaddled himself in clean sheets.

He woke around midnight, sweating from a low-grade fever. He got out of bed and wandered to the window. A blond girl in yellow shorts and a halter was running alongside the pool after a waterlogged puppy. He lowered the shade and turned on a lamp and ransacked a chest of drawers for a change of clothes. Beneath a dark tangle of socks was an accordion envelope fastened with a string tie. Inside were five bankbooks, two in Marlene's name, the rest in Derek's. The accounts totaled close to seventy thousand dollars. He found a pen and some paper in the nightstand, Derek's license in his wallet. At the end of an hour he had the signature down pat.

21

The new deskman wasn't working out. Three times he'd been warned that White was out of the office to everyone but the boys, and three times he'd held him hostage to a taxpayer's quarter. Now Alvorado was asking for help on another case. A shutoff tripped inside White's head, and the words mercifully lost meaning. What the department needed was an unlisted number.

Then a strange voice came on the line, and White could have sworn that he was talking to himself. It was a gravelly baritone spouting cop talk in a no-nonsense military cadence. White forced his ear to listen, and his brain went back to work. He asked the stranger to identify himself again. The voice barked, "Detective Myron Stoneham, Miami Bunco Squad. Am I speaking too low?"

"No," White said. "I hear you fine."

"Lieutenant Alvorado recommends you very highly."

"No one asked him to."

"I did," Stoneham said. "We're involved in an investigation that extends inside your county, and he told us you'd be glad to do whatever you could."

"Tell the lieutenant to mind his own business."

"I will," Stoneham said evenly.

A hand slapped at the mouthpiece, and White heard Alvorado's muffled complaint, then a dull crash, the receiver bouncing on the floor. Then: "Listen to what

Detective Stoneham has to say. This is very important. All that happened before, that's forgotten."

"I haven't forgotten," White said. "It'd be indecent."

"Anyway, you are going to help us again. It is your job."

Stoneham cut in and said, "Lieutenant Alvorado explained about the trouble you had, and your unwillingness to volunteer assistance now. I can just about guarantee that this one's a piece of cake. We're dealing here with people who've never been known to back up the threat of violence. I don't see them all of a sudden getting tough."

"Is that a written guarantee?"

"Hear me out, Sheriff White, and then make up your mind."

"Go on," White said.

"For more than two months we've been trying to run down a Steven and Marlene Derek. She's a.k.a. Marlene Calle. That's C-A-L-L-E. They're a husband-and-wife team working a badger game out of Little Havana. Warrants were drawn in September, but the Dereks dropped from sight before they could be served."

"Do you have a Laxahatchee address for them?" White asked.

"We don't know where they are," Stoneham admitted.

"Then how do I help?"

"Routine checking indicates that they've squirreled away large sums of money in savings banks all over Miami. We requested the banks to contact us when they learned of any new transactions. Yesterday Derek withdrew more than twenty thousand dollars from the Homestead and Old Cutler Road branches of South Florida Federal. We think they're getting ready to blow."

"What do you want from me?" White asked.

"Some time, some patience," Stoneham said. "We're told Derek keeps a sizable balance in the Laxahatchee Station branch. If he isn't cleaning it out this minute, he'll try soon. We'd like you to have someone there when he does."

"Wouldn't recognize him if he asked us to double-count it."

"We'll rush a couple of his old mugs out by messenger if you'll say you want to see them."

"I don't know," White said. "I'm running shorthanded. I can't spare anyone."

"Isn't there any way—"

"Yeah, if I do it myself."

"Will you?"

"I feel mean," White said abruptly. "Too bad this Derek's not a shooter."

The Laxahatchee Station office of the South Florida Federal Savings and Loan Corporation dominated the low country for fifteen miles in all directions, its silvered grid rising out of the Everglades like an unsolvable Rubik's Cube. In the half hour after sunrise, and again at the end of each afternoon, the structure was a certified highway hazard; no fewer than four fatalities had been attributed to its laser-sharp reflection. White homed in on the blue SFFS&L pennant fluttering over the parking lot and left the Plymouth opposite the drive-in teller. The manager was waiting in auto loans, a sleek man with a cough. He showed White inside the stainless-steel vault where a folding chair had been placed next to the time lock on the door.

"You can hide here," he said. "He'll never see you."

White looked at the foot-thick walls and brushed away the moisture beading on his lip. "Can we step outside?" he asked, and led the manager behind the tellers' cages. "He's not expecting trouble, so there's no reason to hide. What I'll do is take a seat in back by the new accounts. That way I can keep the entire room in view."

"Not necessarily," the manager said. "If we crowd up, and we always do on Thursdays, you won't even see the door."

"Then you'd better arrange with your tellers to signal if he shows at their window. Can you do that?"

"Tell me something first. Are you going to shoot him?"

"It's not likely," White said. "Why?"

"If you have to fire, don't miss. A bullet hits these glass walls, I'm not sure the building won't come down."

White placed two of Derek's mug shots on an empty desk and sat down. He dropped his hat on the blotter and stared over the crown at the revolving door. Thursday was payday at the pick-your-own berry farms dotting the eastern county, and the bulk of the bank's customers were field hands, migrants in rough clothing. In the five minutes before noon, the line to the cages tripled in length, and he lost sight of the end.

Another quarter hour went by before the manager came out of his office waving his arms. "He's here!"

White pulled his hat over his forehead. "Where? I don't see anyone looks like him."

"At the drive-in teller, in a Renault with dark glass. I told her to hold him for you."

"Shit. It never occurred to me he'd—"

"You enter through a door behind the other cages," the manager said. "I'll unlock it for you."

"No good," White told him. "He'll take off, and I'll be stuck inside. Have your teller stall him some more. I'll go out to the lot."

He came around the building hugging the wall, his hand heeled to the butt of his gun. Idling beneath the overhang not twenty feet away was a green Renault with rental plates, a Stevie Wonder song pouring from the open windows. A peeling bumper sticker proclaimed FORT LUDERDALE. As he stepped into sunlight it roared off the lot. He lifted the revolver halfway out of its holster, then jammed it down and ran to the Plymouth.

He slammed into gear and raced for the break in the fence. A farm truck sagging under a load of melons got there first. It stalled on the incline, and the driver cranked the engine and threw his hands up in frustration. White left rubber around the back of the lot and came out behind the bank, bruising the bumper on the curb.

He circled the block and headed east out of town, his hood ornament aimed at a speck on the horizon. He nudged the speedometer into the eighties, and the speck grew larger. A car began to take form in the boxy outline of a midsize foreign job. The needle brushed ninety, and he held it there with his toe. He enjoyed high-speed driving, the pleasure still as strong as when it helped him to decide on a police career. But the steel-belted tires under every county car too often proved explosive under extended pursuit. His foot came up a quarter of an inch, and the needle dropped back to eighty. The speck grew indistinct again.

A flatbed truck with two swamp buggies behind the cab crawled out of the scrub and cut him off. He swerved into the westbound lane, rustling the Australian pines that lined the Tamiami Canal. Coming head-on, on shot springs, was an ancient pickup, a Miccosukee war party home from intergalactic video battlefields. Effortlessly he steered back across the yellow line.

He spotted the Renault on a barely perceptible rise, green against the blue-gray sky. He gorged the Plymouth on gas, and the small car moved closer. It was a four-cylinder model, no match for his high performance V-8. He looked hard at the back window but saw nothing behind the dark glass.

Between 30 MPH signs flanking the Billy Bowlegs Indian School, both cars gathered speed. As the Plymouth closed in, the small car fluttered its lights, and White flinched and tromped on the brake. The Renault never slowed. White detected motion in the black window, as if the driver had turned to laugh in his face.

He lead-footed it out of the school zone. Where the highway broadened again, yellow buses backed up traffic in both directions, and he threaded the slender corridor between them, losing sight of the green car. He went another mile without letting up on the gas, till a dust cloud over the high pitch of the levee lured him across a floodgate spanning the canal. Hidden in tall weeds, the Renault limped along the top of the embankment.

The Plymouth jolted through the brush, scraping bottom on gray rock. As White closed in, the other driver slowed and pulled over, and when the big car came abreast, the Renault swung left without warning and broadsided it, dropped back and rammed it again, nearly toppling it into a sawgrass lagoon. As White wrestled the wheel the Renault steered around and showed its rear bumper, then charged back in a riprap hail. Demolition derby for keeps.

White gunned the engine and brought the wheel sharply to the right and bashed in the Renault's door, bulldozed it out of the ruts. The lighter car dropped a tire over the edge and skidded down the embankment. A palm stump snagged the undercarriage and held it for an instant, then flipped it onto its roof in four feet of water.

White stepped out of the Plymouth, rubbing a knot above his eye. He scrambled down the levee with his hand not far from his gun. If anyone was coming out of the Renault, they were taking their own sweet time. It was a luxury he couldn't afford. He tossed his gun belt up the slope and sailed his hat in the same direction. He pulled off his boots and stuffed his wallet in the left one and waded into chest-high water.

An alligator yawned and crawled off the far bank and swam at him in a watery game of chicken. It submerged at the last moment, as he knew it would, bobbing up behind him to beach itself in the sun. White walked into weeds where bubbles percolated to the surface. Ducking his head, he saw the car wedged in a foot of muck, the passenger's door partially bent open beneath the crumpled roof. He peered inside a horizontal opening framed in glass shards and chrome. A man floated facedown across the dashboard, a gashed ear leaking red plumes. For once he was glad to see a driver who didn't use a seat belt.

He broke the surface, took two quick breaths, went down again beside the hood. His hip bumped against the puckered metal and the car shuddered, and so did he, until it settled more firmly into the mud. The murkiness strained reality from the feeble light. He reached through the opening for the first thing that appeared tangible—a white shirt. He squeezed the cloth, and an arm drifted flaccidly over his shoulder. He tugged it out of the car. The body followed part of the way and no more.

He backed away carefully and stood up to taste air again. Then he bellied through the door into the front seat, where the man's ankle was tangled under the cushion. He wrenched him clear and dragged him along the soft bottom, roiling the brown water even more. Using a lifeguard's carry, he brought him up the bank.

He wrapped both arms around the man's waist, letting the head hang down. When the water had drained from his throat, he stretched him on his back and pressed an ear to his chest, then scraped the mud from his face and lowered his jaw, pinched the nostrils shut, and sealed his lips with his own. He inhaled deeply and forced air inside the still body, did it again, pulled away, and stared anxiously at the vacant features, stared at them until his nails cut into his palms.

His throat constricted, and he thought he was going to gag. He wiped his mouth with the back of his hand and then scrubbed it against his sleeve till it stung, tilted his face toward the purifying warmth of the sun. He wanted to walk away, to see justice done as he understood it best. Instead he shut his eyes and tossed back his head to savor the full strength of the vertical rays. Then he filled his lungs once more and breathed color into the blue lips.

A hand pressed weakly against his chest, and White raised his head and sat back on his heels. Norodny coughed and rubbed his eyes, moved his lips wordlessly.

He seemed shriveled, as if his vital fluids had been diluted with canal water. A fit of coughing shook his body, and he fought for breath, hawking gobs of clear phlegm into the brush. In a ragged whisper he said, "I didn't know you cared," and blew a kiss, then rolled onto his side and vomited. He inched away and propped himself into a sitting position, supporting himself with both hands. "You pulled me out?"

"Executioner sent me," White told him.

"Give him my thanks," Norodny rasped.

White swatted him down against the gray sand. "Do it yourself," he said. "Where's Steven Derek?"

"Never heard of him."

"You were emptying his bank account. Trying to."

"Must be some other guy."

"You know," White said, "I enjoyed watching you drown. Enjoyed it so much, I almost kept my distance. Only thing that troubled me was what an easy time you were having. I'm going to love watching you fry."

Norodny puked up more water and shook his head violently, unable to speak. "Won't happen," he mumbled. "Fireproof."

"Not anymore," White corrected him. "We know about all of them, even the limo driver."

"Don't understand what you're say—"

"Alice talked."

If it bothered him, he didn't show it. "To you, maybe," he said matter-of-factly. "It'll be another story in court."

"We don't need her anymore. We have her statement. There's grand juries waiting on you in two counties. We can fry you over and over again, put you on a spit and keep turning it."

"Without a confession? Without Alice's testimony? Where's your case? You don't have the physical evidence."

"You've never gone up against a Laxahatchee jury," White said.

"If I stand trial, I'll be acquitted," Norodny said without

bragging. "If I'm convicted, I'll beat it on appeal. If they send me up, I'll crash out. You must've seen my record."

White's hand went automatically into his pocket and closed around the tin of snuff that was always there. Brown water squirted through his fingers, and he flung it into the canal. "And if we fry you, you won't burn, that right?"

"You think I'm nuts . . . some kind of monster."

"Mind reader too," White said.

"A businessman's closer to the truth. What I did, I did to eat, to eat well. It's not my hobby. Does that strike you as odd?"

When White didn't respond, he forced a laugh and said, "It does to me. I don't get off on it. I'm a lucid, like you, like everyone who counts for something. I like kids, a day at the ballpark. I pay my taxes on time. A lucid."

"Except you know what it feels like to wring the life out of . . . how many women?"

"Wrong," Norodny said.

"Kind of late to cop out of it."

Norodny tousled his hair with his fingers. He looked hurt. "I never felt a thing," he said.

"A lucid, huh? Tell me about the Belson girl." White went up the slope, trying to distance himself from his revulsion. He slipped his wallet in a pocket, sat on a rock and pulled on his boots, whisked the dust from his hat fussily. He put a fresh crease in the crown. "Tell me about her."

"Merry? Merry was terrific," Norodny said. "I was crazy about Merry. She was funny, well educated, a star in the sack. How could anyone not love Merry?"

"Why you killed her."

"They were all fine women," Norodny went on without hearing him. "If they weren't, I couldn't have gotten close. I have no rapport with losers."

"How does someone kill a good woman like her?" White tried again.

"It happened. I didn't feel anything."

"No remorse, no guilt?"

Norodny hunched his shoulders into a shrug. "I don't know what those words mean," he said.

"A lucid."

"Do you think you're any different? You don't move without a gun. What I did is second nature to you."

"I've never killed," White said. "I don't know that I'd have kept this job if I had to. What do they . . . What did you feel?"

"Why do you care so much about what makes me tick?"

"Even an animal would have felt something."

"This is getting to be a drag," Norodny said. "Read me my rights, the part about remaining silent."

"A lucid." White laughed as he came down the slope. "A four-star lucid. Get up," he said. "I'm bringing you in now."

"Give me a minute. I can hardly catch my breath."

"Get up."

Norodny struggled to his feet but stood rooted to the spot, like an old man who had dropped his cane in an empty room. "My ankle's broken," he said. "I need a hand."

White wrapped Norodny's arm around his shoulders, clamping the wrist in his palm. He kept his own arm around the man's waist. Norodny took a tentative step and then another, and then his ankle caved in and he stumbled against White's ribs, knocking him off-balance, shoving him out of the way, latching easily onto the butt of his gun, snatching it from the holster. White tightened his grip on the wrist and reeled him in, sending out a fist to meet the side of his head. It was as hard as he had ever hit a man, the only time he took pleasure in it. Norodny was out before he touched the ground.

He dragged him to the edge of the canal and splashed water in his face. The sawgrass whipped a damp breeze through White's shirt, trapping a shiver between his shoulders. Norodny came around quickly and looked up at him with a childish grin. "You hit like a mule," he said, extending a hand. "No tricks this time."

"No tricks," White said, and pulled him to his feet.

He locked his arms around him, and they moved away in a drunken allemande to unheard music. White bent for his hat but left it where it was. The breeze came up again, and he felt cold all over. Gooseflesh crept along his bare arms as he kicked Norodny's feet out from under him and shoved him into the canal, jumped in after him, wrestled him under.

After what seemed like a very long time he hauled him out by the collar. He went to his car without looking back and raised headquarters on the radio. The new man had wandered away from the switchboard. Pooler picked up.

"Say, Pools," White said, "send an ambulance to the Tamiami Canal about three miles east of the Bowlegs School. I've got a floater here in real bad need of some CPR. Hard to say right now if he's going to make it.

"His name's Norodny, Pools. You might tell them to take their time."